YASMINE

NEW YORK TIMES BESTSELLING AUTHOR

GALENORN

D1528475

CASTING CURSES

A BEWITCHING BEDLAM NOVEL

BOOK 5

A Nightqueen Enterprises LLC Publication

Published by Yasmine Galenorn
PO Box 2037, Kirkland WA 98083-2037
CASTING CURSES
A Bewitching Bedlam Novel
Copyright © 2018 by Yasmine Galenorn
First Electronic Printing: 2018 Nightqueen Enterprises
LLC
First Print Edition: 2018 Nightqueen Enterprises, LLC
Cover Art & Design: Earthly Charms
Editor: Elizabeth Flynn

A Nightqueen Enterprises LLC Publication
Published in the United States of America

Acknowledgments

Thanks to my beloved husband, Samwise, who is more supportive than any husband out there. (Hey, I'm biased!) He believes in me, even at times when I'm having trouble believing in myself. Thank you to my wonderful assistants—Andria Holley and Jennifer Arnold. And to my friends—namely Carol, Jo, Vicki, Shawntelle, and Mandy. Also, to the whole UF Group gang I'm in. They've held my hand more than once this past year as I've made the jump from traditional to indie publishing. It's been a scary, exciting, fast-track ride and I'm loving it.

Love and scritches to my four furbles—Caly, Brighid (the cat, not the goddess), Morgana, and li'l boy Apple, who make every day a delight. And reverence, honor, and love to my spiritual guardians—Mielikki, Tapio, Ukko, Rauni, and Brighid (the goddess, not the cat).

And to you, readers, for taking Maddy and Aegis and Bubba into your heart. Be cautious when you rub a kitty's belly—you never know when you might end up petting a cjinn! I hope you enjoy this book. If you want to know more about me and my work, check out my bibliography in the back of the book, be sure to sign up for my newsletter, and you can find me on the web at Galenorn.com.

Brightest Blessings,
~The Painted Panther~
~Yasmine Galenorn~

Welcome to Casting Curses

I stopped, closing my eyes and holding out my hands as I tried to sense what was going on around me. And then it hit me, full force. A heavy magic lingering from years past. It was ritual magic, structured and ancient, and it was trapped here in this room. I had no idea what we were dealing with, but it set my stomach to quivering, and I had a distinct feeling that we were walking in dangerous territory.

"I can feel it too. I suggest that perhaps we should exit this room—" I started to say, but was interrupted when one of the workmen raced by into the room, screaming at the top of his lungs. His arms were flailing, and the scent of sheer terror lingered in his wake.

"Come back!" I wasn't sure why, but I didn't want him near that table. There was something there that was dangerous, something old and gnarled and twisted. I started to run forward, trying to stop him, when he lurched into the table, crashing against it.

He fell back, sprawling on the floor.

I watched as the urn tilted from the impact and went hurtling down to land next to him. The urn hit the wood and shattered on impact. A plume of black powder filled the air, roiling into smoke, and I screeched to a halt, trying to avoid it. Unfortunately, I was too close and found myself breathing in the acrid smoke that boiled up from the powder.

I scrambled back, trying to get away from it.

The workman was on the floor, flailing and screaming. The next moment, he went limp. I turned to see Leonard snap out of his paralysis. He motioned for me to get out of the way as he ran toward his worker.

Chapter 1

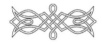

THE WEATHER WAS raging. We were in the throes of a classic November windstorm, with gusts predicted to clock as high as seventy miles an hour, not uncommon during autumn storms in Western Washington. Sustained winds had already reached a steady thirty miles per hour, and outside the trees swayed, lashed by the wind, as rain sleeted down sideways. A number of people didn't believe me when I told them that it rained sideways here, but anybody who had ever lived in the Pacific Northwest could attest to the phenomenon.

I was standing at the counter, staring out into the yard, hoping that all our trees would hold steady. There were several that I was suspicious of, but I hadn't had the chance to have an arborist in to look at their root systems yet. We'd just have to cross our fingers and hope. That was another lovely product of our storms here—downed trees, power outages, and landslides. Every year several people were killed by falling timber when the ground became saturated and the shallow roots gave way.

"Steaks will be ready in ten minutes." Max was out on the back patio, grilling steaks and corn on the cob. He had waved me off when I asked if he wanted to cook them inside. "If I can't handle a little rain, I'm not the weretiger I claim to be," he had said. After ten minutes, he had put on a rain poncho and looked altogether miserable, but he wasn't giving up.

Aegis took an apple pie out of the oven and slid in a pan of biscuits. He was wearing my retro-1950s ruffled polka dot apron that I had bought, hoping to entice myself into cooking more. The apron hadn't proved incentive enough to lure me into the kitchen, but Aegis looked adorable in it. He happily tied it on over his black jeans and muscle shirt, making for one very cuddly goth.

Sandy and I were also in our element. Max and Aegis had designated us the drink department.

"Margaritas?" Sandy asked.

I shook my head. "Hot rum toddies."

She glanced outside. "Yeah, the rum wins out."

As I stirred the base—water, butter, brown sugar, cinnamon, nutmeg, and cloves—she opened a bottle of dark rum. As I moved the pan off the flame to add the alcohol, she shook her head.

"More." She gave me a long look.

I added another splash.

"*More.*" She motioned to the bottle and it jerked in my hand, tipping back into the pan.

I laughed and gave up, upending the bottle into the base. I returned the pan to the flame and gently stirred the contents, then lowered the heat to let it simmer for a few minutes. I ladled the drink into a mug and handed it to her. She sipped and gave me a nod of approval.

For once, she wasn't wearing her usual getup of yoga pants and a crop top. Sandy was a gym bunny, rich enough to buy and sell most of the town. She loved her designer bags and sunglasses, but getting her out of her gym clothes was like trying to keep a fish alive out of water. But given the storm, she had opted for a pair of jeans and a powder blue turtleneck that set off her spun-gold hair.

"So that's enough booze?" I restrained a grin.

"No, but it will do."

Laughing, I turned off the flame and leaned back against the counter. It was true—Sandy and I liked our booze. Our witch's blood gave us a high tolerance to alcohol, though we were also party girls at heart. But the past year, our primary parties had been at home with our boyfriends.

A brilliant flash of lightning split the sky, illuminating the kitchen. I shivered as a crash of thunder began to rumble so long and loud that the windows rattled. It felt like the thunderbolt was never going to end, but when it did, a massive deluge of hail splattered against the deck.

Max let out a curse from the patio. Aegis hurried out to help him carry in the food, and by the time they had carried everything inside, they were covered with tiny chunks of ice.

"Freaking hell, it's coming down out there."

Max's hair was plastered to his head, and he had a couple bright pink spots on his face where the hail had stung him. "The storm's really picking up. I'm going to secure your barbecue so it doesn't go flying across the yard. In this rain, I doubt if the briquettes would start a fire if they fell out on the grass, but there's no point taking any chances."

He headed back outside, moving the grill so that it was resting under the eaves of the house. Short of chaining it down, there wasn't much else he could do.

Inside, Aegis and Sandy arranged the food on the table as I poured tall mugs of the hot buttered rum. By the time Max returned, the biscuits were ready. I grabbed the remote and lit the battery-operated candles in the center of the table. While I preferred flame to batteries, I wasn't betting on having power by morning, and flameless candles were just safer in a power outage.

We were eating in the kitchen rather than at the dining room table, because the dining room table was piled high with linens and china, in preparation for our guests who were coming in tomorrow. But for tonight, the Bewitching Bedlam bed-and-breakfast was ours and ours alone.

Well, that wasn't exactly true. Mr. Henry Mosswood was holed up in his room. Our semipermanent lodger had opted for dinner alone with Franny, our house ghost. The two had somehow ended up in what I assumed was a doomed-to-fail love affair—they didn't talk much about it so I wasn't sure exactly how far it had progressed. None of us understood how they were making it work, but it wasn't any of our business and I did my best to keep my nose out of it.

Another massive lightning bolt forked across the sky. I held my breath, counting. One and two and three and—*boom*. The house shook and I grabbed hold of the table.

"Holy crap," Sandy said.

Outside, hail began to bounce on the ground again.

I picked up my buttered rum, taking a long sip to soothe my nerves. "The storm is supposed to be rough, but I didn't think it was going to be *this* bad. I hope everything's okay up at the school."

Sandy's legal ward, soon to be her adopted daughter, lived at the Neverfall Academy for Gifted Students, a magical boarding school for witches. Children of all ages, from all parts of the country, attended the academy, from *Hexengarten* to grade 12. One of the largest and oldest educational institutions for members of the Otherkin community, Neverfall was also one of the most prestigious.

"Jenna is probably safer than we are. That place was built to withstand an earthquake up to a nine-pointer. So it should be able to withstand a thunderstorm." Sandy buttered a roll and bit into it, a look of bliss washing across her face. "Aegis, if you ever decide to give up the music business, you should open a bakery. I'm not kidding—you are the best baker in town."

Aegis waved her off, but he his grin told me he was gratified.

"I actually worked as a baker, about two hundred years ago. It was ideal because I worked the night shift and baked all the bread before morning. They never figured out I was a vampire, and thanks to my sourdough and rye, that shop made a killing. When I left, they begged me to stay. They offered me twice my salary because they knew they weren't going to find anybody as good as I was. At least not in that area."

As we dug into the steaks, the wind outside grew stronger. The gusts were sending branches sailing through the yard. At one point I glanced out to see a trash can go racing by. I thought I'd managed to secure them, but apparently not.

"It hasn't stormed this hard in a while," I said. "Even the storm that Fata Morgana brought with her wasn't this strong."

"If the weather doesn't let up, you two should stay here," Aegis said. "It's a rough night to go driving around the island."

We lived on Bedlam Island, a small isle out in the San Juans off the coast of Western Washington, near Lopez and Orcas islands.

Bedlam—both the island and the city that pretty much sprawled across it—boasted a population of 6,000, give or take a few. While a number of the other San Juan islands were actually protected from extreme weather, Bedlam was farther north, angled perfectly to receive the brunt of weather coming down through the Haro Strait. The island was like a storm magnet. All the magical power acted like a lightning rod for bad weather. We got heavy snow in winter, and wild windstorms in the autumn.

Founded by witches, Bedlam could cloak up to

prevent too much unwanted attention. But generally, we were open to tourists, though most were
from the Otherkin community, and a ferry ran
from the northeastern part of the island over to
Bellingham, once an hour every hour from five A.M.
until two A.M. But tonight, it wasn't running anywhere, given the rough waves on the sound.

"Did the weather report say how long it's supposed to last?" Sandy finished her dinner, and carried her plate over to the counter. "Anybody ready
for pie?"

At that moment, the lights flickered and went
out.

"Well, at least we got dinner before the power
went out." I crossed to the counter, where I had
already laid out another array of flameless candles.
I used the remote to turn them on, as well. "I'll go
start the fire in the parlor. It's going to get chilly
really quick in this drafty old mansion. Aegis, can
you check with Henry to see if he's all right? I'm
pretty sure Franny's up there with him, but make
sure everything's okay. I gave him a flashlight
and a couple battery-operated candles earlier this
afternoon."

Aegis pushed his chair back and stood. "I'll be
right back. I'll also light the candles in our room.
Do you want regular ones, or fake?"

He didn't seem to appreciate the flameless
candles. They went against his sensibilities. But
I had heard too many reports of houses burning down when careless people left the real ones
unattended. A fireplace was different. They were
built for containing a fire, and a good screen kept

the embers in. Clean it once a year and you were generally home-free.

"Fake, and be glad that we have them. Check on Bubba too, and Luna."

As Max and Sandy cleared the table and cut slices of pie, I found a flashlight and, turning it on, headed into the parlor. After turning on the candles that lined the shelves, I knelt by the fireplace. I had already prepped a fire, and now I reached out, holding my hand toward the wood. I closed my eyes and whispered, "*Fire burn bright*" and the flame flickered to life in the kindling. Within moments, a merry fire was crackling away, safe behind the metal screen.

Max and Sandy carried the pie into the parlor, and then Sandy returned to the kitchen to bring in the rest of the hot buttered rum. We curled up next to the fire, waiting for Aegis. He returned, Franny floating behind him.

Franny had been trapped in this mansion for over 200 years. She had died at a young age, at twenty-four, when she went tumbling down the stairs. We had discovered that she had been cursed—bound to the house—but we still hadn't figured out how to break the hex yet. Meanwhile, she wandered around in her blue muslin gown, doing her best to mesh with our lifestyles. She loved to read so I had set her up in the library with a computer that I kept on twenty-four seven, an e-reader app, an account for an online shopping site that I could monitor, and I had rigged it all with voice software so she could turn the pages and select what books she wanted to read. It seemed the least I could do for her, given her circumstances.

"Henry decided just to go to bed. He's all right. He's got his flashlight and candles. He said to wake him up if anything monumental happens."

Franny let out a disgruntled snort. "This little storm is nothing. You should have seen some of the storms that raged when we first came to the island." She floated over to the window, looking out. "I used to love storms when I was alive. They always made me feel so awake and aware." She turned around, hugging herself. "I miss feeling the rain on my skin. Don't ever take things like that for granted. When you lose them, and you know you've lost them, it can make life seem bleak."

I was used to her angst, but I wasn't used to her being so philosophical. Franny was, in the nicest terms possible, a habitual complainer and a perpetual victim. In fact, sometimes I thought she wasn't happy unless she was complaining.

"Is everything okay?" I scooted over, making room for Aegis. He sat down beside me, wrapping his arm around my waist and giving me a kiss on the forehead. His lips were cool, almost icy, but I was used to it. Dating a vampire had taken some getting used to, especially for *me*.

Franny shrugged, but she didn't turn around. She seemed glued to the storm. "I suppose. I suppose it's as good as it's ever going to get, given my circumstances." She let out a sigh, then glanced back at us. "I think I'll go rest. Good night." And with that, she vanished into the wall.

"Where does she go when she disappears?" Max asked.

I shrugged. "I have no idea, and I've never asked. The question has always seemed invasive to me. She seems awfully solemn, though, not at all her usual self. I wonder if she and Henry had an argument."

"It can't be easy, being in love with somebody when you're a ghost and they're corporeal. I mean, is there any *real* future for them? I wonder if she's beginning to realize the obstacles they face." Sandy paused, then lowered her voice. "Do you think she can hear me?"

I shook my head. "Franny's very good at tuning out. I can't be sure, but I think she has enough sensibilities not to eavesdrop. Why?"

"I had a sudden horrible thought. You don't think she'd ever encourage Henry to kill himself so that he could be with her, do you?" She looked almost ill at the thought.

I blinked. "What kind of late-night horror show have you been watching? *Of course* she wouldn't do that." I paused for a moment, then added, "At least, I don't think she would." I turned to Aegis. "What do you think?"

He held up his hands, leaning back. "Nope. Don't get me involved in this. I am not about to speculate on something so horrible. Franny's a good egg, and Henry's pretty damned smart. That's all I'm going to say about the idea. *And I suggest that we drop it right there.*" Aegis was pretty laid-back but when he put his foot down, he put it down hard.

"Fine," Sandy said. "Just don't blame me if something happens."

"Sandy's been watching a lot of *Ghost Inspectors*." Max laughed. The weretiger was bulky, or rather muscled, and when he laughed, his neck muscles popped. "I swear she's been binge-watching it for the past two weeks. How many seasons of that show have they made, anyway?"

Sandy stuck her tongue out at him. "Eleven. And I'm on season eight, so I have three more seasons to watch. You'll just have to deal with it." Max had recently moved in with Sandy, and even though she owned a sprawling estate, the two were in the throes of growing pains as they learned to live together. They were engaged, but neither one liked to compromise.

I lay down on the rug, staring at the ceiling. I loved this—cozy evenings spent with Aegis, Sandy, and her fiancé. Parties were fun, but I preferred small gatherings of people I loved. My former life seemed far removed—all of my former lives, really.

I was 388 years old, and I had lived a number of lifetimes within that block of time. Some of them blurred together, while others stood out as stark and harsh. But they had all played a part in bringing me to Bedlam. To who I truly was—Maudlin Gallowglass, High Priestess of the Moonrise Coven, witch, and owner of the Bewitching Bedlam bed-and-breakfast. And right now, I was the happiest that I had ever been.

I turned to Aegis. "By the way, how's Bubba? Did you find him and Luna?"

Bubba was the cjinn with whom I had shared most of my life. He was a big fat sassy orange cat. Originally from the realm of fire, cjinns were rare over here. Basically a djinn born into a cat body, cjinns were both delightful and dangerous.

"He and Luna were stretched out on your bed. They didn't seem perturbed by the thunder at all."

I snorted. "It figures. Not much bothers Bubba. I'm glad they aren't freaked, though." After a pause, I added, "Anybody want to play a game?"

"I'd rather just sit here and watch the fire and talk, if you don't mind," Sandy said. "I'm not feeling particularly festive. Or maybe I'm just lazy. After the Samhain ritual the other night, I'm pretty wiped out. I'm surprised you aren't more exhausted, considering you had to lead it."

Sandy was one of the higher-ups in the Moonrise Coven as well. We were expected to lead group rituals for the entire town on the quarter days— the solstices and equinoxes. When it came to the cross-quarter days, the coven celebrated them privately. But that still meant an incredible amount of planning, and energy expended during the ritual itself, four times a year, every year.

"I guess I'm still coming down off the adrenaline rush. Plus, we're headed into the holidays so I don't have time to let my energy flag. We've got nonstop guests booked through the end of the year, starting tomorrow. It will be good for our bank account, but I'm going to be run ragged. Add to that, the coven has to prepare for the Bedlam Yule ritual. I just don't have time to be tired."

But as I started listing off the things on my to-do list, I felt my enthusiasm wane. I loved having a bed-and-breakfast. That was one of the reasons I had moved to Bedlam. But the realities of owning a business proved far more involved than the fantasy. Plus, I hadn't counted on being elected as High Priestess of the coven. And given all that had happened over the past year, including a few dead bodies along the way, it was a wonder that I was still bouncing around as much as I was.

"I take it back. I don't want to play a game. I just want to crawl under the covers and hide." I flashed a smile at Sandy, and she laughed.

"I wondered when you would finally realize how much you've set yourself up for. Maybe you need to hire more help. Kelson does a wonderful job, but even she's going to be hard put to keep up with things if the next few months are as busy as you say they're going to be."

Aegis stretched. He would have yawned, except vampires didn't breathe. "I've been telling her to hire another housekeeper for the past six months. We can afford it—I'll pay for it, and Kelson will welcome the help."

"Why don't you? There are enough people on this island who are looking for part-time work that you should be able to find somebody without any problem. What about Snow White?"

I blinked. "Sandy, the *last* person I want to hire is an ex-porn star who literally jumped out of the pages of a storybook. Although, I have to say, what she's doing now is a whole lot better than what Ralph had her doing."

"Oh yeah? What's Snow up to?"

"She's helping out at the library, reading to some of the younger kids for story time."

The Snow White incident, as we called it, was

better off left in the past. Except you couldn't leave something in the past when there was no way to send it back to where it came from.

When Ralph Greyhoof had summoned Snow White and her band of dwarves out of the storybook, he had roped them into working as porn stars in his cheap homemade movies. Luckily, fate had intervened and Snow White and her band of merry men were no longer part of the sex worker industry. Come to think of it, Ralph Greyhoof had grown up a little bit too, although I never expected the satyr to lose his lecherous ways. It was just part of his nature.

I was about to say as much, when a tremendous crash shook the house. Jumping up, I raced for the stairs. The noise had come from upstairs and I was worried that Mr. Mosswood had taken a tumble, although that wouldn't have been enough to create the shake that we had felt.

Aegis was hot on my heels, and Sandy and Max right after him.

When I got to the second floor, I saw that Mr. Mosswood was standing outside of his room, his flashlight trained on the trapdoor in the ceiling that led to the attic crawl space.

"The noise came from up there," Henry said, pushing his glasses up on his face. He looked like he was right out of the 1950s, with thinning hair and round glasses. He reminded me of an accountant, but he was actually a historian who was writing a massive tome on the history of Bedlam. He was human, but he was born in 1840. Thanks to a curse cast on him when he was twenty-five, he was destined to never find true love, but to live for a very long time.

Aegis motioned for us to stand back. "Let me take a look first."

Max joined him. "I'm coming with you, dude."

Sandy and I stepped back against the wall along with Henry. We cautiously watched as Max gave Aegis a boost up to catch hold of the trapdoor's handle. As he jumped down, holding on to the door, a folding ladder extended to the ground. But the moment the trapdoor was open, I could tell something was wrong. For one thing, I could smell the rain coming through the roof.

Aegis scrambled up, holding the flashlight between his teeth. Once he disappeared through the opening, Max followed him. A moment later, Aegis poked his head back through the hole.

"It looks like a branch blew off a tree and crashed through the roof. A *big* branch. It's a mess up here, with debris everywhere, not to mention a couple puddles that are rapidly increasing in size. It's pouring outside. If we don't get this tarped off, by morning we're going to have a flood."

"I think we have tarps in the basement." Even though I had hired contractors to renovate the mansion when I bought it, we had purchased a number of supplies, given Sandy and I had taken on some of the painting ourselves.

"I'll get them," Sandy said.

"Are you sure? It's pretty dark down there anyway, and going with the flashlight isn't all that easy."

She shrugged. "I'm not worried about it."

As Sandy headed off for the basement, I began to crawl up the ladder, dreading what I was about to see. Roof damage was always problematic, and when I had bought the mansion, the inspector had estimated I had about five years left before I would need to completely replace the roof. Visions of dollar signs floated through my head as I poked my head into the attic. Aegis held down his hand, and I took it, hoisting myself into the crawl space. Sure enough, there was a massive hole in the roof, with a very large Douglas fir branch poking through it. It looked like the wind had ripped it off a tree and aimed the projectile directly at my house. At least it had missed the bedrooms.

"This is not my idea of redecorating," I said, staring at the branch. I reached out and poked it, reassuring myself that it was actually real.

"I suppose we're going to have to look for someone to replace the entire roof," Aegis said. "I want you to let me pay for it. The Bewitching Bedlam isn't quite making its expenses yet."

"That's an understatement," I said, stepping back as the rain began to really pour, quickly enlarging the puddles on the floor. In the dim beam of the flashlight, it was difficult to tell just how much damage there was. I hated accepting Aegis's offer to pay for the roof, but I knew that I couldn't swing it myself at this point. And my boyfriend was flush with money from all his years as a vampire. I hadn't known that when we first met, but it was a nice perk once I found out.

Max returned with the tarp, and together, he and Aegis managed to cover what they could see of the hole, nailing the tarp as best as they could to the ceiling. I held the flashlight for them, praying that Aegis wouldn't slip and impale himself on one of the branches forking off the giant limb. The last thing we needed was accidental death by tree.

Once they had finished, there wasn't anything else we could do. Nobody would be able to get over here in the middle of the night, and with the power out, it would be dangerous on the country roads anyway. I let out a long sigh, more out of frustration than anything else, and scampered back down the ladder. Aegis and Max followed, closing the trapdoor as they exited the attic.

"Well...I'm not quite sure what to do now," I said. "That was quite enough excitement to end the evening on, but I'm almost afraid to go to bed. What if the storm gets worse and causes more havoc?" Right about then, we heard a piercing noise coming from the yard. "Lovely, whose car alarm is that?" I glanced at both Sandy and Aegis. I didn't have an alarm on my car, and I didn't think Max did either.

"I'll go check. Chances are something brushed against the door," Aegis said.

"I'll go with you in case it's mine," Sandy said. She drove what looked like a retro hippie bus, but it was an expensive one and about as green as a car could get—both environmentally and in color.

As they started downstairs, I looked at Max.

"Seriously, you better stay here tonight, given the state of the storm. If it's bad enough to throw a branch through my roof, you know trees are going to be down on some of those roads that lead to your place. The guestroom is all made up, so you guys can sleep there."

"Where's Kelson? I haven't seen her all evening," Max said, following me toward the guestroom.

"I gave her the night off, considering she's going to be busier than hell the next few weeks. I hope she's okay. I haven't heard from her since she took off for the movies." I pulled out my phone, punching in her number. After three rings, it sent me to voice mail and I left a message asking her to call me.

After making sure that there were battery-operated candles in the guestroom, I laid out the bathrobes that Sandy and Max had left at my place. They stayed here often enough that we finally encouraged them to bring pajamas and robes from home and leave them for when they needed to stay.

Aegis and Sandy returned, looking glum.

"Well, my van is trashed. One of the trees lining the driveway toppled over onto it. Damn thing is crushed." She shook her head. "That cost me a fortune to have retrofitted. I'm going to have to have it completely rebuilt. Either that or I just commission a new one."

"How's the storm?" There was no way to console her. That van was her baby, and she had guided the mechanics who worked on it in everything from what she wanted under the hood to the exact color to every single option that she had chosen for it.

"I'm hoping that we're near the peak," Aegis said. "We can't afford much more damage. This is one of the worst that I've seen, and I've seen storms over my lifetime."

"I'd swear those are hurricane-force gusts out there," Sandy said. "It was hard to stand up out there. I think I'll give Jenna a call, just to make sure that she's okay. I know Neverfall is built to withstand a war, but you never know."

As she moved off to the side, I walked over to the window to stare out into the darkness. The entire neighborhood was black. It suddenly occurred to me to report the outage, and I pulled out my phone. I kept the power company's number in my contacts, just for times like these. I placed the call, waiting and punching in the numbers as the options kept coming. Finally, the automated voice on the other end told me that my outage had been reported, and that most of the island was without power. There was no estimated time of restoration.

I was about to tell the others when a shriek echoed down the stairs.

"What the fuck—?" Aegis whirled around.

"Was that Bubba?" I raced toward my bedroom, slamming open the door. But Bubba and Luna were there on the bed, staring at me with looks of alarm on their faces.

"Mr. Mosswood? Are you all right?" Sandy knocked on his door.

"I'm fine," Henry said, poking his head out. "Who screamed?"

"We're not sure. We were worried it might be you." I popped back into my bedroom. Looking at Bubba, I said, "Listen, Bubs, you and Luna stay here. Don't go prowling around, okay? It's a dangerous night."

Bubba let out a purp. "*Murrow.*"

That was Bubba-ese for "Okay, I promise." I shut the door after making sure the doors to my balcony were tightly shut and locked. Then, returning to the hall, I found that Aegis and Max had gone down to the first floor. Cautiously, Sandy and I followed.

Once downstairs, we searched through the house, but we couldn't find anything. But the shriek lingered in my ears. We had all heard it—I knew it wasn't my imagination.

"Maybe it was a cougar—there are cougars in the hills here on the island. Also, plenty of shifters. Maybe somebody is hurt out there in the storm." Sandy pressed up against the kitchen window, staring out into the rough-and-tumble night.

"Possibly." I joined her. "But we're going to have to wait until tomorrow to find out." And right then, I realized we were in for a long, exhausting night.

Chapter 2

BY THE TIME we woke up, the storm had passed. The sky was overcast, but the clouds looked lighter and they lazily drifted past. The house was chilly. The power was still out, but the tension of the storm had broken and it felt like a normal November day again.

Max, Sandy, and I gathered in the kitchen for breakfast at around eight. Aegis was asleep, of course. Sunrise had come at seven, so he had to be in his coffin by then. Vampires and sunlight made for a bad mix. Kelson had arrived home at about three A.M., having to take a few side roads to avoid fallen trees. Mr. Mosswood appeared to be sleeping late.

"What do we do about the caffeine situation?" I asked. I was a caffeine junkie. There was no way I could make it through a day without my fix, and cola just wouldn't work.

"I can run out and look for an open coffee shop, but I can guarantee you that the power's out over a good share of the island." Kelson took off her apron and folded it, hanging it over the back of the rocking chair.

"If you have a pot, I can fire up the grill and make coffee over the flames." Max jerked his thumb outside toward the barbecue, which had weathered the storm. "I've had plenty of experience on camping trips. Don't worry, one way or another you'll get your fix."

"We have bread and cheese. If you start up the grill I'll make grilled cheese sandwiches for breakfast," Kelson said. "We shouldn't trust the eggs or meat, given the power's been out for some time, but the cheese should be fine."

I glanced out the window at the yard. It was littered with debris. Fallen branches carpeted the ground. Electrical lines were probably down all over the island.

"Go ahead, Max. I'm not sure that it's safe out on the road yet. Plus, we need to crawl up on top of the roof and take a look at what happened." I turned to Kelson. "Big branch through the attic. We're going to have one hell of a cleanup job on our hands. Plus, we have guests coming in today. We can't let them stay here if we don't have electricity, so I need you to give them a call and cancel. Assure them we'll refund their deposits as soon as we're up and running with power. We should also check the estimated time of restoration."

I phoned the power company again. As I listened to the automated message, my heart sank. Power was out for more than sixty percent of the island. Crews were out and about, assessing damage, but there was no way to tell how long it would take. It could be today that our power came back on, or it could be a week. Next, I phoned Delia, the sheriff. She might have more information.

"Hey Delia, it's Maddy. I was wondering if you could give me an update on what's going on out there. Power's out here, and I gather over sixty percent of Bedlam's in the dark. Is there anything we should know about?"

Delia sounded harried. "Hey Maddy, good to hear from you. Power lines are down on a lot of the side roads, so be careful if you go out. The power company is doing its best to clear the main roads first, so that people can get out. The ferry's not running right now. The pier was damaged last night and there's no place for it to dock. Crews are on the job, but I can tell you this was one hell of a storm. At least two houses burned down and there are trees down all over the place. No fatalities, though, thank the gods."

"I know. There's a big branch poking through my attic right now. We were just about to go up on the roof and check it out." I thanked her, and asked her to keep in touch.

The others had been listening in on the conversation. I glanced at Kelson.

"That's it, then. I doubt we're going to be open to business for at least for a week." I slumped back in my seat. I hated having to disappoint people, and I tried to keep our reputation for reliability high. Granted, this was an act of nature, but it still sucked.

Max was already out back, cleaning the grill from the night before. Kelson scrounged around and found an old pan that he could use to prepare the coffee in. She also found a cast iron skillet, and went out to help him turn the bread and cheese into grilled cheese sandwiches.

Sandy and I walked out back to assess the damage. First, we wandered over to the cars. Aegis drove a black Corvette, and it looked like it had taken a few scratches from branches skittering across the hood, but otherwise, it seemed to be in one piece. My CR-V had lucked out, escaping without a scratch. But then we came to Sandy's retro hippie mobile.

The van was a bright lime green, with pink and orange and blue flowers painted on it. It captured the spirit of the 1960s, but in looks only. She had had it retrofitted with every comfort, and to make it as ecologically sound as possible. But now, that beautiful shining green van had a massive fir tree lying across the middle of it. The tree had fallen dead center, squashing the van and almost cutting it in half. Luckily, no one had been inside of it.

"I don't think there's much left to fix," I said cautiously, stepping around to the other side.

Sandy let out a groan. "Buying a new car this month wasn't in my plans. And it will take me a couple months to commission another one of these." She sighed. "Lihi, I need you."

Within seconds, a very cute twelve-inch-high homunculus appeared. Lihi and Sandy had forged a contract together. Lihi was at Sandy's beck and call whenever she needed, and in return, Sandy paid her two crystals a month—extremely prized currency in Lihi's realm. Lihi did whatever Sandy asked, and the two were bound to each other for at least seven years. Lihi looked like a winged faerie with a long tail, bat wings, and pointed ears. She wore pink leather hot pants and a matching halter top.

"You need me, boss?" Lihi caught sight of the van and let out a gasp. "Uh oh. That's not good." She flew over to the van and landed on the roof near the front.

"No shit, Sherlock. I need you to go back to my place and see how Alex is faring. Tell him what happened to the van, and have him drive over here in the sedan. Max and I are going to need a way to get home. Also, have him contact my insurance company and open a claim on the van. Let me know when you get in touch with him." Sandy just shook her head as she stared at the van. "Sometimes, Mama Nature can be a bitch."

Lihi gave her a salute and vanished. More than once, Sandy had encouraged me to forge a contract with a homunculus, but given that I had a cjinn and had recently picked up an owl as a familiar who decided that I was his witch, that would be more responsibility than I could handle.

We turned and walked away from the cars, heading into the back yard. I had three acres of land, part of it forest land. I planned to turn the forest into a campground and rent out spaces for people who would rather go glamping than stay in the bed-and-breakfast.

My immediate back yard consisted of an entire lot, with several large oak and maple trees near the house. But the branch that was jutting through my roof seemed to have come from one of the Douglas firs near the driveway. It was massive, but the storm had ripped it off like stripping paper off a signboard. It had punched a hole directly through the roof in what looked to be several places.

"I'm going to need a ladder," I said.

Sandy gave me a sideways look. "Maddy, you do not need to go climbing a ladder. Let's face facts. You're not the most athletically inclined person. Leave this to the professionals."

Frustrated, I gave in. She was right. I was neither adept nor graceful when it came to physical activity, and the roof looked like it had been through a tornado, slick with leaves and branches scattered over the shingles as well as the hole.

"All right. Who should I call? You know anyone who can take down a tree?" I knew the president of the local arborists group, but they met to discuss trees, not fix roofs or do the heavy lifting of removing downed trees.

"Didn't Ralph have a branch crash through his roof last month? When Fata Morgana was here?"

I blinked. Sandy was right. "Yeah. We'll walk over there in a while and ask him who he called. But I will tell you, my idea of fun does not include a morning spent fending off Ralph Greyhoof's advances. Or his digs."

The satyr was constantly ogling every woman he came across, and he was a social nightmare. He and I had a lot of baggage between us, because he had decided that I opened up the Bewitching Bedlam in order to steal his customers. He and his brothers ran the Heart's Desire Inn, ostensibly a small country hotel. But the reality was that they were operating a brothel catering to sex-hungry women just aching to be serviced by horny satyrs.

I had tried to get it through his thick skull that *I* wasn't infringing on *his* clientele in the least. The women—and a few men—who booked rooms at his inn weren't looking for what I was offering, and there wasn't a chance in hell they'd find what they wanted at the Bewitching Bedlam. Ralph and I were attempting to put our animosity aside because unfortunately, the feud he had started had inadvertently led to at least one death.

I looped my arm through Sandy's. "How about we go take a look in the attic, now that it's light?"

"I've got a better idea," she said. "Why don't we have coffee and breakfast first? That will put us both in a better mood, though I'm thinking mimosas might take the edge off even more."

"Yeah, but do you really want to be full of champagne when we head over to Ralph's?"

She grinned. "Good point. All right. Coffee it is."

We were waiting on breakfast when Lihi returned.

"Alex and Mr. Peabody are fine. The house is good. A tree came down in the yard, but it didn't hit anything," the homunculus said. "But Alex won't be able to get here until around five. There's a big tree blocking the main road in front of your house, and it's slow going with the chain saw. He was told that they'd have it clear around four, so expect him after that."

"Thanks, Lihi. Why don't you pop over and tell Jenna that we're okay. The school passed through unscathed except for the power outage, but I imagine she'd be happy to see you." Sandy waved as Lihi saluted her, then vanished. "I hope Lihi never decides to give up this gig. I've come to rely on her a lot. In fact, I've grown very fond of that little homunculus. And Jenna just adores her."

"I can see why," I said, sniffing as the aroma of food and coffee hit me. My stomach rumbled. "Come on. Time to eat."

Good to their word, Max and Kelson had coffee, grilled cheese sandwiches, and a fruit salad waiting. Henry had come down and was eating at the dining room table, his nose in a book. He was always polite about respecting our privacy, and I didn't mind that he had made himself a regular lodger. He paid his rent—I had lowered it because he paid by the month—and never caused trouble. But given the situation, I thought I should offer him the option of moving to another hotel. I sat down beside him and he pushed his book back, marking his place with an embroidered bookmark.

"Henry, we have no clue when the power's going to be back on. And we have to have the roof fixed. Are you sure you still want to stay here? We're not going to be able to provide hot meals or water for at least a couple of days, I think."

He blinked, then shook his head. "That's not a problem. I can always go to the gym and take a shower there, provided they have electricity. And I don't mind eating out for a few days."

I let out a sigh. "Well, I don't feel right taking full rent from you for this time. How about a twenty-five percent discount until we're back up and running at normal operations?"

Henry pushed his glasses up on his nose and nodded. "Don't worry about me. I'm good. Besides, I want to make certain Franny is all right. I hate to say it, but I think I upset her last night. And I haven't seen her this morning."

"Right." I wasn't sure what to say. Whatever they were up to was none of my business, but I could only foresee it ending in heartache. I stood and headed back to the kitchen.

Once we ate and had our coffee, which Max had masterfully crafted, Sandy and I headed over to Ralph's. Kelson and Max had decided to poke around in the attic, and I decided to let them. Both were sturdy as hell, and frankly, I didn't want to just rely on someone I was paying to fix the mess to give me the full picture.

As Sandy and I strolled down the road toward Ralph's place, the evidence of how bad the storm had been was everywhere. Tree after tree had come down, and a few live power lines were buzzing along the side of the road. We called them in, and I was grateful that at least the cell towers were still up and functioning.

The Heart's Desire Inn was picturesque, surrounded by rose bushes and hydrangeas. In summer they were a profusion of color. A beautiful old oak tree had stood in the front yard, but it came down during a storm in October. The inn itself was a two-story house, with siding the color of white mist, and red and gold trim around the windows. Flower boxes containing the last of the autumn marigolds rested beneath each window. The door was bright red, with a brass handle and door knocker.

I had to give it to the Greyhoof boys, they had good taste when it came to decor. Although, come to think of it, a number of the recent upgrades were due to Ralph's current girlfriend, Ivy Vine. Wood nymphs *always* had expensive tastes, and she was rubbing off on Ralph in all the right ways. I just prayed she never found out about the brief tryst he had had with Fata Morgana, because wood nymphs also had nasty tempers and they didn't like to share lovers unless it was *their* idea. All in all, she had been a good influence on Ralph and he was easier to manage since he had taken up with her.

As we ascended the steps, stepping over several broken branches that the wind had flung against the house, the door opened and Ralph peeked out. He was about six-three, with well-defined muscles. The fur on his legs was silky brown and his hair was swept back in a ponytail that hung down to his butt. His eyes were smoky topaz, and he flashed his very white teeth at us. I suspected he'd been to the dentist for a bleaching treatment.

"Maddy, what can I do for you?" He glanced at Sandy. "Morning."

"Hey, Ralph. I need the name of the company you used when the tree came down in your yard." I pulled out my phone, bringing up the note app.

Ralph groaned. "Don't tell me you got hit?"

"Tree on Sandy's car. Tree branch through my roof. Double whammy. So, do you still have his number?" I hoped he wouldn't refuse to help. Ralph's paranoia had calmed some, but he was still one of the most suspicious satyrs I had ever met. And I had dated more than a few in my time.

He stared at us, then stepped back and opened the door. "I'll get his name for you."

When we entered the inn, it was as dark as my house. Apparently they had been hit by the power outage as well. We followed him into the living room and sat on the edge of the sofa while he vanished through a door. I stared at one of the recliners, trying to bleach my brain from the image of Fata Morgana impaled on Ralph's cock. I had accidentally barged in on them, and frankly, that was a sight I could go my life without seeing again.

"You're imagining it, aren't you?" Sandy poked me in the arm. She knew the story.

I stuck my tongue out at her. "Don't even go there."

"Remember, they invited you to join them. You could have been part of that little ménage."

"Shut up. Fata's the one who invited me, not Ralph. And like *you've* never had a threesome with a satyr before." I glared her into submission. We had a long past together, and there had been a crazy time when we partied balls-to-the-wall, hanging out with a group of satyrs and wood nymphs, doing just about everyone we encountered.

Just then, Ralph emerged from the back and handed me a piece of paper with the name, address, and phone number of the tree company written on it.

"They're good. They didn't take too long and they were reasonably priced." He paused, then added, "I'm sorry I seemed so gruff at the door. I just... Ivy found out about Fata," he blurted out.

I groaned. "Yeah, that would do it. Who told her?"

"Me. I was watching *Dr. Phil* and he was talking about the need for openness and honesty in a relationship and..."

Sandy and I stared at him. "*You* were watching *Dr. Phil*?"

Ralph shrugged, blushing. "I thought I could learn how to be a better boyfriend."

"Dude, next time, come to us. Ivy's a wood nymph. They're fucking jealous as hell when they've claimed a man. I've partied down with them—Sandy too—but they were unattached. The moment a wood nymph claims you, you do *not* tell her you boinked a would-be goddess. Even though Fata lured you into it, you just don't blurt that out to your wood nymph girlfriend." I rubbed my forehead. "Did she break up with you?"

He shook his head. "Not exactly. She's decided that I need to prove my love."

Sandy and I locked gazes. That could mean a variety of things, but Ralph wasn't on the swift side, and there was a good chance the wood nymph was having fun at his expense.

"How so?" I asked, pocketing the address.

"Well, I'm working a night job too, now, because she insists on an emerald bracelet. She also forced me to go on a diet, I'm at the gym three times a week, and she won't have sex with me until she says I've learned my lesson. She won't let me take care of my guests, either."

Sandy arched her eyebrows. "By 'taking care' of your guests I'm assuming she means you can't sleep with them."

He nodded. "That's really hurt business. My brothers are good, but not as good as I am."

"You do know that, generally, innkeepers and bed-and-breakfast owners don't sleep with their customers, Ralph. Right?" I said it softly, thinking maybe this was the chance to get through to him how different our businesses actually were.

"Maybe not, but it worked for us. In the past three weeks, we've had four guests check out early, claiming they didn't get what they paid for." His shoulders slumped. The satyr looked defeated. "I don't know what to do. My brothers are pissed at me. My girlfriend is pissed at me. They're all pissed at each other. It's one big pissing contest."

I didn't want to be stuck giving him advice. For one thing, if it backfired I knew full well that Ralph would blame me. For another, it was just such a nasty situation that I really didn't want to get involved. But Sandy stepped up to the plate.

"Ralph, what matters to you most? The inn, or your girlfriend? Because unless your brothers agree to switch directions on how you cater to your guests, you're not going to be able to please them. And if you want to make Ivy happy, then you'll have to change the focus of your clientele."

"I was afraid you'd say that," the big lug grumbled.

"Do you love Ivy? And I'm talking more than *lust* here. Do you truly love her? Can you see yourself making a life with her?" I couldn't imagine Ralph settling down, but stranger things had happened.

Ralph sat down in the recliner and once again, I had a flash of him and Fata. I must have grimaced because he got a big dopey grin on his face. "You wish it had been *you* and not her, right?"

I counted to five before answering. It didn't help.

"You idiot. *This* is why Ivy's pissed at you. You can't even be around another woman without making some lewd comment, can you? Even though your...tryst...with Fata wasn't exactly your fault, the fact is that Ivy knows that a relationship with you has got to be a challenge."

He blinked, looking startled. "What? You mean I can't even joke around?"

"Jokes are supposed to be funny, not creepy. *Telling* another woman that you think she wants to fuck you is slimy. *Especially* when you're supposed to be in love with somebody else." I threw up my hands. "You know what? You want to keep Ivy? You're going to have to pray for a miracle. Because I just don't believe you have the monogamy gene in you. But then, satyrs usually don't, so I have no clue why Ivy thinks you can manage it. That's why most of you aren't married. Thanks for the info on the roofers." I turned to Sandy. "Come on, let's go."

Ralph followed us to the door, a hangdog look on his face. "I'm sorry, Maddy—I didn't mean it. Really."

As I headed toward the steps, I turned around and stared at him. "I'm not the one you need to apologize to. If you really, *truly* want to keep Ivy, you're going to have to decide what matters most to you. And then put your money where your mouth is."

As Sandy and I headed up the road, back to the Bewitching Bedlam, Ralph followed us out and watched us leave. I couldn't help but feel that he was watching our asses rather than mulling over the advice we had given him.

BY NOON, THE tree trimming company—Dev's Tree Service—had arrived. It didn't hurt that Sandy offered to pay for rush service, given we needed to get the tree off of her van so it could be hauled away. Dev Myers and his crew took one look at the downed fir and grimaced.

"I'll set my men to cutting up the tree on Ms. Clauson's van while I take a look at the branch on your roof and the tree it came from." He paused. "Do you also want me to check the other trees in your yard to see if any of them have been damaged or compromised? I'm also an arborist."

I nodded. "Wonderful. Please, do what you need to do. We're entering storm season and I'd rather be safe than sorry."

Visions of dollar bills floated away as he rubbed his hands together and headed out to take a look. He was half-human, he had told us when he arrived. His father was a wood spirit, his mother was human, and so he had a leg up on trees. He was quite capable of talking to them and getting them to answer. A regular tree whisperer. Whether they ever lied to him, I wasn't sure, but I trusted his educated opinion a lot more than my calculated guess.

Kelson had built new fires in the fireplaces. Although grateful the chimneys were away from the area where the tree had crashed through, I still incanted a fire charm to protect the house from any wayward sparks.

Max decided to go up top and watch Dev, so Sandy and I curled up in the parlor, wine in hand and under microfiber throws as we waited for the verdict. Kelson had emptied the refrigerator of questionable food, and set out to see what she could find for dinner. I had thrown money at her and told her to buy whatever was hot and comforting, and make certain to get plenty of it.

"At least this happened before Thanksgiving," Sandy said.

"Yeah, but for us, the holiday season starts this week. Business soars this time of year. We had to cancel three bookings for today and we have more scheduled later this week."

From his perch in the corner of the room, Lanyear let out a soft hoot. The owl had recently come into my life. He was a gift from Arianrhod, the goddess I was pledged to. Not only was the owl her totem, but as a familiar, he was exceptionally astute in the use of magic. We were still finding our way with each other, but he was definitely a member of the house now. It had taken some doing, but I had finally convinced Bubba that Lanyear wasn't a toy. And I had promised Bubba a bright shiny new cat condo if he would keep Luna from going after the owl. While I had a suspicion that Lanyear would win out in a confrontation, I didn't want to test out my theory.

Lanyear was a barred owl, mottled brown that bordered on gray. Now, he flashed an image into my mind, but I couldn't quite make out what it was supposed to be. The image was fuzzy, almost shadowed, but there was an ancient feeling to it, and while I couldn't quite penetrate the origin, whatever it was made me feel queasy and unsettled.

Lanyear hooted again, a warning in his voice.

"Something's wrong, isn't it?" I asked.

He just blinked, then closed his eyes again and tucked his head under one wing.

Sandy stared up at him. "How goes it with him?"

"Slow. We're finding our way. This isn't like Bubba. Bubba's my buddy and companion, but he's not a familiar and he has his own mind about magic. Unfortunately, as you well know."

Bubba was a practical joker, as well as a cjinn. The combo could be lethal, but with Bubba, it just tended to be embarrassing. Rub a cjinn's belly and they might grant you a wish, but like most djinns, they tended to twist it for their own amusement. And they could pluck a wish from your mind—you didn't have to ask them.

Bubba had saved my life with his magic more than once, but he also had a paw in encouraging me to dye my hair blond, even though I had known it was a mistake, and he had been responsible for a very bad fashion fail when I ended up buying a fuckton of leopard print.

Lanyear, on the other hand, was fully *owl*, but since Arianrhod had sent him to me, he was a gift and a tool as well as a friend. I didn't joke around with Lanyear. Bubba, however, I could play with and tease, as long as I could take his teasing in return.

Max suddenly popped his head into the room. "Maddy, you're going to want to hear what Dev has to say. He's got an estimate for you."

Frowning, I sat down my goblet and followed him out, leaving Sandy to snuggle by the fire. I pulled on my jacket as I left the parlor. The old mansion was drafty and without the furnace going, it was as cold inside as it was outside, except for the areas directly around the fireplaces.

Dev was waiting for me on the back patio. He motioned for me to follow him. We hiked over to the massive oak near the side yard.

"The oak is fine. And so are most of the trees, though there's one cottonwood I'd recommend taking out, given it will destroy your house foundations pretty soon. But it's on the other side that you have to worry. The tree that branch came from? It has to come down."

He was talking nonstop, without giving me a chance to get a word in edgewise.

"I think it was unstable to begin with. Now, the wind has almost torn up the roots. If you don't take down the fir, it will topple, and if the tree goes down, so will your front porch and the side of your house. You'll have more than just a hole in the roof to deal with."

"Crap. Okay, well, take both trees down. Anything else?"

He nodded, sticking his pencil behind his ear as he motioned for me to follow him over to the driveway. "Here, you have two options. Most of the trees are fine, except for one of the cedars. It seems to be having problems. There's not enough room for it, and the root system is very shallow. It's small enough that if it goes down it won't hit your house or the cars, but it will fall into the other trees."

"If it hits the other trees, will it weaken them?"

"It could. So I can either take it down, or you can wait to see if it manages to grow deeper roots before the wind catches it."

I frowned. I hated taking down trees unless it was necessary. "How much is this going to run, for everything?"

"Cutting up the tree on the van, taking the branch off your roof, taking down the cottonwood and the damaged fir, altogether you can plan for about two thousand dollars. If we take the cedar too, another five hundred." He showed me the written estimate he had prepared.

I really didn't want to spend that much, but it made sense to bite the bullet and have it all done at once. "You say the rest of the trees around the house are fine?"

"As far as I can tell, they're all fit as a fiddle. We can have this all done by tonight, I think. We've got work stacked up for days, given this storm, so if you want to book us to take down the three trees, best to do so now, or you're going to have to wait."

"Oof, you just hit me where it hurt, dude. All right, get to work. I'll go call a roof doctor so they can get right in as soon as you're done."

I glanced at my phone. It needed charging and it needed it soon. I texted Sandy to meet me at the car, and as I began to call roofers, hoping to find somebody who could get right to work, we charged our phones and drove around the neighborhood, trying to avoid the havoc that littered the roads and yards.

We were almost back to the house when Max texted me.

GET BACK HERE NOW, MADDY. WE FOUND SOMETHING IN THE ATTIC WHEN THEY TOOK THE TREE OUT AND YOU'RE GOING TO WANT TO SEE THIS. I GUARANTEE IT.

With that ominous-sounding message, we pulled into the driveway and headed for the house.

Chapter 3

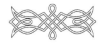

AS I GINGERLY made my way up the ladder and onto the roof, Max reached down to help me.

"Why couldn't I just come through the trapdoor? I don't like climbing on the roof. I'm not all that graceful." I grabbed hold of his hand and clung to the edge as he gave me a good yank, hauling me up and over the eaves. He walked back up the roof, but I wasn't that brave. I decided to crawl up the slope to where the tree branch was being cleared.

"Because they aren't done removing the branch. Debris could fall on you. Come on, I won't let you fall," Max said, coaxing me to stand.

I gave him a suspicious look. "Are you *sure*? I'm not exactly Miss Graceful here."

"I promise. Give me your hand and I'll steady you. It's dangerous for you to crawl. Too many splinters and possible nails." He guided me to my feet and held onto my hand as he led me up the slope of the roof. I tried not to look over my shoulder toward the ground. Two stories and a crawl space high was two stories and a crawl space too many.

"You're doing just fine," he said as I inched my way forward. We reached the place where the branch had impaled itself through the roof. I grimaced, seeing the wide hole it had left. Dev and his men had managed to extricate part of the branch, but there was still a massive amount of debris left in its wake.

"What do I need to look at?" I couldn't tell what the problem was, other than the gaping hole in the shingles.

"Over here. Look." Max led me to one edge of the hole. He pointed to the other edge. "That's the attic, right?"

"Right. And?" I still wasn't seeing whatever it was he wanted me to look at.

"Okay, the wall to the attic stops here." He pointed a flashlight midway into the hole. "But there seems to be another room beyond the attic. That's not just empty space. Do you have two attics?"

I squinted, following the beam of the flashlight. I could see what he was talking about. There was the attic wall, all right, and beyond it, another open space and what looked like a finished wall on the other side.

"What the hell? No, we *don't* have a two-room attic. At least not that I know of." I leaned forward, trying to make out anything I could, but Max grabbed my shoulder.

"You're getting close to a patch of the roof that was damaged by the branch. You don't want to go tumbling in through the shingles."

"No, I meant what the hell *is* that space? There's no door in the attic that I can remember. I'm going down to check." I suddenly froze, unsure of how to get down without stumbling headfirst off the edge. When I was in an ecstatic state, I could sometimes levitate, but it wasn't anything I could control, nor did I want to chance losing my concentration halfway down. "Um, Max...I don't do well looking over the edge of anything high up. How do I get down?"

He frowned. "I suppose you could try crawling, though it's not safe. Or we could lower you into the attic crawl space, but that might further damage the roof."

"How much worse could it get? There's a hole in the damned thing already." I stared at the opening. "How do we do this?"

Dev had been watching our interplay and now he walked over, holding a rope. "Let's tie this around your waist and we can lower you in that way. But my company's not responsible if you break a nail or get a splinter."

I gave him a long, hard look. "Dev, you're good at what you do, but if you patronize me again, I'll fucking show you just how much I care about breaking a nail. I used to be one of the most feared vampire hunters on the Continent, and it wouldn't take long for me to get back into training."

He blinked, then adjusted his tool belt. I couldn't tell what he was thinking, but I didn't give a damn. "I apologize, Ms. Gallowglass. Let me tie the rope around your waist and we'll lower you down."

I held out my arms, letting Dev and Max rig the rope up around my waist. Then, I dangled my legs over the edge of the hole, feeling the shingles beneath me start to cave in from where they'd been weakened. But before they could break through, the men lowered me down into the attic. I managed to find the trapdoor in the dark and opened it, dropping the ladder down into the hallway. I paused to text Sandy, then using the flashlight on my phone, made my way over to the wall that divided the attic from the secret area. Sandy joined me from the hallway, scampering up the ladder, bringing a larger flashlight with her. We began to comb the wall, looking for any sign of a door.

"This paneling makes it hard to see anything," she said.

The wall was paneled in what looked like it had been white shiplap originally. We searched every inch, but found nothing. Up top, the noise continued as they finished removing the last of the branch.

Max peeked through the hole. "Heads up, the hole leading into the other side is big enough for me to get through. I'm going down to see what I can find out. Dev will hold the rope long enough for me to get in and out."

I nodded, waiting. A few minutes later, a rapping on the other side of the wall alerted us. We could hear Max shouting.

"Mark the wall here. There's a door on this side that must have been covered up over on your side. I'll tap around the edges so we can figure out a way to get in."

"Let me get something to mark it with!" I turned to Sandy. "You have a pen on you?"

She shook her head. "No, but let me get one. I'll be right back." She hurried back toward the ladder, but Dev shouted through the hole into the attic and tossed her a pencil. She brought it over and we roughly traced the opening as Max tapped away on the other side. When we were done, we had two-foot wide, four-foot-tall rectangle marked out.

A few moments later, Max joined us inside, dropping down from the hole into the attic.

I glanced at him. "What's over there?"

"I didn't get a good look, but it's an odd room, I'll tell you that. There are a bunch of things over there, and I'm not at all certain what they are. I didn't want to touch anything until we get some solid light going in there. But at least we know where to look." He stared at the shiplap. "Some-body wanted to cover it up, that much is for sure. I'm not sure why, but the energy feels very thick and cloistered. I felt claustrophobic."

"I had no clue there was a room back there. I wonder if it was there when Franny was alive. We should ask her." I stood back, contemplating the roof. "Is Dev securing a tarp over the entire hole? I haven't heard back yet from the roofer I called."

"Yeah, then he and his guys will tackle taking down the three trees. The tow truck's on the way for Sandy's van, now that the tree is off of it."

A moment later, the room went dark except for the glow of the flashlights. I glanced up and saw a deep blue canvas stretched taut over the hole. Another moment and we heard the sound of pounding as Dev tacked down the tarp. It was heavy enough to prevent leaking, and it did help to keep the wind from blowing through. I glanced back at the markings on the wall one last time before following Max and Sandy down the ladder, back into the hallway.

"Well, that was interesting," I said as my phone rang.

Grateful to see it was Alpha-Pack Construction, I answered. While they weren't the best company around, they were quick and usually efficient, if you paid them enough. Leonard Wolfbrane, the owner, promised they could come assess the roof as soon as we wanted, but I needed to make an appointment now before they got totally booked up.

I debated whether to call the insurance company about it. They wouldn't pay for a new roof, and if I only needed a patch, I'd rather not have the ding on my record. Aegis and I had already made the decision this was as good a time as any to have the roof redone, so I decided to just go with the flow. I glanced at the time. It was already two and the power still wasn't back on.

"What about tomorrow morning? Nine o'clock?" I decided I might as well just bite the bullet and get started.

Leonard paused, then said, "It's on the calendar. We'll be there. Thanks, Maddy, for your repeat business. You'll get a ten percent discount for being a returning customer." He disconnected.

I stared at the phone for a moment. I knew Leonard from the Bedlam City Council. He was punctual, that much I could say for him, and his company had done a decent job on renovating my bathrooms when I first bought the mansion.

"Any idea on estimated time of restoration on the power?" Sandy dusted off her jeans. "I hope Alex gets here soon. We should really go home. I need to change. I hate wearing clothes more than a day."

"Oh, don't worry about that. At least not until Aegis gets up. He'll be waking in a couple of hours. Sunset is 4:36 today, and it's almost quarter after two." I didn't want them to go. I hated the fact that there was a hole in my roof, and a secret room I had known nothing about. Without the power on, the mansion loomed large and echoing around me.

Sandy took pity on me. "All right. Alex said it would be after four thirty before he could get here, anyway."

Kelson had returned with several bags of take-out. "The shops that have power and are open, are jammed. The sheriff wasn't kidding when she said over sixty percent of the island was dark. I managed to get a big bucket of chicken, some pot stickers and egg rolls, and a couple dozen doughnuts. I figured that would hold everybody for a while."

"Save some for Aegis. Even though he doesn't have to eat, he likes his food."

Sandy and I helped Kelson lay out the food. She had also thought to get paper plates. I knew we had some, but where they were, I had no clue. And in an emergency, it was just easier to buy new and know you had what you needed.

Max washed his hands, then joined us as we

gathered around the table. I asked Kelson to tell Henry Mosswood that dinner was ready.

"He's not here," Franny said, interrupting as she walked out of the wall. "He asked me to tell you that he decided to go downtown for dinner and a movie, since the cinema has power."

Well, that was one fewer person we had to worry about feeding. Grateful, I changed the subject.

"Hey, Franny, I have a question. When the tree busted through the roof, we found a secret room. We can't get in there yet—it's walled off. But there's a door on the far side of the attic behind the shiplap. It leads to a private room. Do you know anything about what's back there or when it was walled off?" I piled my plate high with mashed potatoes, fried chicken, pot stickers, and a couple egg rolls.

A quiet look of contemplation swept over the ghost's face. "No, I don't. Not that I can remember. When I was alive, the attic did seem larger, now that you mention it. But I never thought to see if there was something behind the wall."

"Maybe someone who owned the mansion after your parents died walled off part of the room? If it seems smaller than when you were alive, that would be the most logical guess." I paused, then asked, "What do you know about any of the owners between then and now? Do you remember any of them?"

Franny tilted her head, absently stepping through the table till she was standing right through the mashed potatoes.

"Could you not stand in the food?" I knew that

she wasn't really touching it, but it still gave me the creeps.

She blinked, looking down. "Oh! I'm sorry. I know that bothers you." She quickly stepped to the side, away from the table, and moved into the dining room corner. "Let me think. I've been here a long time, you know. That's a lot of memories to go through."

"Not a problem," I said, digging into my meal. The food was still hot and it tasted wonderful. Kelson looked exhausted.

"You were in late. You should take a nap after dinner," I said to her. "There's not much we can do till—oh, I forgot to call to find out about the power." I pulled out my phone and placed a call to Pacific Bedlam Power—PBP. The automated voice reported that we should have power back in our neighborhood by seven P.M. "Well, that's better news than tomorrow."

Sandy called as well. "Not such good news for me. Out by my house, it's not supposed to be restored till tomorrow night, around midnight."

"You can take a hot shower before you go home. Or just stay the night here again."

She shook her head. "I may take you up on the shower, but after that, we have to go home and make sure Mr. Peabody's all right." Mr. Peabody was Sandy's pet skunk. He wasn't magical, except when Bubba granted his wish to get his scent glands back, but he was a loving little creature and adored both Sandy and Jenna. He wasn't so sure about Max, but neither did he shy away from the weretiger.

"You know, I remember vague images of people who lived here. As I've said before, most of them never noticed me, or if they did, they left me alone. A few were spooked by my presence. But I do remember one person who stood out. There was a woman here, many years ago—I think it had to be a few years after the turn of the century, 1915 maybe? I don't know, but around there. Anyway, she gave *me* the creeps. There always seemed to be a cloud hovering over the house while she lived here. I remember wishing I could leave, but never being able to. I mostly stayed in the basement because she didn't go down there much. I don't remember a lot, but I do remember there were workmen in the house while she was here." Franny shrugged. "I'm sorry, but that's it. That's the only memory that stands out."

"That's fine." I thought for a moment. "What was she like? The woman? Do you remember anything about her? Why did she give you the creeps?"

Franny sighed, looking put-upon. She was good with melodrama, that was for sure, and she milked it for all it was worth.

"Well, let me think. She felt *dangerous*. I don't know how to explain it, but it felt like she would be a dangerous person to have for an enemy, and an even more dangerous one to have as a friend. She was tall, with long black hair, and really full lips. And oddly enough, she seemed frightened. That's all I can remember." She vanished back into the wall before I could ask anything else.

"I guess she got bored." Max picked up a biscuit.

"I suppose so. Well, that gives me a time frame,

at least. I think I'll look into the previous owners of the Bewitching Bedlam. We know about Franny's family, but I don't know much about anybody who bought the place after them."

There was a resounding thump from the front door. I frowned, then remembered the big old knockers we had installed. With the power out, the bell wouldn't be working.

Kelson jumped up. "I'll get it. You eat." She vanished into the dining room, heading toward the front door. A moment later, the sound of loud voices echoed into the kitchen, and then, before I knew what was happening, an all-too-familiar figure entered the room.

I slowly stood, pushing my chair back as Sandy let out a gasp.

"What the fuck do *you* want?" My stomach felt like it had just been punched in the gut. For the first time in over a year, I found myself staring at my ex—Craig Vincent Astor. And that was one face I'd have been happy never to lay eyes on again.

"CRAIG? WHAT THE *hell* are you doing in my house?" I crossed my arms so I wouldn't be tempted to stab him with my fork. Craig had been my one foray into dating a human. Well, the one foray into *marrying* a human. To say that it hadn't worked out would be an understatement.

He was still just as tall and smarmy looking as I remembered. Five-ten, toned and trim, and with every hair in place on his precious head, and a few fewer wrinkles around the eyes than I remembered, he was wearing an expensive black jacket that I pegged as Armani, and a pair of Italian loafers that probably cost half a grand. Craig was a lawyer, a snob, and an abusive buttmunch whom I had wasted eight years of my life on.

Craig glanced around the room, then his gaze landed on Sandy and his eyes narrowed. The two of them had never gotten along. He had called her a whore one too many times and she had threatened to wither his pecker. However, when he saw Max sitting next to her, he quickly looked away. Max was stocky and fit, and looked every inch capable of taking down someone like Craig. From the scar that traced its way from his left temple to his chin, to the beefy biceps that showed beneath his close-fitting cashmere sweater, Max was an imposing alpha male.

"Can't you live in a normal town? I had to pay someone to bring me over in a boat because the goddamned ferry's out and then rent a fucking car."

I blinked. "Not my problem, dude."

"Whatever. We need to talk." It was a demand, not a question or a request. Craig had always assumed that his demands would be met.

I stared at him, debating on whether to toss him out on his ass, or find out what he wanted. No doubt it was something stupid, but my curiosity got the better of me. But I was going to make him pay to talk to me.

"Say please."

"What did you say?" His eyes narrowed as he swung around to stare at me.

"I said, 'Say please.' As in '*Please*, Maudlin, do you have the time to speak to me?' It's really not that difficult, Craig. At least not for *most* people. I do, however, realize that polite conversation tends to be outside your venue." I moved forward a step. He was in my house and my territory, and I wasn't about to let him have the upper hand.

He clutched his keys in one hand, the tension squaring his jaw as he clenched his teeth. I could sense the impending explosion. I had muted myself for years with him. I had learned to walk on eggshells. But I was done with that. *Forever*.

"Do you have time or don't you?" He tried to lock gazes with me, but I just laughed.

"Even now, even after all this time, you refuse to be civil. I didn't ask you to come here. You didn't call to make certain I would welcome your visit. So you'd better learn how to say please really fast or I'll call the cops and have you thrown off my property." I half-hoped he wouldn't. I wasn't sure I wanted to be alone with him, even in my own house. Craig could be dangerous, and he held grudges for the stupidest things.

A moment later, he let out an angry huff.

"*Please* take some time out of your precious schedule to talk to me," he said.

The ball was in my court. He'd met the challenge. Now I had to talk to talk to him. I glanced over at Sandy and Max.

"Are you sure you want to do this, Maddy? You don't have to." Sandy started to stand, but Craig turned on her.

"I don't need *your* interference, bitch. You already did enough damage."

The words were barely out of his mouth when Craig found himself against the wall, with Max holding him by the lapels.

"I suggest you apologize to both of these ladies before I forget my manners and let my tiger out to play. I haven't played cat and mouse in a *long* time." Max's eyes were burning and even from here, I could smell the anger coming off the were-tiger. The scent of pheromones was overwhelming.

Craig let out a strangled yelp. "I'll sue you for assault—"

"Go ahead, lawyer boy. *I've* got the best lawyers money can buy and they'll whip your ass in court. Now apologize." Max slid him higher on the wall.

Craig squeaked out an "I'm sorry" and Max opened his fists, stepping back. Craig went tumbling to the floor. As he picked himself up, I could see he was stewing for a fight, but he wasn't stupid enough to take on someone who could beat the crap out of him.

"Nice friends you've got, Maud." He turned back to me. "Now can we talk?"

"You've got five minutes. Come into the kitchen." I wasn't about to take him into the parlor where he could shut the door and get me alone.

We entered the kitchen and at that moment, the lights flickered and came on. I let out a long breath. One problem solved. In the sudden brilliance of the overheads, Craig looked less suave than I remembered him looking. In fact, he looked a little rough around the edges. He had a five-o'clock shadow and dark circles under his eyes. And his hairdresser had missed a few gray hairs that were peppered in among the black.

"Five minutes. What do you want?" I set the kitchen timer, then leaned against the counter.

He snorted. "Always so gracious, aren't you, Maddy?"

"Gracious to those who deserve it, yes. You have four minutes, forty seconds. Better hop to it, dude." I wasn't going to let him bait me into an argument. I glanced at the clock. Four thirty-five. One minute and Aegis would be awake.

"I need your magic. You're going to cast a spell for me." Again, a demand, not a request.

I let out a peal of laughter. "Oh, that's rich. Thanks, I needed that laugh. *You* need my magic? You hated the fact that I was a witch. And now you show up at my door demanding I help you? What makes you so sure I'll even *think* about it?"

"Because if you don't, I'm going down in flames and I'll take you with me."

And at that precise moment, Aegis opened the door to the basement, his beautiful brown eyes ringed with crimson, which meant he was in predator mode, and I knew exactly who he was fixated on.

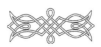

THE NEXT FEW minutes were a blur. Aegis was suddenly behind Craig, and Craig's feet were dangling off the ground again, only this time it was a vampire, not a weretiger, in charge. Aegis looked about ready to toss him through the sliding-glass door when I yelled for him to stop.

"Aegis, wait!" I had no desire to help Craig, but neither did I want him suing us because that's exactly what the little worm would do.

Aegis froze, staring at me, then slowly lowered Craig to the ground and shoved him roughly into a chair. He moved over to slide his arm around me, and gave me a long kiss as the fire in his eyes died down.

"You okay, babe? I heard him threatening you when I was coming up the stairs." Aegis was wearing his bad-boy leather pants, a black mesh muscle shirt, and a gorgeous golden belt buckle in the shape of the sun. His hair hung loose, sweeping his shoulders, and he was wearing both his Apollo ring and the Celtic claddagh ring I had bought for him.

Craig's eyes went wide as he looked up at Aegis, who smiled, deliberately lowering his fangs. He looked wildly from Aegis to me, then back to Aegis.

"What the...vampire? You're mixed up with a vampire?" Craig's voice was raw, and he looked like he might pee his pants.

"Craig, meet Aegis, my boyfriend and business partner. Aegis, this is my ex-husband. I told you *all about him.*" I let my voice drop on the last few words, and once again, Craig blanched. A very small, evil imp inside me was delighted by his response.

Aegis just stared at Craig, not blinking, not moving from where he stood, arm wrapped around my waist. "What the hell do you want with Maddy and why were you threatening her?"

Craig cleared his throat and I could feel Aegis working his glamour on him. He wouldn't be able to look away, no matter how terrified he was.

"I need her to cast a spell to get some thugs off my back. They'll come after her, too, if they don't get what they want from me," he stammered.

I froze. "What the hell did you do? And why would they be after me?"

Craig shifted nervously in the chair. Aegis held his glamour tight, reeling Craig in so tight that he couldn't possibly get away. I recognized the technique, even though witches were immune to the glamour vampires used, at least with their eyes.

"Remember when I signed for the loan on the cabin?"

I blinked. That had been seven years ago, and the cabin had been sold off during divorce proceedings. "Yeah, but I thought that was sold during the divorce."

"Not exactly," Craig said, tugging at his collar. Finally he let out a shudder and said, "Well, it was sold but I didn't pay back the loan. I didn't exactly tell you where the loan came from."

"The bank. Craig, tell me you went through a bank for it? You wouldn't let me see the paperwork, but..." But I had trusted him because, even though things had started getting bad even back then, I kept hoping to make it work. I didn't like giving up so easily.

"No. Not the bank. My credit was falling apart and the only way we could get the loan was for me to borrow it privately. When the judge gave you the condo during the divorce, I decided I deserved something for all those years of being married to you and used the money from the cabin to buy my car and a few other things for me. But now the man I borrowed the money from wants it back and...I put your name on the agreement as well as mine." He slumped back as Aegis let go of control.

I stared at him for a moment, wanting to throttle him. "You fucking took out a loan for five hundred thousand dollars from a goddamn loan shark and signed me up on it too?" Inside, I could feel my fire rising. I reined it in. Craig wasn't going to make me lose my control, even though I had every right to fry him to a crisp.

"How much do you owe them?" Aegis asked, his voice dangerously soft.

"With interest, seven hundred thousand dollars." Craig shifted again, no longer blustery. He seemed aware that Aegis was ten seconds away from poking a drinking straw in his jugular.

I let out a squeak. *Seven hundred thousand dollars?* And Craig was right, if they didn't get the money out of him, they'd be after me. I had no clue whether these guys were part of the Pretcom, or if they were human. Either way, it wasn't good.

Aegis growled under his breath. Then, moving so fast I didn't even see the blur, he was standing beside Craig. He leaned over and grabbed Craig by the hair, yanking his head back.

"Listen to me. You are going to go back to those men and you will tell them to take Maddy's name off of the contract. You'll inform them that you're selling your watch and your Beemer or whatever else you drive and your house in the country and all of your other assets, and you will turn that money over to them even if you have to shit under a bridge and sleep in a cardboard box. Because if you don't do as I say, you're one step away from being a sippy cup for me and my fangy friends. *Do. You. Understand?*"

He let go and Craig slipped off the chair, tripping as he tried to get to his feet. He glanced over at me, and I could tell he was hoping for some sort of intervention, but I said nothing. I decided to let Aegis handle this on his own. I wanted nothing to do with Craig and it seemed fitting that he end up disbarred, or whatever happened to lawyers who made bad decisions.

"Maddy—Maddy? Come on, Maddy, please." He gave me one last pleading look. "I can't afford to pay them back."

"Then maybe you should start offering your legal services free of charge to them. Who knows, they might need a lawyer on the team. Get the hell out of here and never darken my door again. Get back on your private boat and get the fuck back to Seattle. Enjoy the mess you've made of your life, because it's the one you chose." I shook my head, still furious that he had dared to come here, that he had dared to put me in danger, that he had ever even thought of marrying me when he couldn't stand witches.

Max showed up then and grabbed him by the wrist, hauling him toward the front door. As Craig vanished out of my view, I turned to Aegis, breathing hard.

"I can't believe he actually thought he could come here and..." I paused, shaking so hard that I started to cry.

"I know, love, I know." Aegis pulled me into his arms and stroked my face, running his thumb gently down my cheek. He lifted my chin and kissed me, long and slow, and he tasted like cherries and chocolate.

"He's gone," Max said, returning. "Now, maybe we can get on with things."

"Maybe," I whispered. "Maybe he's the last bad luck we'll have this week. Or month." One could always hope, I thought.

Chapter 4

"DON'T YOU THINK we should talk about what to do if those loan sharks come after you?" Sandy gave me a long look, one that I recognized as an *I'm not letting you get out of this* stare.

"That's not necessary," Aegis said. "Because if they so much as set one foot on this island, I'll drain them dry. I have no compunctions about taking care of human scum. And that includes Craig. And I am not entertaining opinions on this matter."

Sandy backed off really quick. "I'm going to call Alex and see if he's on his way over yet."

"Meanwhile, in other news, we've uncovered a secret room upstairs behind the attic," I said. "The only reason we found it is because of the hole in the roof. When Leonard and his team get here tomorrow morning, I'm going to ask them to open up the paneling in the attic so we can get to the door inside."

"What do you mean, 'secret room'?" Aegis fixed himself a plate and sat down at the table.

"I was in there, but I couldn't tell how far back it went, or exactly what was stashed away in there. Even with my flashlight, it seemed far too dark." Max polished off his food, then leaned back, looking tired.

We were all tired, I thought. Except for Aegis, of course. Spending twenty-four hours in a large drafty mansion without any heat hadn't helped, and the time teetering up on the roof during the rain hadn't helped either. I let out a long sigh, staring at my plate.

"You look exhausted," Aegis said, covering my hand with his. "Is there anything I can do?"

I shrugged. "I just want a hot shower, but I think Sandy and Max should take one first. They still don't have power at their place." I glanced over at Sandy. "Did you get in touch with Alex yet?"

"He's on his way. It took some time to get around those downed trees on the roads over there. If you don't mind, I'd love to take you up on the offer of a hot shower. Max and I can take one together, to conserve hot water so you can have a bath. I know it takes time to refill the water heater. Especially after a power outage. Should we use the bath in the guest room?"

I shook my head. "Use mine. It's big enough for two. You know where the towels are. Take as long as you need."

As they trudged upstairs, I picked up a chicken drumstick, waving it around like a wand.

"Honestly, seeing Craig tonight totally sapped my energy. I haven't heard from him in months, and I hoped I'd never hear from him again." I looked up at Aegis, tears in my eyes. "I didn't realize how much I still hate that man. He put me through hell, but I thought it was over. I can't believe he did that." I paused, then shrugged. "Actually, no. I *can* believe it. That's the way he is. That's Craig in a nutshell. He'll do anything to anyone as long as it benefits him."

Aegis took the chicken out of my hand and put it on my plate, then took my hand in his. "Maddy, all you have to do is say the word and you'll never have to worry about Craig again. I'm serious. I will do anything for you."

I realized what he was offering, but I couldn't say yes, no matter how much I wanted to. As much as I hated Craig, I couldn't just order his death. If he had hurt somebody I loved, though, I wouldn't have the same qualms.

I shook my head. "I know what you're offering, but please, no. Don't get me wrong. If he stepped in front of the bus and was squashed flat, I wouldn't shed any tears. But I can't ask the bus driver to aim for him. Do you understand?"

Aegis nodded. "I do. And in some ways, it makes me love you even more. But I won't let him hurt you. I'm serious about that, Maddy. I won't let him do anything that puts you in danger."

"Can we talk about something else? I'm too tired to talk about Craig."

"Of course. Did Kelson reach all our guests?"

I glanced over at the sink, where Kelson was

rinsing off dishes and starting to fill the dishwasher. She still hadn't gone to bed. "Hey, Kelson, did you manage to reach all of our guests and tell them that this week is off?"

"Yeah, I did. Everybody wants us to call them when we're open again. Given that we have power now, do you want to schedule that for tomorrow?"

"Not till the roof is finished. And we don't know how long it's going to take. I don't know if the ferry is running yet either. But I'm glad they want to reschedule. At least that's one thing in our favor. I wish Franny could remember more about the woman who owned the house."

"What's this?" Aegis asked, picking up a doughnut.

I stared at him. "A doughnut."

"No, silly woman. The woman who owned the house?"

"Oh! Right. Franny happened to remember a woman who owned the house around the turn of the last century. We're not certain if she had anything to do with walling off the attic, but that's what we think happened. It's a place to start. The woman spooked her, and when somebody makes an impression on Franny, it's worth looking into."

"How long to fix the roof?"

"I don't know. Leonard and his crew will be here tomorrow morning at nine o'clock to take a look at the roof and assess the damage. I'm going to ask them how much it's going to cost to put on a new roof. If it's too much, or it will take too long, we can just patch it until later."

It had occurred to me that this might not be the

best time of year for a new roof, given the holidays were coming up and everybody would be looking for a fun getaway. On the other hand, if it looked like we were going to be plagued with leaks, we'd want to get it fixed as soon as possible.

"All right. Let me clear the table while you go upstairs and wait for me. I'll come up and rub your back before you go to sleep." He pointed to my plate.

I looked down. Apparently I was too tired to eat, because I had just torn my chicken into bits and left it on the plate. Yawning, I stood and stretched. Grabbing two doughnuts and putting them on a paper plate, I added a napkin and headed for the stairs.

"I'll see you upstairs. Kelson, you get to bed, too. You've had a long couple of days."

And with that, I wearily climbed the stairs to my bedroom, where I found Luna and Bubba curled up on the comforter. As I yanked off my boots and toss them to the side, Sandy and Max came out of the bathroom. They were dressed, but their hair was freshly washed and dried, and they both looked far more comfortable than they had.

"We're heading out. Alex just texted that he's outside, waiting." She dashed across to the bed and gave me a quick hug. "You take it easy, you hear me?"

"I'll see you later, Maddy. Honey, I'll be down in the car." Max waved and left, shutting the door behind him.

After he was gone, I said, "Aegis offered to kill Craig for me." I stared up at Sandy, waiting for her reaction.

She blinked. "The world would be a better place. But I assume you told him no?"

"Yes, I told him no. But there was a part of me that wanted to just say go ahead. Drain him dry. I swear, Sandy. If Craig were to fall off the end of the earth tonight, I'd be relieved. As it is, I'm just going to take a long bubble bath and crawl into bed. I don't think I'm going to have to worry about the loan sharks, though. Aegis seems determined that he won't let me be bothered by that business."

"It would serve Craig right if he had to sell every single thing he owned to pay them back. I wish it would come to light and that he'd be disbarred. All right, I'll call you tomorrow. Wish us luck on getting our power back." With that, she gave me another quick kiss on the forehead, then hurried out of the room.

One hot bubble bath later, I was resting on the bed, on my stomach, as Aegis gently rubbed my back. I thought about turning over so he could rub other parts of my anatomy as well, but I was so tired that I would probably fall asleep in the middle of it. And that wasn't conducive to a man's ego, vampire or not.

Bubba stretched out on the bottom of the bed, Luna curled up back to back with him. As the wind picked up outside, I hoped we wouldn't have another storm. For once, I hoped for a break from the weather. I could happily go for one of those cool autumn days, when the sun glinted on frosty leaves. The kind of day that offered a chance to bundle up and walk down by the water as the breeze nipped at your nose.

As I closed my eyes, curling up beneath the covers, Aegis gently sang me to sleep, his voice resonant and deep. As I drifted off to sleep, I felt him kiss me on the forehead and I thought he whispered, "I won't ever let anyone hurt you, Maddy. I promise."

I HAD GONE to bed so early that I woke up at five A.M., bright-eyed and bushytailed. Aegis was busy in the kitchen, making cinnamon rolls and fresh bread. The hot, yeasty scent filled the air as I clattered down the stairs, feeling much better than I had the night before. Craig could try all he wanted, but I wasn't going to let him get under my skin. As I entered the kitchen, I saw that Kelson was also awake. The kitchen TV—a small one affixed to the wall near the sink—was on, and I saw that they were watching the *Big British Baking Competition*. They also appeared to be arguing over the best way to make a meringue.

"Swiss meringue is best," Aegis said.

Kelson shook her head. "Oh no, I prefer Italian meringue. It's smoother and super creamy."

"Is this what you do when I'm asleep?" I asked, suppressing a laugh. "Watch cooking shows and argue about egg whites?"

"No, sometimes we watch *Pasta World* or *A Baker's Dozen* and argue about the best cheeses for mac and cheese." Aegis stuck his tongue out at me. He was wearing his apron that read, *CAT LOVERS CHEF*. It was black with pink and white kittens printed all over it, and right now it was covered with a dusting of flour. His hands were covered with dough, and he held them away from his body as I leaned up on tiptoe to give him a quick kiss.

"Good morning," I said, bopping him on the nose. Luna and Bubba were right behind me, and both of them set up meowing loud and clear. Apparently, it was breakfast time. Luna fit in with our family perfectly, though I was still worried how Bubba would take it when she started to age. Cats didn't have a very long life span, not compared to a cjinn, or a witch. Or even a human.

Kelson flipped on the espresso machine, preparing to make my morning latte. "What do you want this morning?"

"Make it a quad, caramel and vanilla. Did you get enough sleep?" I pulled a plate out of the cupboard, carrying it over to the freshly baked cinnamon rolls. As I slid one of the fragrant pastries onto my dish, Kelson pulled the eggs and cheese out of the refrigerator.

"I did! Omelet okay, along with bacon?" She rummaged through the cupboard for a skillet.

"That sounds lovely, but weren't the eggs a victim of the power outage?"

"They were indeed," Aegis said. "But I decided to go for a spin around one A.M. and stopped at the grocery store to replenish the food. It looks like the power has been restored to about half the town. I gather the ferries will be up and running again by the end of the week when they have the pier repaired. Oh, by the way, I found out where Craig is staying. I paid a visit to him—don't worry, he's still alive," he added as I winced. "But I doubt that he'll bother us again." He gave me a look that said, *Don't ask.*

I decided to obey for once and changed the subject. "The Alpha Pack will be over at nine A.M. to start work on the roof. Before they actually start patching it up, I'm going to ask them to cut through the paneling in the attic. I'm really curious about what's in that blocked-off room."

"I don't know if I'd do that," Franny said, walking out of the wall.

I jumped, startled. "I wish you'd announce yourself when you did that," I said. "You scared the bejesus out of me."

She giggled. "I'm sorry. By the way, Henry will be down late. He didn't get to sleep until about four A.M. and he asked me to let you know not to hold breakfast for him."

I wanted to ask exactly what he was doing at four A.M. with Franny in his room, but again, don't ask, don't tell. But my curiosity got the better of me enough and I blurted out, "Franny, can you take your clothes off?"

I regretted the words the moment they tumbled out of my mouth. But there was no way I could take them back.

She cocked her head, staring at me like I had just asked her if she was a demon. "Excuse me? You want me to undress?"

"No! I just meant..." I scrambled for a save.

"What I meant is, can you change your clothes? Are you stuck in that dress, or can you change it up?"

"You better stop while you're ahead," Aegis advised with a grin.

"Oh, shut up." I glared at him. I was seriously trying to figure out how I could backpedal.

The frown on Franny's face slowly vanished as a flush of pink rose through her cheeks. I wasn't sure how ghosts managed to blush, given they were bloodless and bodiless, but blush they could. Her eyes widened as she made a little "O" with her mouth. But if she understood what I was asking, she conveniently sidestepped it.

"As far as I know, I'm stuck in these clothes. I'd like to wear something else, but if there's a way, I haven't found it." She rushed on ahead, changing the subject. "I don't know if it's safe to pry into secret rooms and hidden memories."

"Nonetheless, we're going to. This is my house and I want to know everything about it. If there are any skeletons in the closet, I'm prying them out." Even as a little girl, I hadn't been content to go on what people told me. One of my favorite books, written in the 1940s, was *Rebecca*, by Daphne du Maurier. Except I had never understood why the nameless heroine hadn't searched through every inch of Manderley. I know I would have gone prowling through every single room, getting to know every inch of my new home.

"Don't say I didn't warn you." Franny paused, then added, "Can I ask a favor?"

"Of course. What do you need?" I liked to help

Franny out when I could, given she had so many limitations on her.

"I'm almost embarrassed to ask, but I'd like to get Henry a little gift. And I don't know what to get him. Or how, given I'm a ghost and don't have any money."

I glanced over at Aegis, who flashed me the barest of grins. He quickly turned away so that Franny wouldn't see his smile. For myself, I wasn't all that surprised. But nor was I going to let Franny talk me into spending a buttload of money on Henry. I thought for a moment, then snapped my fingers.

"I know. Henry's writing the history of Bedlam, right?"

Franny nodded.

"Why don't we order him a nice leather-bound journal and pen for his notes? He likes to take notes by hand, I've noticed." It was true, I thought. Henry seemed to enjoy the experience of actually writing out the words rather than typing, although I knew he had a laptop in his room. A journal would be a nice, inexpensive gift that he would probably like.

Franny clapped her hands. "That's perfect. Can we go find one right now?"

"Let me eat breakfast first. Meanwhile, why don't you go into the computer in the parlor, and search online. I'm giving you a budget of $100. That's for both the pen and the journal."

"Great. I can check in on STOE, too. I haven't read the forums for a couple of days." Franny also belonged to an online group called STOE, which was short for Spirits Trapped on Earth. It was a support group for ghosts who for—whatever reason—hadn't been able to move on. She stopped. "I think that computer is on."

"Oh that's right, the power outage." I glanced over at Kelson. "I'll be right back. Can you make me plenty of bacon with that omelet?"

"The whole package, if you want." She waved me off.

I headed into the library, with Franny following me. Flipping on the computer, I booted it up in safe mode, given it had shut down so abruptly. As soon as it loaded, I turned it off properly, then once again turned it on, this time normally.

After making sure nothing was wrong, I activated the voice software and brought up Leather Bound, a website devoted to journals and pens. Franny looked over my shoulder. A sweep of cold air rushed through me as she accidentally brushed through me.

"Can you back away a little?" We had had this conversation a dozen times, but she always forgot.

"Oh, sorry." She blushed. "I didn't mean to get so close."

I slid out of the chair, pulling it back so she could have the illusion of sitting down. "When you find one you like, just order it. I added the money to your account. Have fun!"

As I left the library, I glanced over my shoulder. Franny was absorbed in the website, eagerly looking through the myriad journals and pens. She looked content, and for some reason, that made me happy.

When I returned to the kitchen, Kelson slid a

plate in front of me. The omelet was chock full of cheese and mushrooms, and the bacon was sizzling and crispy. I took a deep breath, holding it for a moment before I let it out slowly. It all felt so right, Aegis and me, even Kelson and Franny were so much a part of my world now. I couldn't really imagine being anywhere else. The past felt so far away, almost as if it were a dream.

"PROMISE ME YOU'LL love me forever," Tom said, taking my hands as we stood under the moonlight.

It was 1719, and Tom had my heart in his hands. We had met years before, in 1660, the year after I met his cousin Fata Morgana. She had introduced us at a party, when she caught me watching him.

Tom had caught my eye from the beginning. He was a tall, cool drink of water. With shocking blond hair that he wore in a braid, his eyes were as green as mine, and he was muscled, though not muscle bound. But his voice was what I noticed first. He had a bard's voice, and when he spoke, it was almost as though he were singing. I couldn't take my eyes off of him.

Fata Morgana noticed. "You like him?" she asked, watching me closely.

I nodded. "There's something about him. I can't look away. Do you know who he is?"

She paused, and for a moment I thought she was going to say no. But then she nodded. "Hold on, I'll go talk to him." She hurried across the room, and I considered following her, but decided to wait. Fata pulled him aside, and I saw her point to me, and then whisper something to him. He stared at her for a moment, as though debating, and finally nodded. He followed her back to where I was standing.

"Maddy, this is my cousin, Tom."

I blinked. "Your cousin? Why didn't you just tell me?"

Again, she paused, then the words tumbled out. "Oh, force of habit. In case the witch hunters catch us."

Tom held out his hand, and I placed my fingers into his palm. His skin was warm, and sparks flew when we touched. His eyes met mine, and I was lost.

I BLINKED, SHAKING my head as I shook away the memories. It was all water under the bridge, dark water that I didn't want to tread anymore. I looked up to see Aegis watching me.

"Are you all right?" His eyes crinkled with worry.

I cleared my throat, slicing into my omelet with my fork. "Yeah, I'm fine. Just a stray memory that I didn't expect." I glanced up at the clock. It was seven A.M., and I was starting to regret getting up so early. "I think after I eat and before the Alpha-Pack gets here, I'll go out for a walk to clear my head."

"I'm going to head downstairs. The bread is almost ready and Kelson can take it out of the oven. I don't want to chance being up here when sunrise actually hits. I've only got a few minutes." Aegis folded his napkin and placed it across his plate, standing.

I put down my fork and pushed back my chair, holding out my arms. He pulled me into his embrace, kissing me deeply as his hands wandered over my back. He lowered his lips to my neck, trailing kisses along my skin. His touch chased away the memories of Tom, and of my earlier life. This was where I belonged. Now, in the present, and Aegis's embrace. I rested my head on his chest.

"I love you," I whispered. "You have no idea how glad I am we're together. Thank you for being here." I glanced up into his eyes. "Thank you for being you."

"I love you too, Maddy. I'll always be here for you, as long as you want me." His lips met mine again, so cool against my own warm skin as he kissed me. Finally, he let go, glancing at the clock. "I'd better go. I can feel the sun rising, even though I doubt we'll see it today."

"Actually, it's supposed to burn off the clouds for a while. You'd better get downstairs now. I'll see you tonight, my love."

Aegis gave Kelson a wave, then blew me another kiss as he headed toward the basement door. Another moment and it shut behind him, and he was off to his lair for the day.

I sat back down to finish my breakfast.

Yes, my life had changed drastically. At one time

I had been one of the most feared vampire hunters in the world, rampaging across Europe, staking the bloodsuckers right and left. And now? Now I was in love with a vampire. But I had brought out my tools again, because there was a new danger, one that I didn't want to talk about—didn't dare talk about where people could hear. I had long hoped that part of myself had been put to rest, but sometimes the past caught up to us, and reminded us that we wouldn't be who we were, without the person we had been.

KELSON HAD TAKEN the bread out of the oven, washed the dishes, and was now writing up a new grocery list. I stepped onto the patio, surveying the back yard. Most of the trees were near the house, and the rest of the lot was open grass before hitting the edge of the forest.

I decided that it really was a good day for a walk, and it would give me a chance to oversee some of the work that Aegis had done on creating the campgrounds we wanted. I glanced at my watch. It was seven thirty. I had plenty of time before Leonard and his Pack got here. I slipped back inside long enough to grab a light jacket. Shrugging into it, I headed across the lawn, thinking that we should have a meteor watching party in August when the Perseids streaked across the sky.

The leaves still left on the trees glimmered in the morning light, in shades of burnished bronze,

76

of copper and red and brown, mottled yellow and rust. But there weren't many. The windstorm had stripped away most of them, and now they carpeted the lawn and the forest floor in a quilt of earthen tones.

There was a pungent smell to the forest. It was that deep autumn scent of toadstools and muddy trails, of decaying leaves and moss hanging off the sides of trees. The slow drip of water echoed as raindrops fell from the branches, jarred loose as the sun burned away the clouds.

A slow mist rose, boiling up where the sunlight warmed the chilled ground. The forest felt empty, the way it always did when the leaves were off the trees and winter was on its way. Overhead, a murder of crows swept by, their *caw caw* echoing through the air.

I had let Lanyear out last night to hunt, and now I looked around to see if I could spot him. He hung out here in the thicket, when he wasn't inside with us.

As I looked around, I could see the progress that Aegis had made. He had begun trailblazing through the undergrowth, creating trails into areas we planned to turn into campsites. We wanted to keep most of the acreage forested, but two acres was plenty of room for at least ten campsites. The other acre of my land comprised the house and yard.

I wandered down one of the trails and realized that Aegis had established the way with stone pavers, a nice touch that I hadn't thought of. When I got to the area for the campsite, I saw that he had cleared out a good-size area. I found a fallen tree, a nurse log covered with moss, with toadstools and ferns growing out of the cracks, and sat down, huddling to keep myself warm. I could see my breath, but even though it was chilly, it felt good to be outside.

My phone rang, and I pulled it out of my pocket, cringing as the harsh tone broke the stillness. It was Sandy.

"Hey Maddy, I have a favor to ask."

"What do you need?"

"Now they're saying our power won't be back till tomorrow morning. Do you mind if we come over tonight? And if we bring Mr. Peabody? It's awfully cold here. Alex is going to spend the night with his girlfriend."

I smiled, tracing a ring around the brightly colored toadstool sitting next to me. "Of course you can come over. Aegis made a couple loaves of fresh bread, so we can have bread and soup for dinner. Come over whenever you like. I'm just out taking a walk before the Alpha-Pack gets here to work on the roof."

Sandy paused, and I could hear the hesitation in her voice. Finally, she said, "Have you heard anything more from Craig?"

"No, and don't get me started. I don't ever want to hear anything more from him." I bit my lip, chewing on it for a moment. "Aegis visited him at his hotel. He warned him to back off. What do you think I should do?"

"I think you should trust Aegis. You have to admit, he's far smarter than anybody else we know.

Of course, he's got years of experience under his belt. Well, thousands of years." She paused again, then said, "I hate Craig. I hate what he did to you and what he did to your self-confidence. You've got it back now, but I'd still like to punch him in the nuts."

I broke out into a broad smile. "I'm grinning. I'm nodding. I'll see you when you get here. I might go out shopping for a bit, but feel free to come over when you like. You've got a key in case Kelson and I are both gone."

And with that, I hung up. I leaned back, resting my head against the trunk of another tree. After a moment I took several deep, slow, breaths, letting the pungent tang in the air waken my senses. There was something about this time of year that made me feel so alive and vibrant. Summer was okay, and I liked spring, but autumn and winter were my times of the year. Autumn and winter made every inch of me feel all tingly and energetic.

I glanced at the clock on my cell phone. Eight thirty. With a sigh, I stood and started back toward the house, deciding that I would take this walk every day. It made me feel good, and it made me feel like I was looking more toward the future than staring at the past. And that was always a good thing.

Chapter 5

BY THE TIME I reached the house, Leonard Wolfbrane and his crew had arrived. Kelson had shown them in and they were waiting for me in the kitchen. She had found a package of cookies and spread them out on a platter, and offered the men coffee. Leonard stood up as I entered the room. He was moderate height, well muscled, and had short, sandy hair. His eyes were pale gray, common to many wolf shifters, and he nodded to me, waiting for me to hold out my hand. I extended my hand and he shook it formally.

"I'm so glad you could make it today. There are several things we need to talk about besides the roof."

"Oh?"

"Yeah. First, I need your opinion about whether we can wait on a new roof for a while longer. Ideally, I'd like to wait until spring, but if you think the patch job won't hold, or if it looks like there are other problem areas that are just waiting for a storm, then I suppose we better have a new one now. One way or another, the roof needs to be fixed. I also want you guys to open up something in the attic. When the tree branch punched through the roof, we found a hidden room on the other side of the attic wall. We traced out the area on the paneling that leads to the doorway, and I'm wondering if you could open that up for me today."

Leonard scratched his head. "A secret room? Really? Isn't that a little on point?"

"Didn't you get the memo? All mansions are required to have a secret room somewhere." I laughed, and he joined me.

"I'll remember that next time. Okay, why don't you take me and the boys up to this room, and we'll take care of that before we head up onto the roof. You said you wanted an estimate before we do any work up top?" The tool belt around his waist jangled as we headed upstairs.

"Yeah, an estimate for just a patch job if we can leave it at that, and also what we can expect to pay for a new roof."

I showed them the trapdoor that led into the attic crawl space. They opened it in the blink of an eye, and I slowly ascended the ladder, Leonard behind me. Once we were in the attic, I led them over to the wall, flashing a light on the paneling. "I'm a little afraid to turn on the lights up here. I don't know if any of the wiring was damaged when the tree broke through the roof. So, better safe than sorry."

"We can take a look at that, too. So this is the area that you want cut open?" He traced all around the pencil marks. "That's a short door."

"I know. Actually, if you could just remove all of the paneling, I'd like to see if there's anything else behind there that we should know about."

Leonard motioned for me to get out of the way. "You don't want to be in the way if any nails go flying," he said. Like most werewolves, especially the men, Leonard was a little presumptive, but that was just the way of shifters in general. Werewolves were definitely patriarchal. So were lion shifters, but bear shifters—on the other hand—were matriarchal.

I crossed to the other side of the attic, sitting down on a box to wait. I had to admit, I wasn't comfortable in the attic. I seldom came up here and I used a small spare room on the second floor to store most of my things instead of putting them up in here. We were slowly clearing the basement, and when it was empty we would put the trunks and boxes down there. But something about the attic had always bothered me. Perhaps it was that you had to climb a generally hidden ladder to reach it. Or perhaps I just didn't like the claustrophobic space. There was barely enough room to stand up straight.

The Alpha-Pack made quick work of the paneling, pulling it off the wall in three pieces. When they were done, Leonard motioned for me to join him. I made my way back across the unfinished plywood floor, stopping as I stared at the door that had been covered up. Max had left it open, and

YASMINE GALENORN

now, the pale sun flickered through the tarp into both the attic and the secret room.

"Do you think they built this room as an add-on? Was it originally part of the attic, or can you tell?" I asked.

Leonard and his men examined the wall. It didn't take long before he had an answer.

"Oh, they walled this off after the original attic was built. So yeah, they closed it off sometime after the house was built. Do you want to do the honors, and go through first?"

I took the flashlight from him, and ducked as I stepped through the door.

As I entered the secret room, it was still hard to see into the corners. Even though sunlight was creeping through the tarp, the room seemed to extend back quite a ways. I realized that the attic actually extended the full length of the house rather than half of it as we had originally thought.

"Hold on, wait just a minute." Leonard motioned to one of his men. "John, bring up the LED lantern."

John ducked back into the other part of the attic and returned with a large battery-operated LED lantern. The light illuminated most of the room with a surprising brilliance. I stared at the walls, trying to comprehend what I was seeing.

In this part of the attic, the walls had once been painted a dark blue, with silver trim. There was something at the end of the room, a large table that looked like it might be marble. On the table was a jug, with a narrow bottom, a wide body, and a narrow neck, plugged by a stone stopper.

The floor itself was painted a faded silver, and as I headed for the table with Leonard behind me, I realized there appeared to be paintings on the walls. They were tone on tone—a light blue against the dark, and hard to see, even with the LED light. I couldn't quite make them out, but they seemed to be life-size figures with pictograms or glyphs written between them.

"What the hell?" I asked.

Leonard had stopped a few steps behind me. His eyes were wide and I recognize the scent of fear emanating off of him.

"Maddy, there's some strong magic here. Can you feel it? It's raising my hackles." Werewolves didn't like magic very much.

I stopped, closing my eyes and holding out my hands as I tried to sense what was going on around me. And then it hit me, full force. A heavy magic lingering from years past. It was ritual magic, structured and ancient, and it was trapped here in this room. I had no idea what we were dealing with, but it set my stomach to quivering, and I had a distinct feeling that we were walking in dangerous territory.

"I can feel it too. I suggest that perhaps we should exit this room—" I started to say, but was interrupted when one of the workmen raced by into the room, screaming at the top of his lungs. His arms were flailing, and the scent of sheer terror lingered in his wake.

"Come back!" I wasn't sure why, but I didn't want him near that table. There was something there that was dangerous, something old and gnarled and twisted. I started to run forward, trying to stop him, when he lurched into the table, crashing against it.

He fell back, sprawling on the floor.

I watched as the urn tilted from the impact and went hurtling down to land next to him. The urn hit the wood and shattered on impact. A plume of black powder filled the air, roiling into smoke, and I screeched to a halt, trying to avoid it. Unfortunately, I was too close and found myself breathing in the acrid smoke that boiled up from the powder.

I scrambled back, trying to get away from it.

The workman was on the floor, flailing and screaming. The next moment, he went limp. I turned to see Leonard snap out of his paralysis. He motioned for me to get out of the way as he ran toward his worker.

"Trey! Are you all right?" Leonard started to cough as he entered the smoke-filled area. He leaned over, slipping his hands beneath Trey's underarms and dragging him back away from the table. The other men had fled, running into the other part of the attic. I hurried over to help Leonard pull Trey through the door, then slammed it shut.

"Quick, get him down the ladder," I said, still coughing.

A couple of the men had come to their senses and were standing next to the trapdoor. One of them scrambled down, holding his arms up for Trey. Together, he and Leonard managed to wrangle the unconscious werewolf down the ladder into the hallway. Leonard called for me to head down the ladder.

"I'll shut the door from up here, and go out through the roof. We don't want to leave the trap-door open into your hallway. Robert, go get the ladder and prop it up next to the roof so I can climb down."

Within minutes, I was standing in the hallway, watching as the other workmen carried Trey's un-conscious form toward the stairs. Robert had run on ahead, to do as Leonard asked. I glanced back up at the trapdoor. What the hell had just hap-pened? What was in that room?

My mind filled with questions, I headed down-stairs to join the Alpha-Pack.

THE FIRST THING we did was ascertain Trey's condition. He was still unconscious, and Kelson had cleared off the dining room table so the men could lay him there.

She looked up as I came in. "We'd better call the doctor. He's not coming around."

I nodded, tapping Leonard on the shoulder. "Does he have a doctor? I can call Jordan Farrows. He specializes in magical afflictions. I used to go to a different doctor, but he's extraordinarily compe-tent."

"I'm not sure who Trey's doctor is, so go ahead. Please, hurry. His breathing sounds labored."

I stepped away from the pack and put in a call to Jordan. He had helped us out on numerous occasions now, so I had him on speed dial. He answered on the third ring.

"Maddy? What's up? What happened?"

On one hand, I hated that his first response was to ask me what was wrong. But it had become par for the course.

"The Alpha-Pack came to check out my roof. Long story short, one of the workmen is unconscious. He inhaled some sort of magical smoke." I began to cough, feeling the residue rumble around in my own lungs. "So did I. But whatever it was knocked him out. Can you come over right away? His breathing is shallow and we're worried about him."

"I'm on my way. You said he's a werewolf?"

"Yeah. One of the Alpha-Pack."

Jordan signed off. Returning to the table, I told them he was on his way.

"Should we do anything until he gets there?" Robert asked.

Leonard shook his head. "I don't think so. We don't want to make a bad situation worse."

He glanced around at the men, then over at me. They were milling around, looking mildly agitated. Leonard knew as well as I did that you don't let werewolves get antsy or have too much downtime.

"Why don't you guys head up to the roof and start assessing the situation? Everything should be okay up there. Just don't take the tarp off. Take a look for any other leaks. I'll wait here for the doctor."

"What about Trey?" one of the men said.

"There's nothing you can do until the doctor

gets here. So you might as well get on with the job. That's what we're here for." Leonard shooed them out the door. They seemed relieved to have something to do.

Kelson returned from the kitchen with a cold washcloth, which she laid over Trey's forehead. "He seemed a little hot to me." She motioned for me to follow her into the kitchen. "What happened? I didn't want to ask the men because they seem so freaked."

I told her. "There was something up in that room. I felt it wake up. I have no idea what it is, but I guarantee you it isn't anything good."

"Is it loose in the house?"

I shrugged. "I think so. I'm hoping it was just residue energy that was trapped within the urn. But we need to figure out what the writing on the wall is, and what the pictographs mean. I didn't recognize it, so we should bring in a linguist, I suppose."

"Maybe one of the professors from Neverfall could tell you?"

That was a good idea. Neverfall had a plethora of instructors from all walks of magical life. They had to have someone who specialized in ancient languages.

"I'll give Leroy a call as soon as Jordan gets here and we figure out what's wrong with Trey. Meanwhile, why don't you put on some coffee and get some refreshments for the men. I have a feeling they're going to need something to bolster their spirits. You wouldn't believe how afraid that pack of werewolves was up there." I paused. "Or maybe you would. You're a werewolf yourself. The magic was overwhelming, Kelson. It scared *me*, and I'm used to magic."

She frowned, a worried look in her eyes. "If it's that strong, then I'm afraid we might be in trouble."

"Just watch out when you're around upstairs. Or I guess anywhere in the house. Hopefully, the energy just swooped up and out the roof. But until we know for sure, just be cautious."

She shook her head. "Don't go up there alone, Maddy—you're a powerful witch, but there are some things more powerful than you are."

"Trust me, I know that. I have to think about this for a while." I stopped when the doorbell rang. As Kelson went to answer it, I returned to the dining room, where Trey was still unconscious on the table.

Leonard walked over to my side. He stared at his friend for a moment, then looked at me. "What do you think that thing was?"

I grimaced. "I have no idea, but it scared me, too. Whatever that smoke was, it hit my lungs as well. And I can tell you right now, it didn't feel good."

"Are you all right?"

I shrugged. "I don't know. I feel...unsettled. But at least I'm not unconscious."

Kelson returned, with Jordan Farrows behind her. He set his bag on the table next to Trey. "What happened?"

"Basically, an urn broke, a bunch of black powder hit the floor and smoke rose from it, and Trey was caught in it."

"Anybody else?"

"I got slammed by it too, but didn't lose consciousness." I pointed to the ceiling. "Apparently, we have a secret room in my attic. It looks like it might have been used for some sort of ritual magic, but I can't read the glyphs that are painted on the wall."

Jordan frowned. "Let me examine him, then I also want to check your vitals, too."

Kelson and I retreated to the kitchen, leaving Trey to Jordan. Leonard stayed with them.

"Seriously, how *are* you feeling?" Kelson asked me, firing up the espresso machine.

I tried to assess my state of health, but it was difficult to tell whether I felt off because of what had happened, or because of my emotional reaction.

"I don't know," I said. "I can't tell. I think the storm fried my senses a little bit. Plus, what happened upstairs left me feeling shaky."

She slid a double shot mocha in front of me, adding a dollop of whipped cream. "Maybe this will help."

"Well, it can't hurt," I said.

A few moments later, Jordan entered the room. Leonard had stayed in the dining room.

"What's wrong with him?" I hoped to hell it was fixable.

"To be honest? I don't have a clue of why he's unconscious. Everything checks out. His blood pressure is fine. His blood sugar is normal. His heart sounds okay, his pulse is normal. The man should be awake, but he's not. I'm going to take him back to my office for a complete battery of tests. Now, let me take a look at you."

He took my blood pressure, checked my heart and pulse, and asked me how I was feeling. I told him exactly what I had told Kelson.

"Well, if you start feeling the least bit off, give me a call. Meanwhile I'd like to see that room. I might be able to figure out something if I recognize any of the glyphs on the wall."

"I'm leery of going back upstairs." I really didn't want to go back in that attic again. "Are you sure you want to go look?"

Jordan took my hands in his. "Maddy, I know you're nervous. But you're the High Priestess on this island. You're the leader of the Moonrise Co-ven. I'm afraid the buck stops with you, especially when it comes to your own house."

I rubbed my forehead. I had been promoted to the coven's High Priestess shortly after I first ar-rived on the island. I was still getting used to the responsibility. "I never thought about it like that. But hell, you're right. Okay, I'll go up with you, but I need someone to pull down that ladder. I'm not tall enough to reach it."

"I'll help," Leonard said from the doorway. He was leaning against the frame, arms crossed. "Come on."

We followed him back upstairs, stopping below the trapdoor leading into the attic. Leonard let out a long sigh. "All right, here goes nothing."

He used a chair to reach the trapdoor, then extended the ladder so that it rested on the floor. After that, he cautiously lifted himself into the opening. Jordan followed him, and then I climbed up, steeling myself. Once we were up in the attic, the men on the roof waved down from the roof.

"Hey boss, how's Trey?" Robert called.

"Still unconscious, but he's in stable condition," Jordan answered for Leonard.

"How's the roof look?" I asked.

Robert shook his head. "You definitely need a new one, but I'm pretty sure we can patch it for now until you can make arrangements. Be best to replace it in spring when the weather's better. What about it, Len? Should we start in putting on the patches?"

"Get everything ready. In a few minutes, I'll come up to take a look at what you found." Leonard waved him away. "Be careful up there."

While he was chatting with his men, I led Jordan over to the door to the secret room.

"This was hidden behind paneling. I had no idea it was here when I bought the house. Leonard thinks it was walled off after the original attic was built, and Franny doesn't remember the room being separate, so he's probably right." I handed Jordan a flashlight. "Get ready. I'm not sure if there's anything in there, but I want to be prepared."

I cautiously turned the handle, opening the door. As the hinges creaked and the door swung wide, I tensed, waiting for something huge and horrible to come shrieking at us. But nothing happened, and after a moment, I took a deep breath and plunged inside, followed by Jordan.

Jordan flashed his light on the walls, then walked over to look at the glyphs. While he did that, I slowly crossed to the table in the back. The pieces of the urn were scattered on the ground, along with the remains of the blackened powder. The smoke had vanished and I prayed that meant it was gone for good. I knelt, cautious to avoid touching the powder, and picked up a shard from the urn. As I turned it over, I saw that it was made from some form of pottery, a yellowish clay that looked to be very, very old. There were glyphs on the shard, as well. I had no clue what they meant, but they were very angular and reminded me of Egyptian hieroglyphics, though something told me they weren't.

Jordan was examining the wall. "This is a cuneiform script, that much I can tell you. I have no idea what it means, though. And the paintings are two dimensional, like Egyptian art, but it doesn't have that feel to it."

"That's what I was thinking. The broken urn has the same sort of writing on it." I stared down at the powder. "You may want to take some of this powder for examination."

He joined me, frowning at the black granules. "Yeah, I should. You say the powder spilled out when the urn broke?"

"Along with a mass of black smoke. At first I thought maybe the spilled powder caused the smoke, but I'm thinking maybe that's not actually the case." I didn't want to touch it. There was something greasy feeling about the powder—about its energy. I kept thinking that if I touched it, I'd never be able to get it off my fingers.

Jordan slipped on a pair of plastic gloves, then

scooped up some of the powder into a small container. He closed it, tucking it into his pocket. "I took enough for analysis, but I suggest you leave this until I've had a chance to examine it further. Who knows if I'll need more?" He glanced up at the hole in the roof. "There's something very uncomfortable about this setup, but I can't tell you exactly what or why. It makes me nervous, though."

"It makes me nervous, too," I said. "I don't like the idea that it's here, in my house."

"I understand. Well, I'll get back to the office and start running tests on both Trey and this powder. Hopefully, I'll know more in a few hours." He motioned for me to follow him and we made our way back to the trapdoor.

Leonard had swung himself up on the roof, through the hole. "I'll duck back down to talk to you in about ten minutes, when I've looked over what my men found."

"We'll be downstairs," I waved at him as I turned and began to descend the ladder. Jordan followed me.

JORDAN HAD ORDERED an ambulance to take Trey back to his office. As they headed out, Kelson washed the table and began to lay a cloth on it for dinner. I went into my office, feeling tired and listless. Even the extra caffeine hadn't done anything to pick me up. I glanced out the window. The sun had vanished behind the clouds again, and we looked in for another rainstorm. Usually, I loved the rain, but today it just felt dreary. I finally decided to throw myself into holiday plans since we were guestless, except for Henry, and likely to stay that way for a few days. I pulled up Aegis's notes with the Thanksgiving menu he had planned and looked over it.

Sandy, Max, and Jenna would be here. As would Henry. We'd have guests, the gods willing. I was reading through the list of dishes Aegis wanted to make when my cell phone rang. I frowned, not recognizing the number, and answered it.

"Maddy?" The voice was low but smooth, and the man had an English accent. I had lost my Irish accent decades ago. "Hi. This is Gregory, your brother."

I sat back in my chair, blinking. The last person I had expected to hear from was Gregory.

He was my half-brother, actually. We hadn't even known about each other until a few months ago. Right before my mother died, she broke down and told me about him. Forced to give him up when she was young—five years before I came along—Zara had kept a long-distance watch on him, making sure the couple who took him in raised him with love. But she never reached out to him, terrified of rejection. She had made me promise not to contact him until after she died and I begrudgingly agreed. I had emailed him, and we had exchanged a few letters since then, but we had never talked on the phone, nor had we met. Gregory had needed time to process everything.

"Gregory..." I stumbled for the right words. "Hi, hello—I didn't expect your call." It wasn't the brightest thing to say, but I had to say something.

"I know, and I apologize. But I'm leaving for America tomorrow, and I'll be in the Seattle area for a couple of days before heading to New York for a conference. I thought, if you'd like, we can meet."

Again, my heart thudded in my chest. "I'd love that. Will you be able to come up to Bedlam?" I held my breath, hoping he would say yes.

Gregory paused, then cleared his throat. "If you like, yes. I can take an extra day or two and come visit you." Another moment, then he added, "You're sure you want to meet me, now?"

"Yes, I do! Please come." I wasn't sure why it was so important to me, but all of a sudden all I could think about was meeting Gregory and getting to know him.

"It's set, then. I'll email you my itinerary. I'll arrive in Seattle on Friday, the sixteenth. I'll rent a car and drive up to the island. Email me the details of how best to get to your place." With little more than a quick good-bye, he signed off.

Thoroughly flustered and unable to focus on what I had intended to do—which was balance my checkbook—I jumped up and ran in the kitchen.

"Kelson! Kelson, we need to make sure the place is sparkling by Friday. My brother's coming to visit." I froze, hearing the excitement in my voice.

Kelson watched me for a moment. "What's wrong? I saw that shift in your expression."

I jumped up on the counter, swinging my legs as

I sat there. "It just occurred to me. What if...what if we don't like each other? I never knew I had a half-brother until recently, but I've been thinking a lot about him since then. What if he doesn't measure up to what my imagination has been spinning out for me? What if I don't meet his expectations?"

"That's always a risk. But what else are you going to do? Pretend you aren't excited? Stifle yourself? Refuse to meet him because you're afraid it won't be what you hoped for?" Kelson wiped her hands on a dishtowel and leaned against the counter next to me.

"I hear what you're saying and no, I'm not going to back away because I'm afraid this won't be the reunion I hope it will be. But I *am* scared, Kelson. And I don't really know how to talk about it, because I don't even know what I want out of this relationship."

And there was the crux of the problem. I didn't know what I wanted out of Gregory. Did I want long talks on the phone, brother to sister, where we shared our secrets and hopes? That seemed like something reserved for childhood, but our childhoods were long gone. Did I want an easy relationship, where we sent holiday cards and called each other for a few minutes each month? Did I want him as a friend or as the protector big brothers sometimes were?

The phone rang, interrupting my thoughts. As I glanced at it, half-expecting it to be Gregory, cancelling plans, I saw that it was Jordan. I punched the TALK button.

"Hey, what's up?"

"What's up is that Trey's in trouble. I need to talk to Leonard and I don't have his number. Is he still there?"

Wanting to ask what was wrong, I suppressed the urge. I turned to Kelson and motioned to her. "Can you take my phone out to Leonard? Jordan needs to talk to him, stat."

Kelson nodded, jogging into the back yard with my phone. I walked over to the dishwasher she had been unloading and began to take out dishes. I had set three glasses on the counter and was reaching for a fourth when one of the glasses whipped off the granite counter and wheeled past me, missing my head by less than an inch. Instinctively, I ducked, and it was a good thing, because the other two glasses sailed right past where I had been standing, smashing into the wall.

I slammed the dishwasher closed, breathing hard, as I stared at the broken glass. What the fuck?

"Franny? Did you do that?" I knew it couldn't have been her, but right now, my thinking cap wasn't on straight.

"Maudlin, help me!" Franny came flying out of the wall into the powder room, a panicked look on her face. As she whirled in the air, colliding with the refrigerator and passing through it, a dark form rose up from the wall behind her, emerging in a smoky mist. It looked one hell of a lot like the mist I had seen upstairs.

I held up my hands, intent on creating a wall between it and me, but the next thing I knew, that little zing I got when casting a spell sputtered and died.

The shadow form turned away from Franny, toward me, and began to advance. As I backed up, all I could feel was a wash of fear racing through me. What the hell was this thing, and what did it want?

Chapter 6

I LEARNED VERY quickly just what it wanted. The shadow leapt at me, slamming through me. For a moment, it felt like I was about to be knocked out of my body. I grappled with it, doing my best to shove it away. As it passed through me, I jumped to the side, pulling away from it. But the kitchen wasn't very big, and I ended up jabbing myself in the ribs on the corner of the counter as I ducked.

"Damn it!" I could barely take a breath—the jolt had knocked the wind out of me. But at least I could tell what the shadow was trying to do. It was either trying to take over my body, or render me helpless so it could feed on my life energy.

I held out my hands, summoning up my energy, as I focused on the blur of mist roiling through the kitchen. I needed to disrupt it, and luckily, I knew a pretty good disruption spell.

Bars that break, bars that bind
Shatter now, those of your kind.
Disperse, dispel, scatter wide,
Run in fear, run to hide.

Franny screamed again and I turned in time to see the shadow begin to break apart, but then it reared up, stronger than ever, and the energy that I had pushed toward it came hurtling back. I could feel it rebounding on me, and the next moment, I tripped and fell to my knees, gasping for air. I couldn't breathe. My throat was swelling up, and I struggled, grasping at my neck.

Kelson appeared in the doorway. "What the hell—" She stopped, staring at me as I reached out toward her. At that moment, the shadow aimed for me again and came barreling toward me. Franny screamed, throwing herself in front of me, as Kelson ripped off her clothes, leaping over the table in wolf form, growling and snapping at the shadow creature. She bit through him and he retreated toward the wall.

At that moment, Bubba came racing into the kitchen.

"Get out of here, Bubs—you don't want—" I panted, still struggling to breathe, terrified he'd become the shadow creature's target. But Bubba took a long look at me and flopped on his belly in front of me. I realized what he was offering. I reached out, trying to form my thoughts as coherently as I could, and rubbed his tummy, focusing on the wish that the shadow creature would vanish without any of us being hurt.

There was a shimmer in the air, and then the shadow pulsed and disappeared.

I rolled over on my side, my throat feeling like it was so swollen inside I could barely breathe. Bubba nosed me and turned to Kelson, who immediately shifted back. I barely noticed she was naked. She knelt beside me as Leonard raced in, his eyes wide.

"What the hell was that thing?"

But I couldn't answer. I opened my mouth, trying to breathe, and he jumped up.

"She's having an allergic reaction. She can't breathe. Are witches able to use epinephrine? One of the guys is allergic to nuts and has an injector on him."

I couldn't answer. I just scrabbled, trying to ease my throat.

Kelson glanced at me. "I don't know if she can or not. Let me call Jordan."

But before she could make a move, Bubba leaned down and sniffed my neck. He closed his eyes and flopped over on his belly. Kelson immediately reached out and ruffled his fur.

"Help her breathe, Bubba."

There was another shift in the air, and the swelling in my throat subsided enough for me to gasp down a lungful of air.

Bubba nudged Kelson. "*M-row*!"

"I'm calling the doctor, Bubba. Don't worry." Kelson took my phone from Leonard, who was still clutching it, and flipped to my contacts. She punched a button and the next moment, she was talking to Jordan. "Listen—Maddy needs help really bad. Her throat swelled up... No, I don't know why, but she could barely breathe. Bubba helped a little but I don't think he can clear it entirely. Can witches use epinephrine? ... No? All right, can you—okay, thanks. We'll see you in a few minutes." She turned back to me. "Jordan's on his way over. He said to get you into a sitting position. Leonard, can you help me?"

She was unfazed in her nudity, and Leonard didn't even bat an eye. Together, they gently lifted me and helped me onto a chair. Bubba jumped up on the table, nosing me gently.

"I'll watch her while you get dressed." Leonard motioned for Kelson to gather her clothes.

"Thanks." She quickly slid back into her jeans and shirt. It occurred to me that going commando, without a bra, made sense for her, given she had to take off her clothes in order to shape-shift. She glanced around the kitchen.

"I'm going to sweep up the glass here before Luna or Bubba hurt themselves on it."

"Go ahead. I'm keeping watch." Leonard looked like he had aged ten years in the past half hour.

I tried to focus. The oxygen deficit had taken its toll on me, and I had a raging headache. I needed water, but I was scared to drink in case my throat wasn't wide enough and caused me to choke. I rubbed my head, whimpering, and once again, Bubba leaned down, licking my face. I managed to scratch him behind the ears and whisper a *thank-you* to him.

I wasn't sure how long it took—I was fading in

and out of consciousness—but Jordan was suddenly there, examining me. He pulled out a bottle of a clear liquid and drew some into a syringe, injecting me in my thigh.

It was like a bolt of lightning had just hotwired its way through my body. I jumped, gasping as my throat began to clear up. Within a couple of minutes, I was breathing easily again, and feeling as if I'd been wired with more speed than my body could handle. I felt twitchy and jarred and all manners of jittery, but the important thing was that I was breathing again and able to speak.

"My gods, what happened to me?" My voice was hoarse, and my throat felt raw, but otherwise, it seeped into my brain that I wasn't going to die. At least not right now.

"You went into full-on anaphylactic shock. You were touch and go there, Maddy. If Bubba hadn't done...well...whatever it is that Bubba does, you might not have made it." Jordan wasn't smiling. He was entirely serious and he held my gaze until I had to look away.

I leaned back in my chair. "I'm so thirsty."

"Get her some water, please." Jordan motioned to Kelson. He glanced at Leonard. "Are you coming back with me to see Trey? I'm sorry I don't have better news."

"What news? What's going on with Trey?" I glanced from one man to the other.

Jordan cleared his throat. "Trey's not going to make it. There isn't much I can do for him. He was stable until we got to the office, and then he took a quick turn for the worse and slid fast. His pulse is weak, his heartbeat has slowed, and there aren't any signs of brain activity. It's like somebody just decided to turn off a switch and all the life and energy he had—vanished."

That was more than I could take. It was bad enough something had invaded my home, but it was killing one of the werewolves?

"Crap. Motherfucking pus bucket. What the hell happened? What is that thing?" My voice was scratchy and I began to cough. Kelson handed me the water and I sipped it slowly, almost afraid to even taste it. I didn't know what had caused the reaction, though I suspected it had something to do with my unwelcome guest.

"I'd better get back to the office. Trey's not going to last much longer. Maddy, I want you to come with me so that I can give you another examination. I want to run more tests. We need to find out what happened to you so you can avoid the trigger in the future." Jordan stood, motioning to Leonard. "If you want to see Trey alive, come with me. You say he has no family?"

Leonard shrugged. "He's part of the Pack, so we're all his family, but no wife or kids. His mother lives on the island, but she's on a cruise right now and there's no way she can get back here in time. I'll have to stand vigil in her stead. I need to call one of the Death Singers, too, to come out with me. I'll call them on the way. Kelson, tell the boys to finish up for the day and we'll be back tomorrow to check the patches and how they're holding." He paused. "Maddy, you do need a new roof, but these will hold throughout the winter, I think. I'll give you an estimate later, if you don't mind."

I shook my head. "Not at all. I can barely think and I've got a horrible headache."

"I don't want you driving in this condition," Jordan said.

"She can ride in with me. I won't be leaving the office till Trey's...passed...but that gives you time to line up a ride home."

I nodded, agreeing to anything that would get me into the fresh air. I was suddenly feeling claustrophobic and the last thing I wanted to do was worry about driving. "I'll call Sandy. She can pick me up on the way over to my place." I paused, looking around. "But it's not safe leaving you here, Kelson. Or Henry or Bubba and Luna. Or Aegis. What if that shadow found a way to stake him while he's asleep?"

"Stop worrying." Jordan grabbed a sweater of mine off of a coat hook near the sliding glass door. "Put this on. If you refuse to come with me, I'll tell Aegis just how bad off you were and he'll read you the riot act."

"You can't do that! It's against doctor–client privileges." But I stopped. I had to treat this as serious. I couldn't just blow it off. "Fine, but hurry when we get there, please."

"I'll hurry just enough to be thorough," was his oh-so-not-reassuring answer.

KELSON SHOOED ME out, reassuring me that

she would watch over Bubba, Luna, and Aegis. On the way, in Leonard's truck, I called Sandy.

"Can you pick me up at Jordan's on your way to my house?"

There was a hesitation, then, "What happened. Are you all right?"

I was getting awfully tired of that question. "I am now, and I'll tell you the rest when you get here. But you and Max may want to rethink staying at our place. I'll explain it all when you arrive." I hung up, frowning.

"That room really stirred things up, didn't it?" Leonard said, glancing at me as he turned left on Vans Road, which led to the Bedlam Medical Center.

I wasn't sure what to say. One of his friends was dying because of what happened in my house and even though I knew it wasn't my fault, it still felt like I should take some sort of responsibility for it.

"I'm sorry about Trey. He seems like a nice young man." It sounded lame, even to me, but it was the best I could do at this point.

"Maddy? Don't blame yourself. You didn't know what was in there. And now, whatever it is, is running around your house raising hell. I know you didn't do this on purpose. Trey wouldn't blame you. It was bad luck, nothing more."

The fact that Leonard was being so nice made me feel worse. I stared out the window, a tear trickling down my cheek.

"Tell me about Trey. I feel like I owe it to him to know what he's like."

"Trey's father died when he was young. He was

just a pup, really. He was around eight. I knew Raymond, and he was a good man, but he was a bit of a daredevil. This was before the Pretcom were well-known. Raymond decided to go on a vision quest up in the mountains during hunting season. We tried to talk him out of it, but he insisted he'd be fine. A trigger-happy hunter saw him in wolf form and shot him, thinking he was going to be attacked. Raymond turned back into his natural form and the hunter freaked. It ended up in the pages of the *National Tattle-Tale*. Raymond died, but the hunter also suffered. I gather he spent some time in therapy to come to grips with what he had done, and then turned into an anti-hunting advocate. But the fact is, Raymond caused the problem—he knew that was a dangerous thing to do."

I hung my head. "A lot of people died when we were all closeted."

"Yeah, and a lot of people died when we weren't. Especially your kind, with the witch hunters," Leonard said gruffly.

I nodded. He had a point.

"Trey's mother took two jobs to support her son, and the Pack helped as much as we could. That's one of our most sacred values. If you belong to the Pack, you don't go hungry. You don't worry about rent. You have to make your way, but if you're trying and you need help, it's there. The Pack is always there." Leonard punctuated his words with a nod.

"I've always thought werewolves were more supportive of one another than some of the other

shifters. So what happened to Trey as he was growing up?"

"Ronnie managed to keep a good roof over their
heads. We helped her keep food on the table and
the community created a savings fund to help
should Trey want to go to college. He decided he'd
rather work as a tradesman, so Trey and his mother took that money and offered it to another family
having trouble paying for their kids' education. I
hired Trey about fifteen years ago—he spent some
time backpacking around the country first before
coming back to Bedlam to settle down. He's been
working for me since then, and I've never regretted
taking him on."

Leonard fell silent, staring ahead at the road. We
were at the entrance of the Bedlam Medical Center. He eased into a parking spot and turned off
the ignition.

"You mentioned at the house that you needed to
call a—Death Singer?"

He nodded. "Right. Death Singers are spiritual
mourners for the Pack. They guide the spirit out of
the body and into its next transition. We always try
to have one at a passing. It's our way." He paused,
glancing at me as he lifted his phone to his ear. "If
you don't mind, this is personal."

Feeling very much out of place, I hopped out
of the car and slowly headed into Jordan's office.
Not only did I feel like shit, I felt like I had set into
motion a tragic story that would be told and retold
by the Alpha-Pack members. I couldn't shake the
guilt.

JORDAN HAD ARRIVED before us, but he was waiting by the door. He helped me inside.

"Where's Leonard?"

"He's calling a Death Singer." I shook my head, squeezing my eyes shut. "Jordan, I feel so horrible about Trey. I never meant for this to happen."

"You've been thrown on the rocks, Maddy. I know you feel bad, but you weren't at fault. Come on, we'll see about getting you fixed up. You need a good night's sleep, some hearty food, and then when you put a stop to whatever's loose in your place, you'll feel better." He escorted me into one of the exam rooms. "Go ahead and get undressed and into a robe. I need to take a full battery of tests this time, given what happened. I'm going to go get Leonard situated."

"Jordan?" I caught him by the arm. "Why is Trey dying?"

Jordan gave me a noncommittal shrug. "I wish I knew, Maddy. Something's siphoning off his energy, I believe. But I don't know what, and I don't know how to stop this from happening. I'll be back in a few minutes."

As he headed out of the room, I began to change clothes. I had a massive headache and a raw throat, and I was tired, but otherwise I felt okay. I checked myself for any cuts or scrapes but couldn't see any. By the time Jordan returned, I was on the exam table, trying to keep warm in the cool, hospital atmosphere.

"Is he still alive?"

Jordan nodded. "He's hanging on, yes. Leonard is with him and the receptionist has instructions to put through the Death Singer as soon as she arrives. All right, let's see what's changed since yesterday."

He put me through a battery of tests and I submitted to them without complaint. Given I had suddenly developed an allergy to something, I wanted to know what it was that had almost killed me so I could avoid it from now on. I certainly didn't want a repeat performance.

Jordan listened to my heart, his hand precariously between my boobs. I had big breasts, and they weren't all that fond of gravity, and now as I breathed in and out, they jostled his fingers a bit, even beneath the thin gown. I stared at the ceiling as Jordan cleared his throat and noted something down in my chart.

"We've got to stop meeting like this," I said, trying to lighten the mood.

He blushed. "Yeah, too many exams and Aegis will get suspicious that I've got more in mind than just your heartbeat."

Jordan had a girlfriend, but there had always been a little spark between us. Not enough for me to ever even imagine acting on especially since I was with Aegis, but enough that we both felt the little zings when we were in close proximity.

"Well, your heart sounds good." He hung his stethoscope around his neck. "Pulse is high, but that's to be expected with the medication I gave you. By the way, it's a compound that acts like epinephrine does for humans. You're going to be jumpy for quite some time." He paused, frowning. "What were you doing when the attack came on?"

"I was fighting that damned shadow creature. Bubba helped me, but he couldn't fully take away the attack, and he couldn't fully negate the shadow. The little guy saved my life, Jordan." I ducked my head. Over the years, Bubba had paid me back many times over for saving him when he was a baby. I owed him big.

"What kind of magic were you using?"

"A simple disruption-dispel spell. I've used it before without any issues."

"All right. Well," he looked over my chart. "I can't see much here. I'm going to draw some blood and I'll call you with the results. And in case you have another episode, I'll prepare an injection that you can give yourself or somebody else can give you. You'll need to inject the needle into your thigh—the muscle. Got it?"

I nodded. "I've given shots before. I'm not afraid of needles."

"Good. I'll have it prepared—I'll preload two syringes for you, just in case. Keep them in their container unless you need them." He drew my blood, then prepared the shots. "All right, we're done. I swear, you keep me in business, Maddy." But he said it with a grin.

I smiled faintly. "I wish I didn't have to. Could I see Trey before I go, Jordan?"

"I'd take you to see him, but the Alpha-Pack custom is that once a death vigil has started, nobody goes in except the Death Singer and the witnesses.

No one from outside the Pack or family."

"Then please let me know when he passes?" I let out a slow breath, wishing for all the world that I could walk out of the office to find my life had gone back to normal.

Jordan walked me to the front, where Sandy was waiting. She jumped up, a concerned look on her face.

"What happened?"

"My throat decided to swell shut. I had an anaphylactic reaction and before you ask, I don't know why. Bubba saved me. Oh, also, we have a shadow person in the house. *Welcome to my nightmare*, as Uncle Alice said."

Sandy turned to Jordan. "Her *throat* closed up?"

"Yeah, and she's lucky that Bubba was able to help her." He reached out to take me by the shoulder. "Listen to me. I hope you realize *how* lucky you are, Maddy. Your throat was so swollen when I got there, it's a wonder you didn't suffer oxygen deprivation. As it is, prepare for the headache from hell for a day or two." He shook his head. "I suggest plenty of caffeine, though it's probably a good idea to wait a little for the medication to wear off."

Sandy helped me out to her rental car, even though by now I was able to walk without extra support. But I was exhausted. The adrenaline was beginning to wear off, and I felt raw and jarred and all sorts of jumpy.

"Whatever that thing is, it's dangerous. I'm worried about Kelson and the others, though I think Bubba could probably get his ass out of there without a problem."

Sandy frowned as she skirted a branch that had been left in the center of the road. "I'll call Max and tell him to leave Mr. Peabody at home, but we'll stay with you guys tonight. You're not up to fend off this creep alone if he comes at you again. We'll think of something, Maddy, I promise you that."

"Thanks. You're not my best friend for nothing, woman." I leaned back in the seat and closed my eyes, resting till we pulled back into my driveway.

AEGIS WAS PROWLING around the house, a thunderous look on his face. Apparently, when Kelson had told him what happened, he had gone ballistic.

"I will not allow any fucking creature or person to lay a finger on you. I'm hunting down that freak-show ghost and tearing it to shreds." His eyes were ringed with crimson, which meant his inner preda-tor was out and hunting. He made me sit down in the parlor and wouldn't let Sandy leave me. Max he enlisted to help him search the house. They covered every inch of the place, from the attic and secret room, to the basement. Twice.

I tried to calm him down at first, but quickly realized he needed to vent his worry, so I sat back, cup of peppermint tea in hand, and let him go at it.

Sandy arched her eyebrows. "I wouldn't want to be on the other side of that temper."

"I wouldn't either. I'm thinking about using a

Finding spell to locate that shadow thing. Do you think we might be able to take care of him together?"

Sandy frowned, shaking her head. "I'm not certain that's a good idea. Do you really want to stir it up again while you're still feeling punkish?"

I shrugged. "I guess not. I just want to do something. I want this thing out of my house. I wish the tree branch had never broken into that side of the roof. I usually don't like being ignorant of the facts, but right now, I'd be happy to go back to never knowing that something was hiding in a secret room in my attic." I paused. "Kelson suggested calling Leroy."

Leroy Jerome was the headmaster of Neverfall and he was a fine man, with muscles that had muscles. With smooth black skin and a smooth bald head, he looked hotter than Shemar Moore. He was also brilliant and a damned good headmaster.

"I think that's a good idea. Why don't I give him a call? I have to talk to him about Jenna's new teacher for her Potions class, anyway. She's having trouble and the teacher isn't doing much to help." She pulled out her phone.

While she was talking to him, I got a call from Jordan.

"Hey, Jordan." I waited. It had to be one of two things: either Trey had died, or he had found the answer as to what was wrong with me. I hoped for the latter.

"Maddy? I've got news and it's important that you listen to me and follow my instructions exactly. I managed to analyze that sample of black powder, and I also found out what's wrong with you. Are you listening?" He sounded so worried that my stomach dropped.

"Yeah, I'm listening. Spell it out for me."

"First, the powder is a very powerful Hex-Builder. In other words, it's a powerful cursing powder. When it spilled, it cursed your house and everybody connected to it. Anybody staying in the home for any length of time runs the risk of being cursed. Trey took it full strength, it sounds like, and you said you inhaled it?"

I nodded, suddenly terrified. "Am I going to end up like Trey?"

"I don't think so, but Maddy, you've developed an allergy to magic. Literally, if you use magic, or are near it when it's used, it could kill you."

I groaned, dropping to sit on an ottoman. "What the hell? I'm a *witch*!"

"I'm sorry, but yes, you've developed an allergy to magic. I'm not joking. For now, until we figure out how to break this curse, you don't dare use any more magic, or be near it when it's used. You'll run the risk of going into anaphylaxis." He sounded so deadly serious that there was no doubt in my mind he meant business.

"How do we break the curse?"

"That's the thing. I need to know what kind of a curse it is, and the origin of the magic. It's old and it's powerful. In fact, I'm coming by to gather as much of that powder as possible. I may need it to build a hex-breaking potion."

"When you say magic, do you mean *any* magic?"

"Yeah. And Maddy, I hate to tell you this, but as you know, sex and magic are entwined—they both work through the kundalini. You should lay off the hot stuff for now until we figure out if you'll be safe. I don't think Aegis is going to want you to go into anaphylactic shock during orgasm. And no, before you ask, I'm not joking." He paused, then added, "I have to go. I'll talk to you in a bit."

As I stared at my phone, unable to think of anything to say, Sandy called me back over to the sofa. She smiled.

"I talked to Leroy. He and Professor Weatherhaul, who teaches history and archaeology, will come by tomorrow around two P.M. They're interested in seeing the secret room. Who called?"

I shook my head. "That's great, Sandy. Jordan said the house is under a curse, and I've apparently developed an allergy to magic. I can't use it, can't be around it, and I can't even have sex right now because the kundalini force is too close to the magical energy." I shook my head. "This is so not what I expected to hear. The curse? Yeah, that makes sense, but allergic to magic? If it wasn't so serious, I'd be laughing out my ass right now."

Sandy stared at me. "Did I actually hear you right? You're—"

"Allergic to magic. It can kill me." I grumbled under my breath. "I might as well be a werewolf. Only magic won't *kill* them, they just don't like it."

Just then, Aegis and Max strode in, Aegis looking pissed.

"I can't find him anywhere, and I can't find Franny either. What's wrong? You look like you just ate a frog or something."

"I might as well have." I ran down what Jordan had told me. "This fucking sucks."

Aegis sat beside me and wrapped his arms around me. "Sweetheart, we'll get through this." He kissed me and, of course, because I couldn't, the only thing I wanted to do was yank him down on the sofa and fuck him. Hard, hot, and heavy. He was so hard and...

"Stop!" I tried to shake off my thoughts.

"Stop what?" he asked.

Realizing I had just spoken aloud, I let out a long sigh. "Nothing. I was talking to myself. I can't have sex. I can't work magic. I can handle this for a while, but my mood's going south. Also, if I don't use my magic, after a while it can back up and harm me that way. I'll have to see if Jordan can drain it off me, kind of like giving blood if you have too much iron." I fell back against the sofa in an exaggerated sigh. "At least Leroy's bringing someone out here to look at the room tomorrow. And Jordan's coming by to gather as much of that powder as he can. I hate letting him go up there, though."

"I'll get it for him. I'll go up there now. I can't breathe it in, and I doubt if it's going to affect me." Aegis jumped up and headed for the kitchen.

I started to call him back but Max shook his head. "Let him do this. He's angry that you're in danger, he's angry he can't do anything or find the shadow person, and now I'll give you odds he's freaked that you're hurt and again, he's helpless. Let him do what he can."

I nodded. "I get it. And it's probably safer for him to do this than let Jordan go up there. I don't want him getting hit by this." As I tried to sit back and be patient, a loud thump echoed down from upstairs. I jumped up. "Aegis!"

But as I started to run for the stairs, Franny appeared, looking frantic.

"Help me!" she screamed. "Henry—something's happened to Henry!"

Chapter 7

HYSTERICAL, FRANNY WAS wringing her hands. Max headed for the stairs and I followed, feeling like everything was caving in around me. Sandy was right behind me, and by the time we reached Henry's room, Max was already examining the prone man. Henry was struggling to speak.

"Henry, can you hear me?" I knelt beside Max, then motioned to Sandy. "Call the paramedics."

She nodded, pulling out her phone. Meanwhile, I was trying to get Franny to move. While she wasn't physically interfering, her hysterics weren't helping the situation.

"Franny, back off. Go over there and wait so we can help Henry." I shooed her out of the way. She gave me a tearful sniff and moved.

Max was taking Henry's pulse. "He's alive, but his pulse feels erratic. Get me a blanket."

I grabbed a blanket and a pillow off Henry's

bed. I handed the pillow to Max, then arranged the blanket over him. At that moment, Aegis peeked through the door.

"What are you guys—" He stopped, staring at Henry. "What's wrong with Henry?"

"I don't know. Sandy's called an ambulance. Franny said he just keeled over. He probably had a heart attack or a stroke or something like that."

Franny let out a loud sob from the corner. "He said he felt odd, then stood up and fainted."

Sandy headed for the door. "I'll go downstairs and wait for the paramedics."

Henry moaned, but he didn't open his eyes. I gently removed his glasses, which were still hooked over his ears, and set them on the dresser. "Franny, I know you're upset, but what happened? We need to know so we can tell the paramedics. The more information they have, the better they'll be able to treat him."

She blushed. "We were talking. He was telling me about his life back in the Civil War, and what Althea did to him. I finally told him that I loved him," she said, her voice a whisper. "And he told me he can't love me, because of the curse. I got upset... I accused him of trifling with my emotions. We argued...he stood up and fainted."

I let out a slow breath. "So Henry didn't know how you felt? I thought for sure he did."

Franny stared at the floor. "I think he knew, but he never said anything. I guess I built the whole romance up in my head. He said he was fond of me, Maddy. *Fond.* He insisted that he never told me he loved me. I didn't want to hear it, but he's right. I deluded myself into thinking he was court-ing me, but he wasn't." She paused, then raised her head, a stricken look on her face. "Did I cause this?"

For a moment, I wasn't sure what to say, but then I shook my head. "No, Franny, this isn't your fault. Henry probably hasn't been feeling well for a while. You know how men are, they don't like to talk about their problems."

Here I had been thinking that Henry had been toying with Franny's affections. But *fond* didn't mean love. Franny had led me to believe they were having a romance, but now I could see that it was all built up in her mind. Henry cared about her, but what he had told her was true. He was under a spell that prevented him from ever having a real relationship. In fact, *fond* was probably as close to love as he could ever get.

At that moment, we could hear Sandy on the stairs. She was talking to someone, and when she entered the room, two paramedics followed her. I recognize them as Summer Fae from the fire department. We all moved back, giving them room to work.

"What happened?" asked one of the paramedics as he knelt beside Henry.

"We're not entirely sure, but Franny was with him when he fainted. They got in a debate over something, and Henry stood up and fainted dead away." Technically, debates and arguments could be filed under the same category, at least in my mind.

They took his blood pressure, checked his heart,

and his eyes.

"He's human, right?"

"Yes, but he's under a curse. He was born in 1840, and a witch cursed him to a long life. So he's not exactly your typical human." I didn't like giving away Henry's secret, but this was a medical necessity.

The medic looked up at me, then back at Henry. If he was startled, he didn't show it.

"I'm not certain, but I think he's had a stroke. We'll take him into the hospital. Do you have the name of his next of kin? Or are they all dead?"

I hadn't even thought of that. Anybody in Henry's immediate family—his parents, his siblings—all had to be long dead. Whether he had any distant cousins, I didn't know.

"I suppose we're about the closest thing to family that he's got right now. I'll do what I can to find out if there are next of kin." I glanced over at Sandy. "Do you mind going with Henry to the hospital? I'll go through his room and see if I can find anything pointing to any relatives." I didn't want to say out loud that I wanted to have a talk with Franny, because I didn't want to embarrass her. But Sandy seemed to sense where I was going with this.

"Of course. I'll get my coat. Max, why don't you stay here? I'll be fine. You don't mind if I take your car, do you?"

"Of course not," the weretiger said. He gave her a quick kiss on the forehead. "Take care of yourself, and call me if you need anything."

As they headed out the door to take Henry

downstairs into the ambulance, I looked around the room. Henry kept it neat as a pin. I turned back to Aegis.

"I'm going to have a look through Henry's things. I'll see if he's got an address book. I don't know if I can get into his phone. He might have it password-protected, but I'll check where I can."

Aegis nodded. "I'll go finish gathering that powder for Jordan."

At that moment, the doorbell rang. It was probably Jordan.

"Max, can you go answer the door?" As Aegis and Max headed out for their respective tasks, I started looking through Henry's drawers. I didn't like snooping, but this was an emergency.

Franny had remained in the room. For a while, she didn't say a word, just watched me as I searched through Henry's things. Finally, she let out a choked sob.

"How could I have been so stupid? I truly thought he meant he loved me. When I was a girl, when a man told you he was fond of you, it usually meant he was in love."

I glanced at her. She was sitting on the bed—or rather, partially through the bed—and she looked so distraught that I wished I could give her a hug. I stopped my search and walked over to sit down next to her. The temperature of the air distinctly cooled as I approached.

"Franny, please don't feel bad. It's easy to misunderstand people, especially when you're from different worlds."

"No, don't you see? Henry and I grew up in the

same time. Or close to it. He knows what it's like to live back when I did. I may have been born fifty years before he was, but he understands it."

"Franny, *I'm* older than both of you. I lived through that time period too. So did Aegis, and Sandy, and Max. We're *all* older than you are. What made Henry seem so special?"

She shrugged, staring at the floor. "Maybe he just enjoyed talking about the past more." She paused, then pressed on. "Maybe it was that he really seemed interested in what I had to say. He treated me like I was special. He treated me like I *mattered.*"

Right then, I realized that I had made a horrible mistake. I had been treating Franny like a wayward pet, not like a spirit who had needs and feelings. Oh, we chatted now and then, and I had done my best to make her happy with the computer. But I had never really taken a lot of time to get to know her, and we usually treated her like a wayward child. I closed my eyes for a moment, trying to figure out how to make things better.

"Franny, I want to apologize. You don't have any choice about where you live. You're stuck here, and sometimes I forget that. You're part of our household, and even though I'm still looking for a way to break the curse that holds you here, I think maybe we need to talk more. Hang out a bit more."

She slowly raised her gaze, giving me a hopeful look. "I'd like that. I admit, I get lonely. I do love to read, and I thank you very much for all you've done for me. But it gets lonely in my world. And you and Aegis and Bubba, you all have your lives.

You're all alive. I live in what feels like limbo. I guess Henry paying attention to me just made me feel alive again."

"Can I ask you what the argument was about? I know you argued about feelings, but it might help for me to know when he gets back."

She blushed again. "You're going to think I'm horrible."

"We've all done things that are horrible at some point in our lives. Tell me."

"I don't know what got into me. I would *never* think to say this to anybody, so I don't know why I said it to him." She was beginning to get frantic again.

Puzzled, I cocked my head. "What did you say?"

"Please believe me, I really don't know what came over me."

"All right. I believe you. Tell me what you said."

She blushed a horrible crimson. "Before the argument, I got impatient. I suggested that since he was in love with me, if he were to...*kill himself*... We could be together." She looked up, a fearful expression in her eyes.

"I wish I could take it back. I wish I'd never said it. That's when he told me that he didn't love me, and he said it was a horrible thing to suggest to anybody. When he said he didn't love me, I accused him of trifling with my emotions. He insisted that he had never said the word *love*, and he's right. And then it got nasty. It's like a dark shadow filled the room and we were yelling at each other. And then he fainted."

I wasn't sure what to say. Franny had actually

suggested that Henry kill himself to be with her? That didn't sound anything like Franny. In fact, that was the last thing I'd ever expect to hear come out of her mouth.

"You say a dark shadow filled the room?"

She nodded. "And I'm talking an actual shadow. It felt like we weren't alone. And it seemed to grow as our argument grew. It felt like it was feeding on the anger, Maddy."

I nodded, listening. "I wonder if it's part of the curse that's come over this house. Keep an eye out, if you would. If you notice any strange presences, come tell us."

"Do you want me to stand guard?" She sounded almost proud to offer her services.

While I didn't think we needed to go that far, I realized it would give Franny something to do that would make her feel needed. And who knew, it might actually come in handy.

"That's a good idea. If you get tired, take a break, but why don't you make the rounds? I'd stay away from the attic area, obviously, but just keep an eye out."

She flashed me a faint smile, the first I'd seen since Henry had fainted, and saluted me.

"Yes, ma'am! I'm on the job." As she vanished into the wall, I shook my head. I had had some strange roommates over the years, but Franny had to be one of the oddest.

I resumed my search through Henry's things, finally coming up with a Rolodex. As I thumbed through it, I saw that it was all libraries and universities, as well as a few names. I didn't recognize any of them, and none of them had Henry's last name. They were all out of the area, and I had my doubts that any of them were related to him.

Heading downstairs, I heard Jordan talking to Max in the living room.

"Jordan, has Aegis gotten the powder down for you?" I swung into the room.

Jordan shook his head. He was seated on the sofa, one knee crossed over the other.

"No, but that's all right. I don't mind the wait. Max was telling me that Henry took ill?"

"Yeah, the paramedics took him off to the hospital. Sandy went with him. We're expecting a call when she finds out what's wrong. The paramedics suspect a stroke."

"Damn. Everything seems to be happening here lately."

"It's that goddamn room. The powder, whatever was released when that urn broke... You were right when you said there is a curse on the house. I need to call Garret, and see if he can think of anything. Tomorrow, a professor from Neverfall is coming out to take a look at the glyphs and see what he can figure out. We need to take care of this soon." I sat down beside Jordan, and let out a long breath. "So, this allergy I've got. Do you think it's permanent?"

"I don't think we can know yet. Chances are it was brought on by the curse. Which means, if the curse can be broken, there is a good chance it will lift." He stared at me, giving me a sorrowful smile. "I'm sorry I don't have better news. I know this has got to be difficult."

"I'm just afraid that if I don't use my powers,

they'll back up and cause an overflow. You know how it is."

He nodded.

When I had been with Craig, I had to secretly use my magic because he didn't like it. He knew I was a witch when we got married, but apparently he changed his mind on just how well he could handle a Pretcom wife. And I wasn't Samantha from *Bewitched*, I wasn't willing to knuckle under and try to play the good little housewife to soothe my husband's ego.

Aegis entered the room, a glass jar in hand. It was filled with black powder. "Hi, Jordan. Will this be enough? There is a bit more that I could gather if you like, but this is about eight ounces of it."

Jordan gingerly accepted the jar. Aegis had taped it shut and now he produced a plastic bag, handing it to the doctor.

"I thought you might want to put it in here, just in case something happens and the glass breaks. That's a mason jar, though, so it should be all right."

"Thank you," Jordan said. "I appreciate the thought. The last thing I need is to spill the stuff all over myself."

My phone rang, and I glanced at the caller ID. Sandy.

"Hi. How's Henry?" I asked, hoping that she'd say he was all right.

"He's alive. They say he's had a serious stroke. They want to keep him at the hospital for at least a few days. Right now, he's conscious, but he can't talk very well, and his left side appears to be paralyzed. The doctor says he thinks Henry will regain use of his arm and his leg, but to what degree, he can't tell."

I closed my eyes, taking in the bad news. "I couldn't find any sign of any next of kin."

"That's no surprise. I'll be there for another hour or two to see how he does. He's not fully stable yet, but they're making headway."

As I hung up, I thought that this night couldn't get any worse. Then, quickly, I canceled the thought, not wanting to invoke even more bad luck.

MORNING CAME, AND with it a splash of sun-shine filtered through the windows. I opened the French doors to my balcony, walking out to take in a deep breath of fresh air. Aegis had screened it in a month or so ago so that Luna and Bubba could come out and enjoy the fresh air too, without chancing falling off the edge. Sandy had arrived home at about ten P.M., with news that Henry was stabilized, but in serious condition. The doctors expected him to pull through, but they weren't sure just how much the stroke had damaged him. Aegis had sat up all night, watching over the rest of us as we slept.

Finally, I dressed in a warm turtleneck and a pair of jeans, zipped up my ankle boots, and swept my hair back into a long ponytail. I dashed on a quick base of makeup, and then headed downstairs. Kelson was making breakfast and Max and Sandy were already at the table.

"How did you sleep?"

Sandy yawned. "Like a log, though I could use another couple hours. I've already called about Henry. He made it through the night and they say he's now in fairly stable condition. He's awake, but he still can't speak. They explained to him what happened, and asked if he had any next of kin. He indicated no, so we're pretty much it."

"That's sad, really. But I'm glad we were here for him." I was just accepting my quint shot latte from Kelson when Franny materialized in the center of the kitchen nook. Startled, I almost spilled my drink, but I didn't chastise her this time. Come to think of it, outside of announcing her presence in a non-corporeal voice, there wasn't really any way she *could* prepare us for her visitations.

"You're awake!" She looked delighted to see us. "I have something to report. I know Aegis was up watching all night—in fact, we had a nice conversation at one point. For a vampire, he's actually not too bad."

"You have news?" I gently prodded her. Franny had a way of rambling off onto disconnected subjects and she was the queen of the non sequitur.

"Yes, actually I do. I was hanging out in the basement for a little bit, and I heard a voice down there. It wasn't Aegis—he was upstairs watching the bedrooms. I heard someone growl, and then I heard somebody say 'I'm coming for you' in what sounded like a threatening voice." Franny blinked, twisting her fingers around her handkerchief. "I don't know who he was talking to, and I hope it wasn't me, but it didn't sound friendly."

"You're right. That doesn't sound friendly at all. Did it feel like it was directed at you?"

"I'm not sure. I didn't feel personally attacked, if that's what you mean. But I didn't stick around to chance it, either." She paused, then glanced over at Sandy. "If I may ask, how's Henry doing?"

"He's in stable condition, but he had a serious stroke. He won't be coming home for a few days." Sandy shifted in her seat. I had told her about what happened between Franny and Henry.

"The next time anybody goes to the hospital to talk to him, can they please take my best wishes to him? And please tell him I'm sorry we argued. That I didn't mean anything I said."

"We'll make sure he knows," I said. I didn't want Franny to have to revisit her unfortunate choice of suggestions. I had the feeling she had been prompted by something other than her own conscience. In fact, I had a feeling that the dark shadow she had talked about had instigated the entire argument.

"Thank you. I'm going to go read for a while, if you don't mind. It calms me down."

"Go ahead. I added a couple books to your library that you might find interesting," I said.

"Thanks, Maddy. I appreciate it." She vanished before I could tell her welcome.

I waited for a moment, until her presence was gone from the room.

"I think Franny was influenced by this curse, and by whatever it is that got loose from that jar.

There's no way in the world she would have ever suggested that to Henry without being prompted. So if this creature—or spirit—whatever it is, can influence both mortals and spirits alike, it must be extremely powerful. When did you say the professor from Neverfall is coming over?"

"Two o'clock. So we have some time to fill." Sandy glanced at the clock.

I frowned, accepting the plate of eggs and bacon from Kelson. She set a platter of toast in the center of the table, then joined us for breakfast.

"I don't dare take any bookings until we get this taken care of." My phone went off and I glanced at my text messages. Jordan had texted me. "Trey died."

"Did Jordan say what he died of?"

I quickly texted Jordan, asking him. He texted back.

IT'S AS THOUGH THE LIFE JUST BLED OUT OF HIS BODY. I COULDN'T FIND A DAMN THING WRONG, EXCEPT HIS HEART KEPT GETTING WEAKER, AND HIS BRAIN FUNCTIONS WENT FLAT. SOMETHING ATE HIS ENERGY. I'M GOING TO DO AN AUTOPSY, SEE IF I CAN FIND AN ANSWER. LEONARD ASKED ME TO TELL YOU THAT HE AND HIS CREW WILL BE BACK TOMORROW MORNING TO FINISH THE JOB ON THE ROOF.

I texted back a thank-you. "Whatever it was, it basically ate Trey's essence."

Max offered to help Kelson rearrange the pantry, a big job but it needed to be done before the holidays, while Sandy and I headed out back for a walk. Even though the sun was shining, it was chilly, so we wore our jackets, huddling against the breeze that gusted past. The air smelled clear and fresh, and I realized that I felt much better outside than I did in.

"I've got to get rid of this curse. I didn't realize it was hanging over the Bewitching Bedlam like a cloud. Franny talked about a dark shadow in the basement. I'd love to do a Divining spell, but I don't dare. I can't even be in the same room when it's being done." I glanced over at Sandy, finally expressing my fear. "What do I do if this allergy doesn't go away? How can I be a witch if I can't perform magic? And it's not like the magical energy is gone. I can feel it inside me, pressing. But I don't dare let it out."

"We'll get you through this. You know Jordan is brilliant, and he'll find an antidote to the curse. Have you called Garret yet?"

I shook my head, scuffing through the leaves on the grass. The scent of wood smoke drifted past from a neighbor's house. The thought crossed my mind that we should plant apple trees out here, and make our own apple cider in the autumn.

"I want to wait to see what the professor from Neverfall has to say. Garret may or may not be able to do anything, but if he can, the more information he has, the better." I shivered as a strong gust blew past, swirling the leaves into the air like a whirlwind in bronze and copper.

"Max and I have decided on a wedding date," Sandy said.

Delighted at the change in conversation, I

clapped my hands, then thrust them under my arms again to keep them warm. "When?"

"We've decided to get married on Ostara. Well, not on the actual holiday, since our coven has to lead the town in the celebration, but we thought maybe the day before? And of course, we want you to be the priestess."

I slipped my arm through her elbow, pulling her close. "Of course I will. You know that. I'll do anything for you guys. Have you decided where?"

"What about the grove at the temple of Arian-rhod? Has anybody booked it yet?"

Our temple—dedicated to the goddess Arian-rhod, whom we all served—rented out one of the groves on our land for community events or for private parties, although they had to be spiritually oriented.

"I don't think so. If we haven't, you know that it's yours."

"I'd ask you to be my maid of honor, except you're going to be the priestess. So I thought I'd ask Jenna to walk with me up the aisle."

"I think that's a wonderful idea," I said. I paused, then added, "What about Fata Morgana? Do you think she'll be coming in for it?"

Sandy shivered—I could feel it through her arm.

"Isn't the question really, *Do I want her to come in for it*? On one hand, it wouldn't feel right without her. But given the way she is... I'm a little scared to have her here for my wedding."

I knew exactly what Sandy was talking about. It'd been both lovely and tragic to see Fata again. She was growing into something neither Sandy nor

I could understand. She was becoming a goddess, and in so doing, she had already lost so much of her humanity. It wasn't that she was malignant or evil—although she *could* be cruel and vicious—but she had evolved beyond the life we were living. And she was confused and afraid of what she was becoming, even as she reveled in it.

"I guess we'll have to wait and see. She'll do as she will. I don't know that we can stop her. Anyway, let's talk about more pleasant things. What about your dress? Have you any ideas yet?"

Sandy shrugged. "You know, I always thought I might want a designer dress if I got married again. But the more I think about it, the more I'm thinking I might go simple. When Brad and I started out, we had a big wedding but look how it turned out. Max has been married before, and so have I—several times. I thought you might go shopping with me to see what we could find. I don't want to wear white. For one thing, it's not our tradition, and for another, I think for a spring wedding I want something in pale pink or a sage green."

We chatted a bit more about the decor and themes until we came to the edge of the forest.

"How goes plans for your campground?" she asked.

"Fairly well. Aegis is clearing out a lot of land. He comes out and works during the early morning while there's enough light to see, but the sun hasn't risen yet. We have time. He could afford to have it done all at once, but we decided we wanted to take it at a slower pace—to figure out exactly the way we want it."

"How are you two doing?" Sandy asked. "He hasn't proposed yet, has he?"

I laughed. "You have weddings on the brain, woman. No, Aegis has not proposed and I haven't asked him to. And I haven't encouraged him either. Just like this campground, we're taking things at our own pace. I know he loves me, and he knows I love him. And right now, that's all that matters."

The sky overhead darkened slightly, and we could see an army of clouds rolling in from the northwest. Moisture hung heavy in the air, and it would be raining by noon. But the brief sojourn into sunshine had been welcome. As we turned and headed back to the house, I realized that I almost dreaded going inside. And that wasn't like me at all. I loved my home, I loved my bed-and-breakfast. Yes, a pall had been cast over my house, and I wanted it gone.

Chapter 8

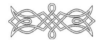

WHEN LEORY JEROME arrived, he brought a welcome breath of fresh air with him. The man could light up the room like a disco ball—tall, with a smooth shaven head, his skin was a rich brown and his eyes flashed with both life and magic. Good to his word, he had brought with him another professor. She was about four and a half feet tall, and looked as old as the hills. She probably was, given that she appeared to be Fae.

"Maddy, Cassandra, may I present Ms. Weatherhaul? She's the professor I told you about." He motioned to us. "Alaysia, this is Maudlin Gallowglass and Cassandra Clauson."

The elderly Fae looked us up and down before nodding. "We actually met, long ago. Let's hope we don't have need to employ your services again like we did back in Europe."

I blinked. We had met Alaysia Weatherhaul before? I had no memory of the meeting, but then a lot of things from that time were a blur. But Sandy stared at her for a moment, then snapped her fingers.

"Back in Kerrville." She glanced at me. "You remember, that tiny little village outside of Dublin? We spent a couple of nights there before we moved over to the continent, when we first started hunting."

I blinked. *Of course.* Alaysia Weatherhaul had been working in an inn, and I remembered that she had led us to our rooms. She had looked younger than she did now, although she had probably been old as the hills even then. The Fae only looked old when they were ancient—and they aged rapidly toward the ends of their lives.

"You warned us about the witch hunters staying in the inn. I remember now. You helped us get away early in the morning before they were up and scouting around." I held out my hand. "I don't know if we thanked you properly back then, but I'd like to now."

Alaysia smiled, nodding graciously as she shook my hand. "Aye, girl. That was me. I knew who you were. Rumor ran quickly through the grapevine back then. And I knew where you were headed and what you were going to do. I couldn't let them catch you."

I felt faint for a moment, as the past suddenly collided with the present. "It's amazing what a few hundred years will do to bring people together."

"Why don't you tell me what your problem is? Unfortunately, I have a class in a couple hours."

Her eyes crinkled at the edges, as her lips slightly tilted into a smile.

As we let them upstairs, Sandy and I ran down what had happened. Max followed, and he opened the trapdoor and pulled down the ladder for us. I didn't really want to go back up those stairs. I was growing to hate my own attic, but somebody had to show them what we were talking about. Before I set foot on the first rung, I turned to Sandy.

"You stay down here. There's no need for both of us to be in the line of fire."

She nodded, backing away as I began to ascend the ladder. Behind me Leroy and Alaysia nimbly followed. For such an old Fae, Alaysia was pretty damned spry. I led them to the attic, gauging how much of it had already been patched as we went. It looked like Leonard's crew had finished for the most part, but I knew that within a few months they would be tearing the whole thing up again. Hopefully, they wouldn't find any other hidden surprises.

I opened the door to the secret room and stood back for them to enter.

Leroy went first, and then Alaysia. I ducked in behind them and turned on as many of the lights as I could that Max had set around the room.

Alaysia gasped. "I haven't seen this in years. Centuries, in fact." She slowly made her way to the walls, not touching them, peering closely at the glyphs.

"You recognize the language, then?"

She nodded. "Yes, definitely. This is Sumerian cuneiform."

"Then you can read what it says?" I held my breath.

Finally, something went right. Alaysia nodded.

"Yes, I can translate it for you. It will take me a little time, and I have to use magic to do so, but I can probably have a rough translation of all of these glyphs for you within an hour. I may be old, but my memory is fully intact."

I cleared my throat. "I can't be up here, if you're using magic. Before you begin, please do understand that this is some sort of curse—Jordan Farrows has determined that. And I got hit with the brunt of it. Well, me and one of the Alpha-Pack. He's dead now, and I've developed an allergy to magic."

"Then go downstairs and wait for us," Leroy said. "We'll be all right. I'm a shadow witch." He shooed me away. Shadow witches worked on the astral, more than with any one particular element. They were extremely powerful, and they were few and far between. Sandy and I suspected that Jenna was going to be a shadow witch, but we hadn't been able to have her tested yet.

I scrambled down the ladder, getting as far away as I could from the attic. I explained to Sandy and Max what they were doing up there.

"Why don't you go downstairs?" Sandy suggested. "I'd feel better if you had plenty of distance between you and the attic. Max and I will wait here."

I thanked her, and then headed downstairs to wait. Kelson was busy cleaning the kitchen, so I decided to pop into the library and see how Franny was doing.

Franny looked up as I entered. "Hi, Maddy. Did you want something?"

I shook my head. "No, I'm fine. I just need to be away from the attic while the linguist is up there. She's using some spells to translate the language. Apparently those glyphs are ancient Sumerian in origin."

"How interesting. You know, that rings a bell. The woman who lived here around the turn of the century? The one I said I kind of remembered? There's something about her that makes me think about ancient civilizations. Something I caught in passing, but I can't remember what. I'm sorry. If I can think of it, I'll let you know."

I decided to hop on my laptop and do some sleuthing. "You said she left here around 1925?"

Franny nodded. "Yeah, it was somewhere around that time."

I pulled up City Hall records that were open to the public, and began to search on my property. In 1920, a woman named Lilis Spencer had bought the house. She sold it in 1932. That gave me something to go on.

I brought up another browser and typed "Lilis Spencer." I didn't expect to find much, but was surprised when a string of entries and links appeared. She even had an entry on Witchapedia, a site devoted to witches and witchcraft. I scanned through the entry.

Lilis Spencer, of British and Assyrian birth, was born August 2, 1655. She is the daughter of Sir Reginald Alfred Carter Spencer and Arbella

Nadir. A witch on her mother's side, she later went into her father's profession—archaeology. Lilis Spencer was one of the early pioneers for women in the field. Little is known about her except that she worked on an early excavation of Kish, an ancient tell, in Sumer (Mesopotamia). She was under the supervision of Henri de Genouialloac. She worked with the excavation from January 1912 through April 1912. She vanished from the archaeological scene shortly after her time spent on the Kish excavation. She was next seen emigrating to America in 1920. She vanished around 1932 and no one knows where she went, or if she still lives.

I printed out the entry. If Lilis had been at the tell, and she had owned this house, there had to be some connection between her and the upstairs room. I did a number of other searches, trying every possible combination I could in order to find out what had happened to Lilis, but the entry on Witchapedia had been correct. It was as if she had just vanished off of the earth.

I looked up to see that Franny had disappeared. Wondering where she went, I called out, "Franny? Are you still around?" But there was no answer. Figuring she had gotten bored, I headed into the kitchen where Kelson was making lunch. I began to help her when there was a scream from upstairs, and both of us dropped the sandwiches we were making and ran up to the second floor.

"What's wrong?" I looked around, half expecting to see someone dead on the floor.

Sandy shook her head. "I'm not certain. Alaysia screamed. Max was about to go up there to make sure they're okay."

Max started up the ladder, but as he did so, Alaysia's legs swung over the trapdoor opening. He jumped down, and then helped her down the ladder, Leroy quickly following.

"Shut that door," Leroy said, glancing at me. "Maddy, get back. I need to throw a spell and you shouldn't be in the area if you are having a problem with magic."

I raced toward the stairway, fuming that I couldn't help out. As I dashed down the stairs, I stopped when I heard a loud *poof* from the hallway above. I could feel the energy sparking off my aura, making me prickle and tingle. Luckily, it didn't seem to do any more than that. I hesitantly started to ascend the stairs again, but they were coming down—all four of them.

"What happened?"

Alaysia looked nerve wracked, and it was unusual to see one of the Fae her age looking frightened. "I translated it, all right. I almost wish I hadn't. Who the hell owned this house?"

"Apparently, a witch who was also an archaeologist back in the early 1900s. Her name was Lilis Spencer, and she was part English, part Assyrian, I think—her mother was a witch. She worked on a dig in an ancient tell from Sumerian days. What did you find out?"

"Can you get me a glass of sherry?" Alaysia asked.

Kelson hurried off to bring us drinks. Sandy and

Leroy led Alaysia over to the sofa and helped her sit down. She looked shakier than a house of cards. Kelson returned with the sherry bottle and several cordial glasses. Sandy poured, handing them to everyone, as I leaned forward, anxious to hear what Alaysia had to say.

"I also looked at the pottery shards you left. From what I can tell, the writing on the wall is a hymn to Ereshkigal, the Sumerian goddess of the Underworld. It's a plea to keep the person in the urn locked in there."

"If Lilis was praying to the goddess of the Underworld to keep somebody locked up in that urn, I kind of hate to ask who the hell it was. And I assume that breaking the urn freed whoever it was?" I didn't like to make assumptions, but this seemed a pretty sure bet.

Alaysia nodded. "Oh yeah. It released him. If I am correct, the person in the urn was named Etum. He was a sorcerer. An ancient sorcerer who was incredibly powerful. He was trapped because he was treacherous and apparently had used his powers for his own gain and killed a number of women and children. He tried to defy death, so Ereshkigal cursed him to a half-life. He's neither living nor dead, but caught between the worlds. And he was trapped inside the urn for who knows how many thousands of years. Now, he's free and running around your house."

Holy crap. I couldn't believe my luck.

"Let me get this straight. An ancient sorcerer who was so evil that the goddess of the Underworld cursed him is free in my house?"

Alaysia gave me a shrug. "That's about the size of it."

"Can he leave my house? Is there a chance he *will* leave my house on his own?"

Leroy shook his head. "It looks like this Lilis created a magical barrier in the walls. He can't get out."

Kind of like Franny, I thought. But Etum was a most unwelcome house ghost. Or spirit. Or whatever the fuck he was.

I rubbed my head. "I have a headache."

Sandy laughed, rubbing my shoulders. "Well at least we know what we're dealing with now. That's something. And if we know what we're dealing with, we can find an answer to it."

I patted her hand, grateful for her support. "I love that you're so positive in the face of all this crap. I need that. All right, what do I do about this?" I asked Leroy and Alaysia.

Leroy said, "I might be able to help. As a shadow witch, I am used to dealing with things on the astral plane. The first thing we have to figure out is *how* to get rid of him. And we can't get rid of him till we destroy that magical barrier that Lilis created."

"I'm afraid I'm out of my repertoire here," Alaysia said. "But what I can do is research some of the ancient texts and look for any mention of breaking a curse set by Ereshkigal. You see, when you broke the urn, that curse was unleashed on your house not because of Etum, but because you set him free."

"Oh my gods. Then the curse is actually from

Ereshkigal?" Even better! My stomach was knotted up like a tangle of spaghetti.

"Again, about the size of it."

"Maddy! Maddy! I need you out here." Kelson was calling from the living room.

Wondering what could have gone wrong now, I jumped up and ran into the living room, followed by Sandy and Max. Kelson was standing there, pointing at the painting that I had hung up a few months back. I had found the painting of Franny in the basement. It had been painted by an unrequited love of hers while she was still alive. She had been overjoyed that I had decided to hang it up, and it fit the decor, giving a pastoral feel to the room.

I gasped, stumbling back, at first thinking that Franny had come to life in the painting. But then I saw that it was really Franny—not the image of her, but her spirit. She was pounding on the glass, mouthing something, and I realized that she was trapped inside.

"What the hell? How did you get in there?" But even as I spoke, I knew the answer. Etum. It had to be him. If he could chase her like he had earlier, maybe he could drive her into the painting and trap her.

"Can you hear me? Nod twice if you can." I pressed up close to the glass, and enunciating my words as clearly as I could. I hope to that, even if she couldn't hear me, she could read my lips.

Luckily, she nodded. She seemed to be calming down a bit.

"Franny, is he in there with you now? The shadow figure?" I was worried about him having access to her, and what he could do to her. A powerful sorcerer could disrupt a spirit, and the last thing I wanted was to see Franny obliterated or sent somewhere horrible.

She straightened her shoulders, then shook her head. But she looked terribly frightened and I wondered how long she could keep it together.

"You're trapped in a picture frame. Can you see the picture behind you?" It was as if her image was superimposed over the painting of her. I wondered how far her world went in there.

She turned around, to look. Then she turned back, and shook her head.

"Can you see me?" I was trying to get a better handle on what had happened.

She nodded.

"Can you see anything else there behind the glass with you?"

She shook her head.

"Try to keep calm. We'll do everything we can to get you out of there. For now, stay where you are— I know that sounds ridiculous, but just do it—and we'll check back on you every once in a while to make sure you're still alone." I turned back to the others. "What the hell are we going to do?" Then I realized Franny might be able to hear me, and I motioned for them to follow me into the dining room. I didn't want her freaking out any more than necessary.

Alaysia was frowning, thumbing her chin. "I've heard of these types of spells before. Trapping someone's soul or spirit inside of a mirror or a picture. I'm trying to recall of a way to break that sort of spell."

Leroy leaned against the doorway, his arms folded over his chest. "I have to say, this is the nastiest set of circumstances I've encountered in a while. I might be able to free her from the picture, but I'd have to prepare myself. Meanwhile, Alaysia, why don't we head back to Neverfall so you can see what you can dig up? I think we can cancel class for a day or so, given the gravity of this situation."

I didn't want to see them go. They felt like a lifeline in what was rapidly becoming a deteriorating situation. But then I remembered I was going to call Garret. Dirt Witches were extremely powerful, and he might be able to do something to hack into Etum's magic.

"Please, do whatever you can to find out a way to help. I'm going to call Garret James and get him over here."

Leroy raised his eyebrows. "You know Garret?"

"We're actually friends. And don't give me any guff about hanging out with a Dirt Witch."

Leroy just laughed. "Maddy, I wouldn't think of giving you guff over anything. Not with your background. Alaysia and I will be in touch as soon as we can find out anything that might help." He steered her toward the front door. Kelson saw them out.

I turned to Sandy and Max. "This is getting out of hand."

"I think that's an understatement," Sandy said. "What do you want to do?"

"Well, obviously I can't cast any spells. I'll call

Garret. What can either of you do? Do you have any ideas whatsoever?"

"Possibly," Sandy said. "Lihi! I need you!"

A moment later, Lihi appeared. The homunculus glanced around, then shivered as she landed on the dining room table.

"What's going on? What on earth do you have loose in your house, Maddy?" She looked at me with wide eyes, and I could see the glimmer of fear within them.

"We've got a nasty shadow spirit on the loose," Sandy said. "But what I need to ask you is if you can do anything about a situation. You know who Franny is?"

Lihi nodded. "I've been around enough that I know who most everybody is."

"Franny is stuck inside of a picture. Come on, I'll show you. I want to know if there's anything you can do about it."

Lihi hopped on her shoulder, and Sandy headed back into the living room. Meanwhile, I pulled out my phone and punched in Garret's number. He answered on the first ring.

"Hey Maddy, what's up?"

"What's up is I've got an ancient Sumerian sorcerer loose in my house, and apparently Ereshkigal cursed him to live a half-life. I've developed an allergy to magic, Franny's trapped in a painting, and I'm just about at my wits' end." I let out an exasperated sigh. "I'm calling to see if there's anything you might be able to do to help."

"That's a lot of information to take in at once. Suppose I come over and you begin at the beginning?"

"I was hoping you'd say that. Thank you."

"Don't thank me until I see if there's anything I can do." He paused, then added, "I'll be over in about fifteen to twenty minutes. Meanwhile, try to keep anything else from happening."

As I put away my phone, I realized I was breathing a little easier. Whether Garret could do anything or not, I didn't now. But just the feeling that he was going to try seemed to calm me down. I settled back at the table to wait.

GOOD TO HIS word, twenty minutes later Garret was at the door. Garret James was from the Blue Diamond Copperhead Clan. He'd grown up in the Blue Ridge Mountains of Kentucky, and he was a snakeshifter. A lot of people were afraid of him because not only was he a Dirt Witch, but he was an actual copperhead.

He entered the house, his silver dreads a startling contrast to the brown of his skin. He was lithe and had a sinuous quality, and his eyes were a rich hazel, molten and beautiful.

"What the hell have you been getting yourself into, woman?" He glanced around the foyer as he followed me in to the living room. "I could feel the pressure around your house as I walked in the door. Even as I walked up on the porch." He froze as he saw Franny in the picture frame. "Holy crap." He slowly approached the painting as Franny pressed her hands against the glass, staring out. I could tell she had been crying even though we couldn't hear her.

"Our Sumerian sorcerer chased her in there and got her stuck. Luckily he's not in there with her. Take a seat and I'll tell you what happened." I explained everything that had gone on, for what seemed like the twentieth time. I told him about Leroy and Alaysia, and what they were planning.

"I can't do anything, because the magic could kill me. I've never felt so helpless in my life." That wasn't exactly true, but it didn't matter. The one other time I had felt this helpless was when the vampires had attacked Tom and me, and I hadn't been able to save him from them.

"I'm afraid this is probably outside of my alley. But let me see if I can help Franny, at least. I suggest you leave the room, if you can't be around magic."

I headed into the kitchen, wondering what he was going to do but deciding not to even ask. Kelson was there and without a word, she handed me a mocha. I sat down at the kitchen table, feeling exhausted. I wasn't sure where Max and Sandy had disappeared to, but they could probably take care of themselves better than I could at this point. Kelson joined me, carrying a cup of coffee and a plate of cookies.

"You look absolutely beat. Is there anything I can do to help?"

I shook my head. "No, but I appreciate the offer. Just help keep an eye on Bubba and Luna." I glanced around, suddenly afraid. "Where are they?"

"Last I saw, they were hanging out in the library. Do you want me to go check?"

"Would you? I'd feel so much better if I knew they were all right." It felt like I could barely move. I was tired, and it felt like something was sapping the life out of me. I briefly thought back to Trey, wondering if I was somehow undergoing the same effect.

Kelson dashed out of the kitchen, returning a few minutes later. Bubba and Luna followed her, and Bubba jumped up on my lap, rubbing the top of his head against my chin. Luna curled up on an empty chair, and Bubba jumped over to join her, spooning around her.

I let out a breath of relief. "Thank you so much for checking. I know Bubba's a cjinn, and no doubt he can protect himself, but seriously, so many things have gone wrong the past few days that I'm jumpy." For a moment, I thought about rubbing Bubba's belly and making a wish. But Bubba had already done his best to help protect me, and hadn't been able to fully negate Etum. He was a powerful cjinn, but I had a feeling that Etum was far more powerful than all of us put together.

Garret entered the kitchen, a frown on his face. "Sorry, Maddy, but there's not much I can do. I can work you up a bundle of roots that will help protect you and the rest of the household, but I don't know how long it will hold against the sorcerer's magic. Whoever he was, he's extremely powerful, and works in ways that even dirt magic can't touch." He sat down beside me, the pupils of his eyes mere slits, and I could see the snakeshifter in him reacting to the magic.

"I was afraid you were going to say that. But I had to try. I'd be happy to accept any help you could give us. I need to get this freak out of my house." I leaned back, disappointed. I had been putting more hope than I should have in Garret's abilities. I had to remember that some of the ancient ceremonial magicians and sorcerers reached almost godlike status. Unfortunately, a number of them fell on the darker side of magic.

"I really wish I could help. But I'm afraid I might just make things worse. I'm leaving town for a few days—I'm heading out tonight on a red-eye back to Kentucky. I'm going to go visit my family. But I'll drop off the protection hex for you before I leave." He glanced at the clock. "If I'm going to get it worked up, I'd better go. Good luck, Maddy. And be careful." He slapped the table, then winked at me and headed out the kitchen door.

Sandy entered the room, dropping into a chair. "Lihi and I have tried everything we can think of. Her magic won't work against this curse, either." She paused, then looked at me. "Why don't you try Auntie Tautau? If anybody can help, it will be her."

I let out a snort. "Why the hell didn't I think of her in the first place?"

Of course, Auntie Tautau!

The Aunties were a group of powerful witches who stood outside of time and space. As far as we knew, they were immortal, on par with the gods. They weren't omnipotent, but they could often see the future and affect it. Whether they would or

not depended on the situation. Nobody was even
sure if they were witches in the proper sense of
the term, but they were powerful beings, and they
kept to themselves for the most part. In fact, they
blended in with society in such a way that it was
almost impossible to pick them out unless they
wanted to be known.

"That's a wonderful idea. I'll head over there
now. I hope to hell she can help me." I stood up,
sliding my purse over my shoulder. I glanced at the
clock. It was almost six P.M. All of a sudden it hit
me that Aegis wasn't up yet. "What the hell? Aegis should be awake by now. He should have been
awake an hour and a half ago." I dropped my purse
on the table and headed toward the basement
door. Sandy followed me.

As I turned on the light and started downstairs,
holding on to the new railing that Aegis had put
up a few months ago, I realized the room seemed
more shadowed than usual. In fact, it felt like there
was a dark mist down here.

"Sandy, can you see the mist?"

"Yeah, I can. And I don't like the way it feels.
Maddy, there's something wrong."

At that moment, Aegis's voice boomed out from
the shadows below.

"*Stay back, Maddy.* Stay up there on the stairs
in the light."

"What's wrong? Are you hurt?" My heart was
beating a mile a minute. I wanted to race down
the stairs, but when Aegis warned me about something, it was usually for a reason. It took everything I had to stand there, frozen on the stairs,

holding tight to the rail.

"I'm having a hard time controlling my predator tonight. That's why I haven't been upstairs yet. I couldn't text you because I forgot my phone in the office last night." He sounded frantic, but beneath that I could feel the glamour in his voice, the seduction oozing out.

"Crap. What do you want me to do?"

"Get back upstairs and lock the basement door. I'm trying to hold on. You should put a silver barricade across the door. Hurry. I don't want to hurt anybody."

The angst in his voice hit my heart, and I turned around to find that Sandy had already run up the stairs. I followed, slamming and locking the door behind me. Sandy was calling to Max.

"He can still get out through his secret entrance, but I don't know if he's thought of that. Max, can you grab his phone out of the office? I want to slide it down the stairs to him. Then at least we can communicate. Kelson, in the storeroom you'll find the box with the silver chains. Bring them, quickly."

We worked frantically. Max and Kelson took some of the silver chains out to bar the secret entrance that was near the driveway. I quickly opened the basement door again, setting his phone on the first step, then slammed it shut and locked it again. Sandy and I crisscrossed the door with the rest of the silver chains, locking them into place with the system we had rigged up some time back, just in case of an emergency like this. Even if Aegis broke through the door, the silver would drive him back.

At that moment, I got a text from him.

I'M STILL DOWN HERE. I STILL HAVE ENOUGH CONTROL TO TEXT YOU.

DON'T TRY TO GET OUT YOUR SECRET ENTRANCE. WE BLOCKED IT WITH SILVER. WE'VE ALSO BARRICADED THE BASEMENT DOOR.

I LOVE YOU, MADDY. I DON'T KNOW WHAT'S HAPPEN-ING, BUT I WOKE UP SO THIRSTY THAT ALL I COULD THINK ABOUT WAS DRINKING. AND I'M NOT TALKING BOTTLED BLOOD.

I THINK IT'S THE CURSE. WE FOUND OUT A LOT TODAY. I'LL TELL YOU IN A BIT, BUT I NEED TO GO SEE AUNTIE TAU-TAU NOW. I LOVE YOU. HANG ON.

I LOVE YOU TOO.

I turned to the others. "I've got to go see Auntie Tautau. If for any reason you feel unsafe, get out of the house. Take Bubba and Luna with you. There's not much more we can do at this point for Aegis, but I think I'll have a talk with Essie, too. Maybe she can help."

I didn't want to involve Essie or leave the others to the mercy of Etum and his curse, but I realized I had no choice. I turned and, grabbing my purse again, ran out the door, heading to my car. I could only pray that Auntie Tautau would be at home.

Chapter 9

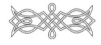

AUNTIE TAUTAU LIVED in a cottage set off from the road. It was on a big lot, covered with a tangle of vegetation. Huge overgrown trees, huckleberry bushes, waist-high ferns, and rosebushes filled the yard and shrouded the path to the porch. You could barely see the house through the knotwork of green, and the smell of growing things filled the air. Even in November, when all the flowers had died back and the leaves had fallen from the trees, it was like walking through a ghostly jungle to get to her place. The ivy was still green, though, and it covered the walls of the cottage.

The pathway was lighted by grinning jack-o'-lanterns on stakes, and her porch was outlined with orange and purple faerie lights—her nod to the season. Using a stick, I brought down the spiders that built their webs between the bare branches of the trees, covering the sidewalk. There were always a plethora of the orb weavers here, and I had a feeling Auntie Tautau encouraged them to keep strangers away. I brought down web after web, shaking the spiders off onto the sides of the path. I wasn't afraid of them, but neither was I fond of the creatures.

As I knocked on her door, I could hear the rustle of movement inside, and then she was peering out, her eyes twinkling.

"Why, Maddy, what brings you here this evening?" She opened the door and let me in.

I breathed a sigh of relief as I stepped into the cottage. It was filled with bric-a-brac, but it didn't look cluttered. It reminded me of an Irish grandmother's home, filled with keepsakes and pictures. And I had known plenty of Irish grandmas over the years.

Auntie Tautau herself was a squat, sturdy woman. Most often she wore a Hawaiian muumuu, but tonight she was dressed in a tidy floral shirt dress, with a checkerboard apron tied around her waist. Her hair was long and gray, and she had braided it back and tied it off with a pretty bow. She wore her straw hat, as always, and on the brim perched a crow. The crow was alive, and his name was Merriweather. He let out a squawk when he saw me, but I recognized it as a greeting rather than a threat.

"Auntie Tautau, I need your help. I'm in serious trouble, and so is my family." The frantic mess of the past few days hit me full force and I dropped to the sofa, bursting into tears. I was tired, and the magic that was pervasive throughout Auntie Tautau's house was making me queasy. I felt sick to my stomach, and tingly around the lips.

"What's wrong, girl?" Auntie Tautau sat down, reaching across to stroke my hair out of my face. "Oh my, you are in trouble, aren't you?"

As I looked up, I see the worry in her eyes. I stammered out my story, punctuating it with an occasional flood of tears. I finally finished, adding, "Have you ever heard of Lilis Spencer? Did you know her when she lived here?"

Auntie Tautau leaned back against her chair, folding her hands on her lap. "I believe we need some tea for this."

I didn't want tea, but I knew better than to rush her. You never could rush the Aunties—they worked in their own time, on their own schedule, and I had learned that sometimes it didn't matter how long it took. What went on in an Auntie's house often happened outside of time as we knew it. Sometimes I would leave Auntie Tautau's house and find that it had been merely moments since I had entered, even though it felt like hours.

I started to follow her into the kitchen, but she motioned for me to sit down. "Breathe. Just breathe."

I curled up on the sofa, sliding my shoes off so I could sit cross-legged. I tried to do as she said, breathing deeply, clearing my head. But the incessant tingle of magic made me jumpy, and my throat felt raw and slightly swollen. After a moment, Auntie Tautau returned and handed me a cup full of something that smelled like woodland mushrooms and moss.

"Drink this," she said. "It will help you handle

the magic in my house for now."

Even though it smelled like pungent dirt, I gulped down the liquid, eager for anything that would help. It tasted as bad as it smelled, but a moment later I began to notice a decrease in my agitation. I could breathe better and focus better.

"Thank you, I needed that."

"There are reasons that you can find no more mentions of Lilis after 1932. She vanished into the Witches' Protection Program, for her own safety."

I groaned. "Please tell me that you know how to break this curse. I was hoping she would be able to tell me what to do if I could find her, but if she's in the WPP then there's no hope for that, I suppose."

"Not necessarily."

"Not necessarily what? That you can help me break the curse, or that there's no hope to meet her?" Even though my agitation was decreased, I was still stressing like crazy. But the moment I said it, I realized how churlish I sounded. "I'm sorry. I didn't mean to snap."

"Oh my dear, if you think that's snapping, then you haven't met the true definition yet. Let me go get the cookies and the proper tea now. I'll be back in a moment."

As she headed back into the kitchen, I forced myself to breathe. I felt like I was on pins and needles, as though every second was working against me. Once again, I reminded myself that time worked differently in the presence of the Aunties.

She returned, carrying a tray with the teapot and two teacups on it, along with a plate of sandwich cookies. I accepted a cup of what smelled like peppermint tea, along with several of the cookies. Sugar seemed like a good idea, and I realized that I was hungry.

Auntie Tautau settled back into her chair and then, taking a sip of her tea, set her cup and saucer to the side on the end table next to her. Once again, she leaned back, folding her hands across her stomach, staring at me.

"As to whether I can break the curse for you, no. Once a curse is given by a god, only the god can break it. As to whether you can talk to Lilis, that I might be able to swing. It's been so long, she might be willing to come back for a visit."

I stared at my cup, at the steaming pale green liquid. "Then you're saying that Lilis can't break the curse either? Because Ereshkigal cursed Etum?"

"Yes, my dear, that is what I'm saying. However, Lilis may know the proper way to petition the goddess. And she can answer the question as to why she set up a shrine in what is now your house."

My heart sank. Right now I didn't care about the *whys*, I just cared about the *hows*.

"Auntie Tautau, what am I going to do? Aegis needs help. His predator is fighting him for control."

"Essie might be able to help you. I would consult her about that. As to Lilis, sometimes knowing *why* something happened can lead you to the knowledge of *how* to take care of it."

I glanced up at her, a sheepish grin on my face. I swear, sometimes I thought the Aunties could read minds despite their protests that they couldn't.

"Please, get in touch with her. And I do have Alaysia Weatherhaul and Leroy Jerome on the case as well."

Auntie Tautau brightened up, a smile springing to her lips. "If Alaysia Weatherhaul is helping you, then all I can say is that you're in good hands. I know her from a long time back."

That made me feel better. "How long before you can contact Lilis for me?"

"It will be sometime. Perhaps half an hour. Perhaps a day. Perhaps longer. It depends on whether she decides to answer. No one is at the beck and call of the Aunties, regardless of what you may think." She urged me to eat another cookie. "You look tired. Why don't you take a nap?"

I shook my head. "I can't afford to take a nap. I have to get back to the house and make sure everything's okay."

Auntie Tautau laughed. "You know that time isn't a factor when you come visit me. I will make certain that you don't lose more time than you can afford. Lie down now, and rest."

Her words made me tired. My eyes began to flutter, and slowly, I sank down on the sofa, resting my head on one of the throw pillows. The last thing I remembered was Auntie Tautau covering me with a soft blanket as I fell into a comfortable, deep, dreamless sleep.

WHEN I OPENED my eyes, Auntie Tautau was

sitting there, a wide smile on her face. I wasn't sure if she'd even moved, or how long it had been, but I noticed the tea and cookies had been cleared off of the coffee table.

"How long was I asleep?" I asked, sitting up. I felt slightly stiff, as though I'd slept for a long time, but I also felt refreshed and full of energy.

"You slept as much as you needed to. But no worry. As I told you, time works for the Aunties, the Aunties don't work for time. Meanwhile, I contacted Lilis. She's willing to come back for a brief visit to tell you what happened. She can't get here until tomorrow, so why don't you come back at around noon?"

I thought about Aegis, and hung my head. "There's no chance she can get here tonight?"

"I'm sorry, Maddy. But no, Lilis can't get here until tomorrow. Go talk to Essie. She may have something to help your situation with Aegis." She guided me to the door, and patted me softly on the back as I left the house.

Once back in my car, I reluctantly put in a call to Essie.

Essie Vanderbilt was the queen of the Pacific Northwest vampires. She had been born in New Orleans in 1844, and had been an active part of the Voudou community. She had studied with Marie Laveau, commonly known as the Queen of Voodoo, and later on with Marie's daughter. Essie had reached the peak as one of the most powerful Voudou priestesses ever, but Philippe, the Vampire King of the Southern States, had fallen for her.

He had turned her, expecting her to bend to his

will, but Essie had a surprise in store for Philippe, waging war with him until she managed to stake him in front of his own court. She had taken the crown, and then moved on up in the vampire hierarchy, coming to the Pacific Northwest later on. Once here, Essie had taken her throne by assassination. She was constantly trying to increase her influence in Bedlam, and she skirted the edge of the law set by the Moonrise Coven. Somehow, over the past year, she and I had managed to become friends—well, as close as I could be a friend to a vampire, other than Aegis.

Shar-Shar answered. Shar-Shar was Essie's personal lapdog, as I liked to call her. Sharlene was Essie's secretary and she liked to think herself above most of the other humans in the area. How she got her job I had no clue, but she was officious, pretentious, and altogether an offensive figure. Essie knew exactly what I thought of Shar-Shar, and I had a feeling that she was amused by it, but she did her best to protect her assistant.

"It's Maddy. I need to talk to Essie. It's important."

As usual, the protests began.

"Essie's busy right now. May I take a message?" That was code for, *I want to make you wait and squirm a little.*

"As High Priestess of the Moonrise Coven, I can command your mistress's attention anytime I want. Put me through to Essie right now. I'm in a bad mood, and you don't want to make a witch mad." I wasn't in any mood to cope with her petty pretensions.

Shar-Shar let out a huff, but all she said was, "One moment, please."

Exactly thirty seconds later, Essie picked up the phone.

"Maudlin, I see you're back to needling my secretary. What's going on?" Essie wasn't one for small talk and that suited me just fine.

"I need to come talk to you. I need your help."

There was silence on the other end, and then, a puzzled, "My help? Did someone in my nest do something that I should know about?"

"Nothing like that. It's easier to explain in person. Are you at home?" I was usually more polite with Essie, but I was feeling at my wits' end. At least I wasn't exhausted like I had been before I arrived at Auntie Tautau's.

"I'm at home. Come on over. Leave your boy toy at home." Essie didn't like Aegis, primarily because Aegis wouldn't kowtow to her and refused to join her nest.

"I'm alone." I hung up and put the car into gear, heading out toward Essie's.

ESSIE HAD DECKED out her Victorian house and yard to out-goth the Addams family. She was even encroaching on Munsters territory. I parked in the driveway, pausing for a moment before heading toward the door. I made sure I was wearing my silver pentacle. It was uncomfortable, because it was magical, and I was already developing a rash from the metal. But right now, it would save my throat in case Essie went off her rocker. I didn't expect her to—harming the High Priestess of the Moonrise Coven would be tantamount to vampire suicide—but you never knew when somebody was going to go fucknut crazy.

As I dashed up the stairs, the front door opened. It was Ruby, one of Essie's personal assistants. Ruby was actually a fairly pleasant vampire, and she and I got along all right. She wasn't someone I would want for a good friend, but we were pleasant to each other and seemed to have a sort of rapport.

"What, Shar-Shar isn't going to greet me?" I couldn't help but laugh.

Ruby suppressed a smirk. "You shouldn't be so mean, Maddy."

"I'd like to know why not," I said, giving her a big smile. It was the first laugh I'd had in a while.

"You're bad. Follow me, Essie's waiting in the parlor."

I looked around. The new decor had held, surprising me. While the outside of the house looked like it was straight out of a horror movie, Essie had renovated the inside, and now it looked very New England Cape Cod. I wasn't sure exactly what mood she was going for, but it was better than the heavy black drapes and red tapestries the place had sported earlier.

Ruby led me into the parlor, where Essie was sitting near the fireplace, waiting for me. A fire crackled merrily in the hearth, though when I looked closer I saw it was gas and not actual wood. But I welcomed the warmth, and the cheer that the flames brought. I loved fire. It was my element, and I had a sudden pang as I wondered if I would ever be able to conjure it again.

I curtsied briefly in front of Essie. It was proper, given she was a queen.

"Maudlin, sit down, please. You sounded frantic on the phone. What's going on?" Essie eyed me evenly, but I could hear the curiosity behind her voice. She liked to be in on everything that was happening, and though I didn't want to tell her about this, I needed her advice.

"Yeah, frantic is the word, all right." I glanced over at the desk where Shar-Shar was sitting. Her back was stiff, and I could tell she was eavesdropping. "Can we have some privacy?"

Essie motioned to Ruby, who tapped Shar-Shar on the shoulder and led her out of the room. Shar-Shar shot me a dirty look as she went.

"Why the secrecy? What happened?" Essie relaxed in her chair, leaning back. I had the feeling I was one of the only people she could actually let down her act for.

"I need some advice about Aegis. There's a curse on my house, and it's causing his predator to come out. I've got him locked in the basement, at his own request. Do you know something that can calm a vampire's predator instinct? Is there some sort of temporary medication for this?"

She stared at me like I had lost my mind. "You're truly asking *me* this?"

"The curse is affecting all of us, including Aegis. Until we can corral the spirit running around the Bewitching Bedlam, I've got to help Aegis find a way to control himself."

Essie shifted in her chair, staring at the fire for a moment before looking back at me. "Tell me everything. I can't help you unless I know what you're up against."

I realized I had no choice. I started at the beginning and told her what had happened. By the time I finished, she was leaning forward, and I realized I had grabbed her interest.

"You're actually *allergic* to magic right now?" Her pale eyes flickered over me. I felt like the prize cow at a slaughterhouse. Witch's blood was an aphrodisiac to vampires, and I knew she could smell the life force pulsing through my veins.

"Yeah, so I'm going to have to double down on my *physical* protection." I had forgotten my silver dagger, but she knew that I had one, and she knew just how many vampires I had killed with it over the centuries.

"Warning noted." She eased back in her chair, resting her hands on the armrests. "There are ways to temper a vampire's inner predator. Of course, we don't talk about them with mortals, but if you trust me, I can give you something that will act like a sedative for Aegis."

It was my turn to pause. How much did I trust her? How much would I trust that she wouldn't give me something to harm him, or to make the situation worse?

She laughed. "It's not that easy, is it? Trusting someone who—for all intents and purposes—could be your enemy? I find the irony amusing, although the situation is not. The great Mad Maudlin, the greatest vampire hunter ever known, come seeking my help for her vampire lover."

I was starting to get pissed. I stood, saying, "If you're just going to gloat, tell me now and I'll leave. There's nothing that says you have to help me."

Essie frowned, waving me back in my seat. "I'm not gloating. Although if I were, I'd feel I have the right. I'm simply stating that this is an ironic situation. Don't you think?"

"Call it whatever you like." I continued to stand, unsure of what to do.

"Do you want my help? If so, you're going to have to trust me."

I slowly eased back into my chair. "You have to understand how difficult it is to trust you. I know you don't like Aegis."

"Whether I like him or not is moot. Don't you think it would be stupid for me to do something that would kill him or harm him when he is connected to the High Priestess of the Moonrise Coven? The coven on whose goodwill my entire livelihood in Bedlam depends? Do you really think that I'm stupid enough to let my personal feelings interfere with what's best for my reign here?" She let out a harsh laugh. "If I let my emotions control my actions, I would have been staked by now."

Relaxing a bit, I caught her gaze. There was no subterfuge in it, nor any attempt to glamour me.

"You're telling me the truth, aren't you?"

Essie shrugged. "I seldom lie. I seldom need to. And yes, I am telling you the truth. I just find it ironically amusing that we're in this situation."

Biting my tongue, I tried to keep my ego in check. "Well, you're right about that. I suppose irony hasn't had its fill of us yet, has it?"

"I guess that settles matters. As to what I can do, there are three options. One—I can give you a powder that will put him into a deep sleep until you give him the antidote. It won't kill him, it won't hurt him. But until you administer an antidote, which I do have, it will knock him out. The second choice is a collar. You lock the collar around his neck, and with a code word you can incapacitate him. Unfortunately, the collar can be quite painful. I use it for punishment."

The first option seemed possible, the second made me cringe. She noticed my reaction and laughed again. "Would you like to see the collar in action?"

I quickly raised my hand. "No, thank you. You described it quite well. What's the third option?"

"If he pledges himself to me, he'll have to take my authority to heart. And if he won't, he'll be destroyed."

"No—for the sake of the gods, no. I don't want him destroyed. Neither do I want to see him kowtowing to you. I'd say no offense intended, but I doubt you'd believe me."

"I'm glad we can be so open with each other," she said, her eyes glowing around the rims. Oh, she was enjoying this game of cat and mouse, that much was apparent.

"I suppose the first option is the best. You're sure you have an antidote?"

"Quite sure. I'll make certain you have some

when you leave. Both are powders, and you have to blow it in his face. It's only good close up, obviously, and it can't be injected into his system. It has to make skin contact with his nose. Regardless of the fact that vampires don't breathe, the powder will enter his body that way." She rang a bell, and Ruby entered. "Get me one package of Xanafeeb, and a package of the antidote."

Ruby raised her eyebrows but disappeared out the door without a word.

"Essie, I want to thank you for this. I know that we're on opposite sides, and I know that you'd rather not even have to bother with me, but I truly appreciate it." I realized just how much trust she was placing in me. I had never heard of the drug before—in fact, most people thought there were no drugs that worked on vampires. But apparently we were wrong. If this got out, vamps everywhere would be in danger.

"I like to think we're more than adversaries. We may not be friends, but we each have our place in the scheme of things. And all power systems must have a check and a balance."

Ruby returned, carrying a plastic bag with her. I peeked inside. There were two small containers filled with powder. One had a big "A" printed on the top.

"The one with the 'A' is the antidote?"

Ruby nodded. "All you have to do is open the container and blow it in the face of whoever you're fighting. If they're a vampire, it will immediately knock them unconscious." She paused. "Do you need some help?"

I considered her offer, but then shook my head. "No, but thank you. I think I'd better do this myself." I accepted the bag, and stood. "I need to get home. I don't want to be gone too long."

Essie stayed seated, but she looked up at me and I thought I almost caught a sympathetic glance in her eyes. "Let me know how things work out. I'm truly curious to see what happens."

With that, I took my leave and headed back to my car.

I GOT HOME to find things just about the same as I'd left them, with Aegis still in the basement. I thought about my next step. While Aegis had just texted me again, I wasn't sure how much I could trust him. If his predator had taken over, it would be easy for him to text me whatever he thought I wanted to hear. And while I trusted Aegis implicitly, that predator inside was another matter.

"Well, what do you all think?" I asked Kelson, Sandy, and Max. "I've got to blow this powder in his face. I have no clue if he's still in control of himself."

I shuddered, staring at the basement door. If Franny wasn't trapped in the picture, I could send her down there to find out. Briefly regretting that I didn't know any more ghosts, I hesitated, trying to figure out how to best go about this.

"You could ask Bubba for help," Max suggested.

I shook my head. "No, way too fraught with variables. Even if Bubba didn't do anything to mess it up—and I doubt he would—just his very nature could throw a monkey wrench in the business. And I don't want to put Bubba in danger. No, I have to go down there. But I can load myself up with silver. Kelson, can you run upstairs and grab my jewelry box?"

Sandy shook her head. "I dunno, Maddy. Are you sure you want to take the chance?"

I shrugged. "I have no choice. Because his predator is running so high, there's always the chance it could break through and take over. Aegis wouldn't hurt us for the world, not normally. But once a vampire's predator gets free and takes control, you can't trust them. And as much as I love him, the very fact that he told me his predator was trying to take over shows me that he wants us to be careful."

Kelson returned with my jewelry box, and I quickly sorted through it, putting on as much silver as I could. Wearing gloves, she handed me a thick silver chain that served as a belt.

"Won't the magic of the powder affect you?" Sandy asked.

I frowned. I hadn't even thought of that. But she was right. Since it *was* a magical powder, being around it when it was released into the air could cause an adverse reaction.

"Let me do it," Max said. "I'm stronger than either of you—and I'm stronger than even Kelson. And I can wear silver, whereas she can't."

Silver affected werewolves just about as much as it affected vampires—meaning *very bad*. It was like iron was to the Fae.

"You make a good point and I can't argue it. All right, let's get you all dolled up here."

Between Sandy and me, we blinged out Max, including my silver belt. It barely fit around his waist, but that didn't matter. As long as it was on his body, it was going to help. Another thought hit me. I turned to Kelson.

"Doesn't Aegis have some edible silver leaf in the kitchen that he uses for fancy desserts?"

"I think he does. Let me go look." She returned with a small container filled with silver powder. For a long time I had thought gold and silver leaf were both just colored sugar dust, but I had found out they were both created from minute bits of the metals.

"I need a brush. I'm going to brush this around his neck and his wrists."

She vanished again, returning with a basting brush. I dabbed it in the silver leaf and quickly covered every square inch of Max's skin that was showing. He looked like he was getting ready for a low-budget costume party.

He picked up the packet of powder that Essie had given me. "So I blow this in his face, correct?"

I nodded. "You have one chance. She only gave me that one packet. It should knock him unconscious."

"Then unlock the door and let me go down. Shut it after I go in. I've got my phone and I'll text you when it's safe for me to come out again. I'll text you the code words 'The tree fell' so you'll know it's me. I doubt if he'll be able to do much damage to me, as covered in silver as I am."

Taking a deep breath, I unlocked the door, and Sandy and I unfastened the locks on the chains. Max prepared to dash through the opening.

"Remember that there are stairs leading down. You're not running onto a landing. So if you just charge through, make certain you don't go tumbling down the steps." Sandy gave him a long look. "You come back to me, you hear?"

At that moment I got a text message. It was from Aegis.

WHAT'S GOING ON UP THERE? I CAN HEAR YOU GUYS DOING SOMETHING.

I stared at it for a moment, tempted to text him what was going on. But he could be in predator mode, just trying to take me off guard. Not knowing was hell. I didn't answer, just turned back to the door and nodded at Max.

"He can hear something going on, so be prepared in case he's lying in wait."

We opened the door, and Max ran through. I could hear him clattering on the stairs as we slammed it behind him and locked it again. We prepared the silver chains, holding them ready to fasten just in case Aegis tried to break through. There was a loud noise from below. We waited, Sandy looking on edge. I didn't blame her. Regardless of how much silver Max was wearing, Aegis was still an incredibly powerful vampire. We waited another beat, and then Max texted me.

HE'S DOWN FOR THE COUNT. I'M COMING UP. THE TREE FELL.

I breathed a sigh of relief. "Max did it."
Then I texted back.

CAN YOU GET HIM INTO HIS COFFIN AND CLOSE IT?
THERE'S A LOCK THERE THAT CAN KEEP IT SHUT. THE PAD-
LOCK IS IN HIS VALET BOX.

10-4. WILL DO.

Five minutes later, Max exited the basement.
"He's in his coffin, and it's locked. He was hiding in the shadows, but when he saw me, he came out. I could tell by his eyes that his predator was really pushing him, but he managed to hold himself in check. I'm not sure what he thought I was going to do, but he stood still as I got close enough to blow the powder on him. Sure enough—he fainted immediately. At least he didn't try to fight me."

Relieved, I slumped into a chair. I hated pulling a trick on Aegis, but at least it would take care of that part of the problem for now. And he couldn't get out of his coffin with the padlock holding it shut. We had talked about the possibility of something setting off his predator before, and he had ordered the coffin built to be strong enough so that he couldn't break through if it was locked. That alone showed me how much he trusted me. We had never told anyone else about it, and now only Sandy and Max were privy to his secret.

"Don't tell anybody else about the coffin and the lock. It makes him vulnerable, but it's a safeguard that he wanted me to take. And now I'm glad he did."

"So what do we do next?" Max asked as he began to remove the jewelry and the belt. Kelson brought him a wet cloth to wash off the silver leaf.

"I guess we wait until I can talk to Lilis. And for Leroy and Alaysia to come up with some sort of solution. I feel beat down, I can tell you that. I'm exhausted, even though I took a long nap at Auntie Tautau's. And my chat with Essie wasn't a barrel of laughs, either. Oddly enough, I think she and I have developed a mutual respect for one another."

"It helps to have somebody in the loop with the Vampire Queen," Sandy said. "So tomorrow, you talk to Lilis?"

"Yeah, and my brother comes into town. He would show up right in the middle of all this mess. But I want to meet him. I just hope it goes better than everything else has gone lately." And with that, Kelson called us into a late dinner, and we straggled into the dining room.

Chapter 10

SANDY AND MAX opted to stay the night again. I told them they didn't have to, but given they were still out of power, and I was grateful they had volunteered to help me, it worked out for the best. Alex had texted that he and Mr. Peabody would be fine. They had the fireplace, treats, and a generator that powered his tablet.

I had disturbing dreams, seeing Aegis coming at me, eyes flaring crimson, fangs descended, laughing as he bit deep into my neck and feasted on my blood. I woke out of the nightmare to find Bubba patting my cheek with his palm. He nosed my face, and I realize Luna was standing on the other side. They cuddled up next to me, one on either side like stalwart protectors, and I tried to get back to sleep, but it was a long time before I was able to close my eyes again.

When morning came, I felt like I had barely

slept at all. All the rest from my nap at Auntie Tautau's had vanished. I stumbled into the shower, rinsing off quickly, and then brushed my hair back into a sleek ponytail. I had deep circles under my eyes, and I made full use of my concealer and foundation, doing my best to give myself a *not dead yet* look.

Finally, I stumbled to my closet and stared at my clothing.

What did I want Gregory's first impression of me to be? I sorted through my clothes until I found a pretty blue halter dress with a matching shrug. The shrug was lace with silver trim. I changed into a strapless bra, then slipped into the dress and belted it. I slid on the shrug and laced up my knee-high granny boots. Finally, I added a silver bracelet. I didn't get to wear my silver often, given I lived with Aegis, so I might as well take advantage of the situation and wear a few of my favorite pieces. Standing back, I looked in the mirror. Sexy but not overt, pulled together but not tailored. It worked.

As I headed toward the stairs, I could hear Kelson singing down in the kitchen. She often sang when she made breakfast, and I liked the sound of her voice. I had suggested once that she join Aegis's band, but she shook her head and told me the last thing she was willing to do was sing on stage.

"Good morning," she said, looking up as I entered the kitchen. Sandy and Max were at the table, already drinking their coffee. Kelson pressed a mug into my hand. It was a quint shot mocha, topped with whipped cream and chocolate sprinkles.

"Oh, I need this," I said, sipping the nectar of the gods. The hot chocolate raced down my throat, fueled by the bitter undertones of the coffee. My body responded and I let out a satisfied sigh as I joined Sandy and Max at the table. I glanced over at Bubba and Luna, who were eating their breakfast. Everything seemed so normal, and yet it wasn't.

"Did you sleep?" Sandy asked.

"Some, but not well. I had nightmares about Aegis attacking me." I felt like a traitor for even voicing my dreams, but I knew in my heart that it was just fear talking.

"I checked on him this morning. He's still in his coffin. And of course, once the sun rises, he would naturally be out for the day. Maybe we'll be lucky and be able to take care of this by tonight." Max raised his coffee cup to me. "Here's hoping."

I clinked my mug against his. "Amen to that. Thank you, guys, for hanging out. It makes me feel better having you here."

"We're family. Family of choice is stronger than blood." Sandy blew me a kiss from across the table. "Speaking of blood, when does Gregory get in?"

I checked my texts. Nothing. Then I checked my email. There was a note from him that he would be here around four P.M. He was renting a car at the airport and would drive up. Luckily, the city had found an alternative dock for the ferry and it was back in action.

"I'm due at Auntie Tautau's at noon. I'm not sure what to do until then. Is Franny still stuck in the picture?" I felt a little guilty for not checking on her when I first got up. But there were so many things going on that it was hard to remember everything.

Kelson nodded. "Yeah, she's still in there. Etum hasn't managed to follow her in there, at least as far as I can tell. I'm wondering if he can."

"Hopefully, we won't find out." My phone dinged and I took a look. There was a text from Garret.

I'M SORRY I DIDN'T GET BACK TO YOU YESTERDAY. IT TOOK ME LONGER THAN I EXPECTED TO FIND THE ROOTS I NEEDED. CHECK ON YOUR PORCH—I LEFT IT IN A BAG ON THE PORCH SWING BEFORE I TOOK OFF FOR THE AIRPORT.

As Kelson set breakfast on the table, I hurried out front. Sure enough, there was a paper bag sitting on the porch swing. Inside was an intricately woven charm about the size of a dinner plate. The note enclosed said to hang it on the front door. My fingers itched and burned just touching it, reminding me that magic and I weren't getting along too well right then.

Not one to waste time, I hung it on a nail beneath to the autumn wreath by the front door. As I did so, a quiet hush flowed around me, caught on the wind, and a sense of peace settled in my heart. Hoping for the best, I entered the house. I closed my eyes and reached out, trying not to immerse myself in the magic. I could still sense the dark shadow, but it felt like Etum was behind a barrier of sorts. I didn't know if he could break through, but I felt like I had a little breathing room.

As I entered the kitchen, breakfast was being served on the table. Bowls of oatmeal thick with raisins and brown sugar were on the table, along with the jug of cream. I licked my lips and sat down, drowning the cereal. I loved oatmeal, but we didn't often have it because we were always on the run. A plate of sticky buns sat in the center of the table. I glanced up at Kelson, questioning.

She gave me a sad smile. "No, Aegis didn't make them. In fact, we've gone through all of the goodies in the freezer. But I thought I'd pick them up at the store this morning. Mornings just don't feel right without some sort of muffin or pastry on the table."

I nodded, my heart sinking. Aegis had come to be such an integral part of my life in the year we had been together. I couldn't imagine *not* being with him. Having to keep him unconscious for safety's sake shook my confidence in the future. Sandy noticed my expression, and she leaned over and wrapped her hand around mine.

"It will be okay. I promise you, everything will be all right."

"But we don't know that. We have no clue how to deal with this." Then, trying to muster my spirits, I added, "At least I get to talk to Lilis today. If anybody can help, she should be able to."

"Eat your breakfast," Max said. "You need your strength to deal with this."

We were just about finished when Leonard and his men pulled up. They were back to work on the roof.

I slipped into my jacket and headed outside

to talk to them. Lanyear landed on my shoulder. I was worried about how the curse might be affecting him, but so far he seemed to be okay. As I stepped into the back yard, the owl flew up, circled around and took off to go hunting.

I waited until they were next to the house with their gear. "Hey, Leonard!"

He set down his tool box and placed the ladder he was carrying against the side of the house.

"Hey, Maddy. We're back to finish the patching. My men took a look at the entire roof, and it does look like you need a new one, but it can wait until spring. I know the holiday season is coming up, and that's got to be a busy time for you."

I nodded. "Good. Yeah, as soon as I can get this curse lifted, I need to start booking people. We'll be busy through Thanksgiving and into the beginning of the year. I'm glad to hear it can wait. When you finish today, if I'm not around to pay you, ask Kelson. She can cut you a check for the patch. Again, I'm sorry about Trey. I never envisioned anything like this happening."

"It wasn't your fault. I just hope you can take care of this and get it off of your back. How are you doing?" While werewolves didn't like magic very much, Leonard had always been friendly to me.

I gave him a faint smile. "As well as can be expected. I'm hoping to have some answers after today. Anyway, I got things to do, so I'll leave you to your work."

As the Alpha-Pack switched into full gear, I headed toward the back acreage of my home. Lanyear was overhead, gliding down to greet me.

And then, I was seeing myself, from the air. It was exhilarating, soaring and gliding on the breeze, as I felt my mind touch Lanyear's. It was as though I was seeing out of his eyes, and he could sense my joy. He swooped and turned and glided, taking me with him, before settling in one of the fir trees near the trail.

I blinked, shaking my head. That was the first time that it happened, and for a moment I was terrified, wondering if it would set off a reaction, but it didn't seem to. I wasn't exactly certain who had instigated it—whether it was Lanyear, or some part of my subconscious—but whatever it was, the experience was beautiful and calmed my fears.
I raised my hand to the owl as I headed into the woods.

The day was crisp and clear, the pale sun rising. We were due for rain by afternoon, but for now I thrust my hands in my pockets to keep them warm and perched myself on the stump of the tree trunk. There was something different in the air. The faint scent of ozone crackled down, making me think of snow. I glanced up at the sky again, searching for clouds. They were there on the edge, coming in slowly, with a silver glint to them. My breath formed in puffs in front of my mouth, and my nose began to tingle from the chill.

Lanyear swept by, in hunting mode, and I didn't bother him. He was beautiful, and it still amazed me how Arianrhod had sent him to me. We were still working out our relationship and I hadn't the faintest idea of what it would become, but for now that was perfectly fine. I still wasn't even sure of my *own* place in the world. I was finding my way as High Priestess, day by day and month by month. Since moving to Bedlam, I had become exceedingly aware of how true the old saying was that everything happened in its own time.

I was trying not to think about Aegis locked in his coffin, or about Trey, now dead and gone, or even the fact that I couldn't use my magic. I cleared my head as much as I could, letting the chill of the day and the quiet rustle of the woods soothe me.

After a while I realized that the tension had eased up in my muscles. I pulled out my phone and glanced at the time. Another hour and a half until I was supposed to meet Lilis. Deciding that I could use a little retail therapy, I stood and headed back to the house to see if Sandy wanted to go shopping with me.

Sandy declined. She was on her laptop, taking care of business concerns with her restaurants. "I would love to go, but I have three hundred and fifty-two emails waiting. Max and I will probably have to head home tonight, but we'll stay here until you get back to keep an eye on things." She blew me a kiss.

I grabbed my purse, returned her kiss, and headed out.

MOST OF BEDLAM seemed to have recovered its power and the roads had been cleared. As I navigated my way through the downtown area, I saw an open parking spot across from McGee's Apothecary and snagged it. I was the queen of parallel parking.

Andy McGee—the owner—was out, and so was his daughter Beth. But the new clerk looked familiar, and I introduced myself to her.

"I'm Maddy. Maudlin Gallowglass. I'm a regular customer. You new here?" I leaned against the counter, smiling.

She burst into a bright grin. "Mad Maudlin! It's really *you*? They told me you shopped here, but I didn't think I get to meet you." She thrust out her hand. Taken aback, I accepted the rather enthusiastic handshake.

By now I was used to people recognizing me, whether it was for running the coven or because of my past. But it still felt odd and awkward to realize I had my own set of fandom.

"Yes, it's me. And you are?"

"Oh! I'm sorry. I'm Penelope Johnson, Andy's niece."

"Well, Penelope, I need three ounces of valerian root, and three ounces of chamomile." I knew that I didn't dare buy Andy's special teas since they were infused with magical energy, but I could brew my own soothing mixture with just the plain herbs.

She scurried to gather my purchases as I glanced around the shop. There were a number of things that I could use, but I was afraid to buy them or even touch them. I paid for the herbs, said goodbye, and left.

Downtown Bedlam was a beautiful place. It

had all the charm of a quaint village, but with a number of modern conveniences. In the center of town was Turnwheel Park, right next to the town square, where the Moonrise Coven led the quarter day events. Turnwheel Park was also used for the winter carnival and the autumn fair. The farmers market had a permanent spot as well. The week before Thanksgiving, city workers would hang the lights for Winter Solstice and put up decorations. And during Thanksgiving itself, Bedlam always held a massive community dinner for those who had no place to go, or who simply wanted to take part in a communitywide celebration. It was a pot-luck, although the town supplied the turkey and mashed potatoes.

As I walked along the sidewalk, watching people bustle by on their way to work or to the shops, I realized how much I had come to love this town. And how much it had become a part of me. I stopped in at Dugan's Donuts, a retro coffee shop, and ordered a double mocha, a maple bar, and a chocolate glazed cream doughnut. As I settled into a booth by the window, a familiar voice caught my attention. I glanced up to see Delia Walters standing there.

Delia was Bedlam's sheriff. She had taken over in 1998, when her grandfather died. Her grandfather had taken over from her father, who was killed under mysterious circumstances in 1980. Delia was as upstanding as they came, a fair and just woman. Even though she was a werewolf, she didn't shy away from hanging out with the witches of Bedlam.

"Hey Maddy, I haven't heard from you lately. Can I sit down?" She was carrying a cup of coffee and a piece of pie.

I motioned for her to take a seat. "Things have been a little crazy since the storm. Well, more than a little crazy."

She laughed, shaking her strawberry blond shag. Her eyes were a bright blue and she was a sturdy, athletic woman. "You can say that again. I swear, the next time we have a storm like that, somebody *else* can take over answering calls. You would not believe how many people called into the sheriff's office for things that we can do nothing about. It pissed me off."

"I bet!" As I bit into my cream-filled doughnut, I began to tell her what had happened. "Have you ever heard of Lilis Spencer?"

She frowned, thinking as she sipped her coffee. "I don't think so. Who was she?"

"She owned my house in the 1920s. And I think she's the reason that I now have a cursed Sumerian sorcerer running around as a shadow form, causing havoc."

She snorted her coffee out her nose. "Oh, *this* I have to hear."

I told her everything, between eating my doughnuts and drinking my mocha. When I finished, Delia sat back in the booth, staring at me incredulously.

"You know, I used to think Ralph Greyhoof got himself in more damned trouble than anybody on this island. I think I can now quite comfortably give you the honor of being named the Queen of

Mayhem."

I stuck my tongue out at her. "Please do not tell me you're actually comparing me to Ralph."

"You have to admit, since you moved to Bedlam, you've been in one jam after another."

"Yeah, and I didn't start any of them."

She grinned, finishing the last bite of her pie. "That's all I'm going to say on the subject. I have to go, but let me know how everything's going," she said, finishing on a serious note.

She tossed a ten-dollar bill on the table and headed out toward the patrol car. I glanced at the sky. The clouds were beginning to sock in. I added fifteen dollars to hers, and set all of the money on both of our checks. Then, gathering my herbs and my purse, I headed outside.

I still had forty-five minutes until I needed to be at Auntie Tautau's, so I dropped into the French Pair, a lingerie shop that stocked my favorite bras. They were one of the few places that carried my bra cup size. The clerk waved at me as I came in.

"I ordered a red gingham bra and panty set about three weeks ago. Has it come in yet?"

She went to look and came back with a box. I examined the lingerie, nodding. "This is what I wanted. Please wrap it up and also, I'll take one of those." I pointed to a Santa teddy in stretch burgundy velvet, with white trim and a black belt. I decided that once he was back to his usual self, Aegis deserved a naughty Santa's helper. Paying for the lingerie, I headed back to my car.

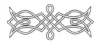

AUNTIE TAUTAU WAS waiting at the door when I arrived at her cottage.

"Is Lilis here yet?" I was nervous, hoping she hadn't backed out.

But Auntie Tautau gave me a broad smile, her eyes twinkling. "She's here. Come on in."

She led me into the living room. There, sitting on the sofa, was one of the most striking women I'd ever seen. As I entered the room she rose, and I was struck by how tall she was. She must have been almost six feet tall, and she had long raven black hair, the color of my own. But her bangs were cut straight across and her hair was smooth and shining, as sleek as mine was wavy. Her eyes were pale brown, and she was well proportioned, looking sturdy and yet with an hourglass figure. She was wearing a long gray robe over a white dress.

"Maudlin Gallowglass? I'm Lilis Spencer. Auntie Tautau tells me you are looking for me."

I let out a sigh of relief. "I'm so glad you're here. I need to talk to you about my house. I bought the house you lived in. The other day, a storm brought a tree down on it, and it destroyed part of the roof. I found your secret room and unfortunately the urn broke and now we have a freakshow sorcerer running around, causing trouble." I sat down on the sofa next to her.

She gasped and slowly buckled, landing on the sofa beside me. Her face was pale.

"I had hoped no one would ever find that room. I meant to dismantle everything before I had to leave, but then things snowballed and I had to run. The best I could do was to have a wall built across the door."

"So you *know* what was in that urn?"

She pressed her lips together, nodding.

"Unfortunately, my household is now under a curse, thanks to you. I need to know everything about Etum, about the curse, and how I can break it. I've developed an allergy to magic because of this. My boyfriend is locked in a coffin to keep him from going crazy. My house ghost—who was there when you were there too—is trapped inside of a painting." The words came out sharper than I intended. I realized that the tension hadn't disappeared, I had just pushed it away for a while.

Lilis glanced over at Auntie Tautau, who just stared at her. She turned back to me.

"I'm so sorry. I didn't mean for any of this to happen. I suppose I owe you the truth."

"The more I know about this, the better I'll be able to handle it."

She shifted her shoulders, then settled back. "Auntie Tautau, can we have some tea?"

Auntie Tautau rose and silently exited into the kitchen. Lilis watched her go.

"All right. The truth. I don't know if it will help you, but I certainly hope so. What do you know about me?"

"That you were an archaeologist who worked on a site in Kish, and that you have English and Assyrian blood lines." I didn't add, *and you left me a mess to deal with*, because I had already made that abundantly clear.

"Yes, that's all true. My father got me interested in archaeology. My mother has ties back to Sumer. I was doing some research into her family tree when I noticed that there was a gap. A relative from long ago had been expunged from every document I could find. I couldn't help but wonder why. The name had been marked out in every single family document. So I did some digging and I found out that the person who had been cut out of our history was a man named Etum."

"Etum was your ancestor?"

She nodded. "Unfortunately. But I couldn't find out what he had done wrong. I asked my mother and she wouldn't talk about him—she said it was bad luck to even speak his name and to leave it alone. But I couldn't get the thought out of my head that maybe he had been wrongly accused of something. I don't know why that kept hammering at me, but it did. I was already interested in archaeology and when they started to make inroads into excavations in the mid-1800s, I began to study on my own. Finally, in early 1912, I was offered the chance to go to work for one of the most preeminent archaeologists from France. I assume you read about him?"

I nodded. "A bit. I read that you helped out on his excavation of Kish."

"I wish to hell I'd never taken that offer. But something drew me to it. I loved the work, but it felt as though I had being summoned. I was absolutely ecstatic to go on the excavation. My mother didn't want me to. Neither did my father. They both forbade me to go, but I didn't listen."

"You were being summoned, weren't you?" I was beginning to get an inkling of what had happened.

She let out a long sigh. "Yes, but I didn't realize it."

"What happened?"

"When I arrived in Kish, I felt an incredible déjà vu, as though I had been there before. I *knew* the area even though I had never laid eyes on it. I knew exactly where to look for some of the artifacts. Henri didn't question it. He just used me like a hunting dog. I was his bloodhound. We made discovery after discovery, thanks to me."

"And I imagine he got all the credit?"

"Most of it." Her eyes darkened. "But that was the way of the times, you know. Then it happened. One night, I was sitting on a sand dune, staring at the stars, when I heard a voice calling to me. I'm not certain what name he called out, but I knew it was *my* name, and I had no choice. I answered."

"Was it Etum?"

She nodded. "I followed the voice into a valley not one hundred yards from where we were camped. Under the stars, I began to dig. Henri didn't realize what I was doing, so I dug through the night with my hands, bloodying my nails. By first light of dawn, I had discovered an entrance into an underground catacomb. When he found out, Henri was horrified by the state of my hands, but the medic wrapped them up, and I begged him to let me be the first one in. For once, he played fair. I wish now he hadn't. He said that since I had discovered the opening, I would be allowed to go first."

"I have a feeling it didn't end well." I rubbed my head.

Lilis laughed, her voice bitter. "Does it ever? Once I was inside what turned out to be a catacomb, I heard my name again. I followed the voice, breaking off from the main group. They were so astounded by the discovery that they didn't notice I had disappeared. I found myself near a trapdoor, and opened it, to find a ladder going down." She closed her eyes, as though reliving the moment.

"I was surprised the air was still fresh. It wasn't like there was any ventilation as far as I knew. I still think there had to have been a shaft leading to the surface that brought in fresh air. Anyway, I cast a light spell and headed down the ladder. When I reached the bottom, I found myself in a small room. There was a well in the middle of it. I couldn't see the bottom of the well, but I could hear water down there. And hanging over the well was a basket containing an urn."

"Let me guess, this urn was the one in the secret room? The one holding Etum's spirit?"

She nodded. "But I didn't know that at the time. All I knew was that the basket had a variety of charms and words written on it. I didn't pay attention. I grabbed hold of the basket and pulled it to me. I heard a laugh, but I didn't pay attention to that either. I took the urn and the basket. I was planning to give it to Henri, but something came over me. If I showed it to him, he would put it with the rest of the artifacts and I couldn't allow that.

This urn was *mine*."

"What did you do?"

"I'm a shadow witch. I created a portal to my home, took the urn and the basket there. Once I got there I realized that if Henri found out what I had done, he could accuse me of theft. So I disappeared into the countryside."

"Did your parents know what happened?"

She nodded. "Yes. My mother was horrified when she saw what I had done. She knew what was in the urn. She told me about Etum. About how he had destroyed so many lives, and then defied Ereshkigal. The goddess sentenced him to an eternal half-life. And he had used me to free him from that half-life. Luckily, I hadn't opened the stopper to the urn."

"Thank gods. But why you?"

"I'll get to that in a moment. It's why I vanished into the WPP. Anyway, my mother told me that now I was responsible for keeping the urn hidden forever. She suggested that I go to America, to get as far away from Kish as I could. The more distance I could put between myself and his homeland, the less Etum would be able to pull on me. And my mother couldn't take the urn because she was bound by a promise to *her* mother."

"But why didn't she tell you this from the beginning? Wasn't the story passed down from generation to generation? It sounds like it should have been." I didn't understand the secrecy. All secrecy led to was danger and misunderstanding.

"She never thought anything would happen. The family thought it was long enough in the past to just bury old bones and leave them alone. Apparently they didn't count on how much power Etum still had. And there's one other thing that I haven't told you yet. When my mother gave birth to me, one of the Aunties warned her that I was the reincarnation of Etum's lover. I was the woman he was planning to marry and I had promised that I would free him, then took my own life. When I was born into this body, I had no memory of that. But the instinct was there. The promise held me. And he was able to communicate with me because of it. We were going to ravage the world and rule it by force."

Holy crap. This was getting far more complex than I first thought.

"So let me get this straight. In a past life you were Etum's lover, and you and he were out to rule the world. He was cursed by Ereshkigal and you killed yourself to come back in the future and save him. That about right?"

"Pretty much," Lilis said. "Now you know why I'm in the Witches' Protection Program. Etum could make use of my powers. The Aunties see an unbalance arising if I stay in the same world as him. Even now I fear that if I stay here he'll sense me. Auntie Tautau promised me that he wouldn't, as long as I stay inside her house. Until he is fully destroyed, I have to live outside of this world. Otherwise, everything could crumble."

"What can he do without you?"

"Until he's gathered enough strength, there's not much he can do except make life miserable for the people around him. But if he got hold of me, he could fully bring himself back into this world. And that would put everyone in danger."

I leaned back, floored by her story. The fact that I had a being capable of terrorizing the world in my house made me want to throw up.

"All right then. So, what do I do to get rid of him?"

Chapter 11

LILIS LOOKED BOTH relieved and worried. "First, realize you're dealing with an extremely powerful sorcerer."

"The fact that the goddess of the Underworld cursed him to a half-life tells me that much. It also tells me he's not a very nice man. What else you got?"

"There is a ritual you can perform to appeal to Ereshkigal. You can petition her to curse him to oblivion. Put the blame on me if you want. She may be terrifying, but she is a fair goddess. You must follow the descent of Inanna. I don't know the exact ritual, or I'd tell you in a heartbeat. But it *is* written in some of the ancient texts. I believe there is a book called the *Journey of Ereshkigal* that may have the instructions. It's a translation of an ancient scroll. The book is so old that I don't even know if there's a copy left in existence. But if you can find it, I think it should contain the ritual that you need."

I held her gaze. "Can I do this without magic? Your beloved Etum—"

"He's no beloved of mine! It's not my fault that my ancestor decided to come back in my body to wake up her lover. I don't remember her, I don't remember *being* her. I don't want to follow through with her plans."

I relented. It really wasn't Lilis's fault. "I'm sorry. I'm just on edge, given all that's happened to my family. But can I do this without magic? Etum's curse ended up giving me an allergy to my magic and it could kill me if I try to use it."

Lilis closed her eyes for a moment, hanging her head. After a moment she whispered, "I don't know. I'm not sure. I'm so sorry you and your friends have been dragged into this."

At that moment Auntie Tautau reentered the room. She was carrying a tray filled with tea and sandwiches. I shook my head as she offered me a plate.

"I ate before I came, thank you." I paused, then turned to Lilis. "Is there anything else you can tell me? Why did you create the secret room? Why the paintings on the walls?"

"It was an attempt to keep the room from ever being discovered. The paintings and glyphs were my plea for protection. I thought about trying to approach Ereshkigal over the years, to beg her to destroy Etum, but I couldn't bring myself to. As the years went on, I began feeling urges to break open the urn. When I realized the urges were becoming stronger, I knew I had to seek help. So I had the room walled off. I came to Auntie Tautau and begged her to put me into the WPP. I told her I needed to live in a different dimension. But I didn't exactly tell her why."

"It is not the place of the Aunties to always ask why," Auntie Tautau said. "In this case, I wish you would have told me, child. But the damage is done and we must do our best to rectify it. Etum must not be allowed to go free."

"Then I have to figure out how to petition Ereshkigal." I hung my head. "Fuck."

Auntie Tautau motioned to Lilis. "It's time for you to return to your home. I can keep him from sensing you for a while, but he's powerful, and will soon know you are here. If you leave now, he will never suspect that you returned to this world."

She turned to me. "Maddy, warn your friends who know what's happened to keep their silence. The politics stretching out from this are myriad, and not all of the players will appreciate Etum's destruction."

"But how can I tell the entire Alpha-Pack to be quiet? They were there when it happened. I'm sure they've already told their families about it. Word will get out and I can't stop it. I can shut my mouth about it, and Sandy and Max of course, and of course Aegis and Kelson will listen. But I can't stop anything that's already transpired."

"Then we must hope that word never reaches the wrong ears. Now go, and ask your professors to find that book. Tell them to keep their silence. Tell them Auntie Tautau said so. They will listen to me."

For the first time since I had known her, Auntie Tautau hustled me out the door, not even giving me time to say good-bye to Lilis. As the door shut behind me, I shivered. Hurrying to my car, I locked myself inside and held tight to the steering wheel. This was just getting worse and worse, and somehow I didn't see us emerging from this totally free and clear.

I HEADED TO Neverfall next, to talk to Alaysia and Leroy. Luckily, I found Leroy in his office. I loved Neverfall, with its vast winding hallways, stone towers, and the electrified scent of learning in the air. Unfortunately, the school was also rife with magic and by the time I reached Leroy's office, I was breathing heavily. Luckily, I had the injections in my bag that Jordan had given me, just in case I needed them.

Leroy took one look at me and hustled me into a back room where I suddenly felt better.

"This is a magical stasis room. No magic can be performed in here. It should make you feel better while you're here."

I nodded, breathing deeply. "It already is. Thank you so much."

"Alaysia will be here in a moment. Do you have any answers?"

"Actually, I do, although I'll need your help." I leaned back in the chair, trying to relax until the elderly professor got there. Leroy rested his chin on his hands, staring quite openly at me.

"You confuse me at times, Mad Maudlin. It's so hard to imagine you rampaging across the countryside, stabbing vampires right and left."

"If you ever saw Sandy and me during one of our party-hearty evenings, you'd understand a little better. I've mellowed a lot, but to be honest, I recently pulled out my dagger again. I don't trust that things will remain calm." I wanted to tell him about the Arcānus Nocturni, but for his own safety, I bit my tongue.

Leroy paused for a moment, then asked, "Speaking of vampires...I don't want to step on toes here, but how serious are you and Aegis? Is there...an opening?"

I blinked. That was the last question I had expected. Leroy Jerome was a handsome man, and he was smart and funny. But I had left my *party-hearty with the satyrs* days behind. I was a one-man woman now.

"We're pretty serious. We've been together for a year. I don't know how much I believe in soul mates, but if I have one, I think it's him. I never expected myself to fall for a vampire. It seems like an oxymoron, considering who I am. But one thing I've learned through the centuries is to be open to the unexpected, and to be flexible." I paused, then added, "But thank you. I'm flattered, if you're asking what I think you were asking. If I were free, I'd definitely say yes. If I'm mistaken, then I just made myself sound like an idiot."

He let out a sigh and gave a shrug. "I was asking

what you think I was. I can't say I'm not disappointed, but I respect your directness, and I wish the two of you a world of happiness." He paused as Alaysia tapped on the door, then peeked inside. "Come on in. Maddy has some information for us."

Alaysia took a seat beside me, giving me the once-over. "How are you doing?"

"I've been better. But Leroy is right. I do have some news." I told them as much as I could without revealing that I had met Lilis, or who she was. "I have to ask you to keep your silence on this. Auntie Tautau was adamant about that. Etum is a danger we can't afford to let into the community. I would tell you more, but I wasn't given leave."

Alaysia made a clicking sound with her teeth. "I think I know what you're not telling me, but I'm not going to press it. I did some research. As far as the book you are talking about—*Journey of Ereshkigal*—I do have a copy of it. Parts of it are blurry. It was hand-copied over and over, and then in the modern day, someone finally photocopied the scrolls, and that's what I have. But there's enough still clear that I should be able to glean what we'll need for the ritual. I'll get on it as soon as we finish here."

"Is there anything else I can tell you that will help?"

She shook her head. "Knowing the nature of the ritual and having a copy of the book are our two best bets."

My phone rang at that moment, and I glanced at it. It was from Kelson. I excused myself to take the call.

"Maddy, I need you to get home now. Something's happened."

"What now?" My heart sank.

"Max went into the secret room to look around, to see if he could figure out anything. I asked him not to, but he insisted. He came bounding down the stairs in his tiger form. He can't seem to transform back. Sandy said she's worried that he might fully fall into his tiger nature and go ballistic on us."

"Crap. Double crap. The last thing we need is a rogue tiger running around. I'm on my way. I'm at Neverfall so it will take me awhile to get home. You and Sandy be careful, you hear me?"

"I hear you. We'll see you when you get here." She hung up, and I shoved the phone back in my pocket. As I turned to Alaysia and Leroy, I saw they were both staring at me.

"Bad news?" Leroy asked.

I nodded. "It seems that Max has been affected by the curse as well. He's now running around in his tiger form and he can't change back. We're worried that he might just go all jungle boy on us."

"Tigers are more often found in the savannah and rocky climes than in the jungle," Alaysia started but stopped when I glared at her. "But I guess it doesn't really matter, in this case."

"No kidding. This tiger happens to be inside my house. I've got to go. Call me as soon as you can, please. I'm relying on you, because I don't know any other way to deal with this."

"Go on, head home now. And don't let your worry push you into reckless behavior."

"I think I passed that point a long time ago," I muttered as I left the office.

I CALLED JORDAN on the way, using my Bluetooth. "Do you have anything that can knock out a tiger? A weretiger?"

"I like that you didn't even start this time with a 'Hello, how are you,' " he said, laughing. But he quickly sobered. "What happened?"

"Max is in tiger form and can't seem to turn back. Hence, I figure that—like Aegis—it might be a good idea to put him down for the count. He gets nervous when he's a tiger and around a lot of chaos. And that's one thing we aren't lacking for."

"I'll be over as soon as I can. How are you doing?"

"Feeling nauseated. I've been around too much magic today and it's only going to get worse. Do you have anything else that can help me?"

"I *have* developed something, but it will temporarily totally suspend your powers. It will make you immune to the effects of magic in terms of the allergy, but you won't be able to cast any spells at all while it's in your system. And it may take a few days to filter out of your bloodstream."

"I'm desperate enough that I'll take it. Bring it with you, please." I ended the call, trying to focus on the road. It was true, my stomach felt like it was about ready to hurl, and I was tingling all over. I really didn't want to have to give myself one of those shots, but I sure as hell didn't want to go into anaphylactic shock.

By the time I arrived home, Max was running around the yard, with Sandy chasing him, trying to get him to slow down. He leapt into one of the trees, and was clawing at the bark.

"He's upset. And when he gets upset, he gets a little bit twitchy."

"We're all a little twitchy by this point. Jordan is headed over with something to put him down for a nice long nap. We're about to be down both Aegis and Max. And I don't have use of my powers. In fact, Jordan is bringing along a shot that will totally suppress my magic. It will also suppress the allergy. I won't be able to cast any spells, but at least I won't die from being around magical energy."

"Motherfucking hell," Sandy said, sputtering. "Once we take care of this, girlfriend, we are going on a week-long binge. I don't know how much more of this I can take. And I can't imagine how you feel."

"I feel ready to shit a brick." I stood back, watching Max climb the tree. At least he had picked one that was sturdy enough to hold his weight. He was gorgeous, a beautiful massive golden Bengal, big enough to strike down just about anything that gave him trouble. And yet, he was graceful and delicate as he climbed the tree, his dagger-sharp claws digging into the trunk.

"Well, he's gorgeous, I have to say that much."

"You should see it when we go up in the mountains and he turns into his tiger self and goes running. It's breathtaking to watch. It makes me wish I could do the same. The freedom that he must feel…" She paused, watching him, her eyes warm and loving. "And yet, Maddy, he's one of the most gentle men that I've ever known. When I first met him he was a mess as far as dating was concerned. He wasn't used to it. He loved his wife so much, and her death hit him incredibly hard."

As we waited for Jordan, I couldn't help but say, "Isn't it hard to fill the shoes of a saint?"

She shook her head. "Even though he'll always love Gracie, I know he loves me. What we have isn't the same as what they had. We finally figured out that's the easiest way to look at it. And that works for me. I'm glad that he loved her, and that she made him happy. He doesn't have lingering resentments."

She paused, then asked, "What about Aegis? Does he have any old flames who worry you?"

I shrugged. "I wonder about the woman he was in love with, the one Apollo cast him out because of. I think I remind him of her. I'm not sure what it is, but ever since we met, we've both felt this connection that seems to go into a past life. But we haven't figured it out yet. So…no. I don't feel threatened by anyone he's talked about. Sometimes I *do* worry that one day, he'll want to be with one of his own kind."

"I think if he wanted to be with a vampire, he would have stayed with Rachel. But you saw how well that worked out."

I laughed. "Yeah, just about as well as things worked out between me and Craig."

At that moment, Jordan arrived, pulling up into the driveway. As he got out of his car, carrying his bag, I walked over to greet him. Sandy stayed where she was, to keep an eye on Max, who was still having fun up in the trees.

"As you can see, we've had a bit of an incident."

"Lovely. I do have a shot I can give him. It should transform him back, but he won't be able to shift again for a while. It's the same base as the shot that I've prepared for you." He paused, looking at me for a moment. "Maddy, are you sure you want this? It will mean you can't perform *any* magic until it wears off. That could be a couple days, or it could be a week, or even longer, depending on how long it reacts in your system."

"Right now, that has to be better than constantly worrying whether I'm going to end up gasping for air. Go ahead." I held out my arm as he set his bag on a bench and rummaged through it. He brought out a long-needled syringe, holding it up and flicking the side of it with his fingers.

"This may sting a little bit."

"I'm sure I've felt worse over the years." I closed my eyes as he stabbed the syringe into my biceps. As the medicine filtered in, I grimaced. He was right. It *did* sting, but I handled it just fine. As Jordan pulled the needle out and wiped the area with a cotton ball, I felt an odd wave of dizziness rush over me. I sank down to sit on the bench next to his bag, rubbing my head.

"Dizzy?"

I nodded. "Yeah. Is that normal?"

"Very. Oh, one other thing. A positive side effect,

you might say. I'm lifting my prohibition on sex.
Now that the kundalini channels are effectively
closed, you should be safe to scratch any itch you
get."

"Well, that's good." I closed my eyes as the drug
seeped through my body. All over, it felt like senso-
ry channels were shutting down, and I felt smaller
than before. That was the only way to describe it.
I felt like I was *less* than I had been. Part of myself
seemed to vanish in those few moments. I burst
into tears, not realizing just how intertwined my
magic was to my being.

"It's only temporary. Just remember that. I've
used this before and I've seen the same reaction
from every single witch I've used it on."

I sniffled, wiping my nose on my sleeve. "That
makes me feel better. It just took me by surprise. I
guess we'd better get Max under control. What are
you going to do? I'm not sure how to coax a full-
grown Bengal tiger down out of a tree."

"I thought of that. I brought my tranquilizer
gun. I'm going to shoot the medication into him.
So I advise you and Sandy to move away, because
he's probably going to come leaping down out of
the branches at me. But it works so quickly that
everything should be all right by the time he hits
the ground."

"I hope you're right, for everybody's sake."

I called Sandy over as Jordan headed toward the
tree. He had what looked like a small-gauge shotgun, and he fitted the drug-laced dart into it.

"Will that hurt Max?" she asked.

Jordan shook his head. "The dart will probably

fall out of his skin as he transforms. It does sting, but it's probably not going to leave a bruise. At least not a big one."

He got near enough that he could aim at Max's haunches. He leveled the shotgun, holding it steady to his shoulder, and then pulled the trigger. His aim was true, and the dart landed right in the hindquarters of the tiger.

Max let out a roar and, as Jordan predicted, came charging down out of the tree. Jordan took off running toward his truck, with Max was bounding after him. But not more than five yards from the tree, Max froze in mid-air, then fell to the ground, transforming quickly back into his natural shape. Jordan skidded to a halt.

"Are you all right?" Sandy asked, reaching Max's side first. She knelt, stroking his hair out of his eyes.

As he pushed himself up into a sitting position, he groaned and yanked the dart out of his right butt cheek and tossed it on the ground. I grimaced, thinking that must have hurt like hell, and then as Max began to stand up, I suddenly blushed, realizing Max was fully naked. The wayward thought crossed my mind that Sandy was a lucky, lucky woman.

"What the hell just happened?" Max shook his head, glancing around at the three of us.

"Do you remember changing into your tiger form?" Sandy asked.

Max staggered to his feet, not seeming to realize he was naked as jaybird. "Not really." He suddenly looked down, and let out a little groan.

"That would explain why I'm standing outside in forty-degree weather without any clothes on." He glanced at me, and let out a choked laugh. "Eyes to yourself, woman."

"You haven't got anything I haven't seen hundreds of times over. How are you feeling?" I asked, stifling a laugh. But I couldn't hold it in and ended up belting out a loud guffaw.

"That's right, chuckle it up." He snorted. "How do I feel? Like I got hit by a sledgehammer. What did you do to me?" He turned to Jordan. "The last thing I remember is…I don't remember."

Jordan nodded. "Let's go inside and get you into some clothing. I'll explain there."

As we headed into the Bewitching Bedlam, it occurred to me that we were very quickly losing our power players. Aegis was down for the count. I couldn't cast any magic now. And Max wouldn't be able to turn into his tiger. Pretty soon, we would be left with only our wits, and that was a scary thought.

MAX TOOK A quick shower and changed clothes as Kelson fixed a pot of tea. I glanced at the time. It was almost three thirty and my brother was scheduled to arrive at around four. It occurred to me that maybe I should rent him a hotel room so he didn't get hit by the curse as well. I hated not being able to offer him my hospitality, but it might be safer that way.

As we waited for Max to come down from the guestroom, my phone rang. I glanced at the caller ID. It was Alaysia.

"Maddy? I figured out what ritual you need to do. It's daunting, and it's not going to be easy, but I'm calling you now because we have to do it tomorrow night. Rituals to Ereshkigal must be done on Saturday night—the seventh night. And we need to do it at your house, because that's where the curse is. I'll have to come out and set up tomorrow afternoon, if that's all right with you. Leroy is going to join us as well."

"Good. But I have to ask you something. Jordan Farrows gave me a shot that suppresses all my magic. Will I be able to go to the ritual even though I can't do anything magical?"

"Oh, you can go through the ritual, all right. I don't guarantee how you'll fare without any magic, but it certainly won't stop you from trying." She paused, then added, "Really, this is the only solution if you want to break that curse. I know more than you think about it."

"Let's go for it. Why don't you come over around three tomorrow? That will give you plenty of time to set up. Should we clear the house of everyone else?"

"Actually, anybody affected by the curse should be there. At least, anybody you can manage to have around."

"Henry won't be able to. And it's probably a good thing, because if this ritual is to remove curses, it might affect the curse that's keeping him alive. Besides, I have a feeling the stroke was brought on by something other than the magic." In fact, I knew it had been. Not everything was magical in origin.

"All right. I'll see you then."

I hung up, breathing deeply. "Tomorrow night, Alaysia and Leroy are coming over. Sandy, you and Max need to be here. Aegis needs to be here as well. She's managed to figure out a ritual that should break the curse."

As Max entered the kitchen, the doorbell rang. Reeling from everything that it happened, I headed to answer. As I opened the door, a tall lanky man stood there, wavy brown hair down to his butt. As I stared into his eyes, I saw my mother's reflection staring back at me. It was Gregory, my brother.

Chapter 12

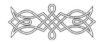

GREGORY OAKSTONE MIGHT be my half-brother, but I could see my mother in his eyes. At first, he seemed at a loss for words as he stared at me. And then, it was as if the gulf between us vanished. He set down his suitcase and his backpack, and held out his hands. I took them, squeezing them tight.

"I'm not sure what to say," I said. "I'm not used to situations like this. Please come in." Even as I spoke, I realized I was nervous, wondering what he would think of me and of the house, and of Aegis.

But as Gregory crossed through the doorway, he broke into a wide smile, an almost goofy grin. "What the hell am I doing?" he asked, grabbing me into a bear hug. "You're my sister. I still can't believe I have a sister!"

"I know," I said, a wave of joy sweeping over me. "When Zara told me about you, it felt so surreal.

I've had a half-brother my entire life and never known. Come in. Please, come into the kitchen. I'm afraid you've caught us at a very difficult time."

We entered the kitchen, me dragging him by the hand. "Look who's here! This is Gregory Oakstone. He's my half-brother. Greg—may I call you Greg?"

He nodded. "That's fine with me."

"I want you to meet my best friend Sandy, her fiancé Max, and Jordan—who happens to be one of the best doctors around." I motioned over to Kelson. "And this is Kelson. She's my manager for the Bewitching Bedlam."

There was a flurry of greetings as they all said hello, and I noticed Greg looking at the remains of the sandwiches on the table. "Are you hungry?"

"Actually, I am rather peckish. The food on the plane wasn't exactly filling."

"I'll make you a couple sandwiches if you like. Roast beef all right?" Kelson asked. "And would you like some coffee, or a latte, or tea?"

"Tea would be fine. Black, with lemon if you have it. And roast beef sounds delicious." He sat back, and I could see his shoulders relax.

"Was it a rough trip?"

"It wasn't exactly a pleasurable jaunt. There was a lot of turbulence, and the airplane seats are getting tighter and tighter. I swear, the next chance I get to learn how to open a portal, I'm taking it. You know we could make a fortune if we set up portals between various cities, though I suppose the Society Magicka wouldn't care for that."

I laughed. "I'm pretty sure they wouldn't appreciate us price-gouging humans for easy travel, and neither would the airplane companies or airlines. I'm so glad you're here. How long can you stay?"

"I have to leave Sunday morning to catch my flight. I wish I could stay longer, but I have a business meeting back east."

"What do you do?" Sandy asked.

"Well, by magical practice I'm a bard. I parlayed that into my business. I run a small recording studio in London, and I'm also the manager for several groups. I'm over here to make a deal for one of them to record their demo album."

I stared at him. "You've got to be kidding. My boyfriend is in an indie band. They were with a recording company, but the rep kept coming on to the bass player and wouldn't leave him alone. The owner of the company didn't want to hear it—he said that it wasn't sexual harassment if it was a woman bothering a man."

Gregory arched his eyebrows. "That's not good. What kind of music do they play?"

"Celtic industrial goth, I suppose you'd say. They update a lot of the old folk songs and write their own as well. They're most like Corvus Corvax or Faun."

"I'll have to hear them play when I get a chance." He paused as Kelson set his sandwiches and tea down in front of him. "That looks really good."

"We better get going," Sandy said. "We haven't been home in a couple days and we need to see what's going on there. We'll be back tomorrow evening for the ritual. Let us know if there's anything you need, Maddy. And please be careful. Even though Jordan shut down your magic, I still think you're in danger."

Gregory glanced at me, a questioning look in his eyes, but he didn't say anything.

I stood, giving Sandy a hug as she passed by. "I promise I'll be careful. If I need you, I'll call. See you tomorrow—why don't you come around three o'clock? That's when Alaysia will be here." I waved as she and Max headed out the back door, then turned to Gregory. "As I said, there's a lot going on right now, and you walked into a hornets' nest."

"Why don't you tell me about it while I eat?"

I stared at him for a moment, then smiled. "Wow. I actually have a *big brother* to talk to." And so, I began to tell him everything that had gone on over the past week.

WHEN I FINISHED, Gregory still hadn't said anything. He had listened avidly, though, a couple of times spilling a drop of mustard on his shirt because he was so intent on what I was telling him.

"I wish I could help somehow," he said finally. "I'm a bard. I weave my magic through my music and song. But unlike you, I don't have any control over elemental magic, nor am I a shadow witch. My parents—my adoptive parents—knew I was a bard from birth. Apparently, Zara told them. Unfortunately, bards are like the country cousins of the witch world. I don't know if you knew that or not, but we don't have as much primal power as you do. We're mostly good for charming people out of their money, which is why most bards tend to be entertainers."

I actually hadn't known that about bards. Tom had been a witch who happened to be an excellent singer, rather than a bard. Other than that, I really hadn't had much to do with them.

"I wasn't holding out hope that you could do anything. This is been an extremely taxing situation and I just want it done and over with. Anyway, what do you think? Do you want to stay somewhere else? The last thing I want to do is see this curse come down on your head as well."

He laughed. "I could use a little excitement in my life. You have to understand something about me. I've led an extremely sheltered life. Oh, it's been good. My adoptive parents are wonderful and I never wanted for anything growing up. I wasn't spoiled, but I led a pretty privileged childhood. Even into my adulthood they have always supported my choices. They even supported me coming to meet you. So if you're wondering if they know about this, if they know about you, the answer is yes. In fact, they want to meet you."

I blinked. I hadn't expected that at all. "That's nice of them. What are their names? Do you have any brothers or sisters? I mean, besides me."

I suddenly found myself hoping he didn't, and then immediately felt bad. It wasn't that I wanted him to be lonely, but I realized that I had missed having a family all these years. Until the very end, my mother—Zara—and I had always been at odds, and I hadn't seen my father in decades. In fact, after what Zara told me before she died, I wasn't sure I wanted to see him again. He wasn't a bad man, but he hadn't been supportive to my mother, and that's why she had become so hostile to everybody over the years.

"My mother's name is Missy Oakstone, and Father's name is Drake. They're both earth witches. I do have one little brother. He was adopted too. His name is Rica and he works with air magic. His parents were killed in a plane crash on the way home from a conference in Germany. And by little, I do mean little. He was only two when he came to live with us, in 1954."

"What does he do? Or has he chosen a path in life yet?"

"He decided to study aviation. He was in the plane crash, you see, and survived. Only a handful of passengers made it through, and while he doesn't remember the actual crash, he has an almost morbid fascination with planes. He's researching airplane safety." Gregory shrugged. "I guess even if you don't remember a trauma, it can still affect your life. He works for BAE Systems, in Farnborough."

"Well, I hope he's happy. Now tell me more about yourself. You've been very circumspect in your emails. Now that you're here, I want to know all about you." I stood up, motioning for him to follow me. "Leave your suitcase here and come on in the parlor. Unless you're tired and want to rest for a little first. I'm sorry, I totally forgot you're just in off of an international flight."

He yawned and stretched. "Actually, I am fairly beat. If I could just take a hot bath, then we can talk. It would relax my muscles. Those narrow airplane seats don't help my back."

"In that case, grab your suitcase and follow me. If you want to stay here, then we'll get you settled right in. Just be careful, okay? The spirit that's running around has no qualms about hurting people. I've got a protection spell from a Dirt Witch, but I don't know how much it will protect us."

Gregory picked up a suitcase and followed me up the stairs. I put him in the second guestroom—the first being Henry's room—and showed him the adjacent bath. I made sure there were plenty of towels, and then left him to freshen up.

I decided I could use a little freshening up, too and went in my bedroom. I changed into a wrap dress in heather gray. It was a jersey knit with a low V-neck, and a wide skirt. After touching up my makeup, and brushing my hair, I walked over to the bed where Bubba and Luna were sprawling across the quilt. Bubba was lying on his back showing his belly. Luna was licking it.

I groaned. "Please don't tell me you're making a wish."

That was the last thing I needed. I could just imagine what she might be wishing for—giant mice to chase, opposable thumbs to open cans of cat food, a mechanical petting machine... There were *oh so many* things a cat could want to make life more interesting.

I ruffled Bubba's fur, cautious to avoid his belly. Then, scratching Luna's chin, I gave them both a kiss on the nose and headed back downstairs. I could hear Gregory singing from his room, and I paused to listen. He had a beautiful voice, and he was singing a song that reminded me of one Aegis sang to me. Humming the tune under my breath, I quickly clattered down the stairs to the kitchen where Kelson was getting dinner under way.

By the time Gregory came down, pizza was ready, and I was opening a bottle of chardonnay.

"I don't know if you're hungry again, but I'm famished. You're welcome to join Kelson and me in some pizza if you like. Would you like a glass of wine?"

He stared at the pizza, then shook his head. "Save me a couple pieces, though, if you will. I'll probably be hungry in another hour or two. The wine, however, sounds good. I'd love a glass."

I poured him a goblet of wine, and then, picking up my plate filled with pizza, I motioned for him to follow me into the parlor. Kelson had laid a fire, and it was crackling merrily. I set my plate down on the table next to one of the armchairs along with my goblet, and motioned for Gregory to sit wherever he wanted. He sat next to me on the sofa, taking off his slippers before sitting cross-legged.

It felt odd, sitting here with a man I had never met but with whom I had such a close connection. It hit me that if Zara had never said a word, I would never have known about Gregory.

"Is there anything you'd like to know about our mother? I told you most everything I could, but I might have left something out."

Gregory stared at his hands for a moment then looked up.

"I hope you don't take this the wrong way, but

the fact is, my mother is the woman who brought me up. I never knew Zara. I'd like to know about health issues, or anything along that vein, but you told me the circumstances surrounding my birth already. I understand why she had to do as she did. But...her life had no connection to mine, other than she gave birth to me. But you—you're my half-sister, and you're alive and you're interested in forging a connection. So I want to know about *you*, Maddy. Tell me about your life."

I had half expected the answer that he gave me, and I really wasn't offended. Until the very end of her life, I had hated our mother. She had treated me like crap, and I hadn't ever known about her past until shortly before she died. I had forgiven her, given the circumstances, but it hadn't wiped away the years of pain and of thinking that I could never do anything right.

"Do you know anything about me?"

He was trying to suppress a smile, I could tell that much.

"Actually, I do. I looked you up after your first email. What I found was quite...amazing. My little sister is a famous vampire slayer who now owns the Bewitching Bedlam together with her vampire boyfriend. I'd say that you've had quite an eventful life."

I coughed. "I suppose you could put it that way."

I paused, then told him about Tom and Sandy and Fata Morgana, and how after Tom's death, we hunted our way across Europe.

"But those days were long time ago. I still have my hunting knife, and I still..." I stopped.

"You still what?" he prompted.

I shook my head. "Never mind. Doesn't matter. Now I own the Bewitching Bedlam and yes, I'm in a serious relationship with Aegis, who used to be a servant of Apollo until he got turned into one of the Fallen. He's a great guy. He loves kittens, he reads murder mysteries, he does jigsaw puzzles, and is the best baker in town."

"When do I get to meet him?"

"Hopefully before you leave. Right now I've got him locked up in the basement in his coffin because the curse is affecting him as well. But I'm hoping tomorrow night will put an end to it." I told him about the ritual that Alaysia was creating for me.

As the evening wore on, we slowly got to know each other. I found out that his favorite food was roast beef, and that he absolutely loved sticky toffee pudding, and he was addicted to cola. His favorite color was green, and he didn't have a girlfriend at the moment, although he had been married twice though it had never worked out. In return, he learned that I just plain liked to eat, especially fried chicken and pizza and sweets and booze. My favorite color was purple, and I told him about Craig and what had recently happened.

The fire crackled into ashes, and by two in the morning we were both ready to turn in. It felt like we'd been talking forever, and in a sense, we had. We had covered over three hundred years in our conversation, touching on the highlights and occasionally the low lights. But as we headed up the stairs, I paused at his room and gave him a long hug.

He patted my back and hesitantly kissed my forehead.

"You know what? I'm glad I have a half-sister. And I think I'll just drop the 'half' off of there, if you don't mind. You're my sister, regardless of whether our fathers were different. I think I'm going to like this. And someday, you're going to come over to England and meet my parents and my little brother."

I hugged him back and left him to get some rest. In my room, I realized I was lonely, missing Aegis. Even though he was downstairs, safe in his coffin, the house felt empty without his laughter and his touch. But Gregory had buoyed my spirits, and as I settled under the covers, hoping for an easy night, I couldn't help but smile. I had a big brother. And he cared about me.

I WOKE UP to the sound of my phone ringing. Blurry eyed, I fumbled on the nightstand, finally managing to hook my finger through the O ring on the back of my phone. As I pulled it toward me, rolling over so I could see the screen, I came face-to-face with Bubba, who was curled up on the pillow next to me. He raised one eye, glaring at the phone as it jangled, then indignantly padded down the side of the bed to curl up next to Luna.

I was surprised by the caller ID.

I hadn't talked to Scarlett Wells in well over a

YASMINE GALENORN

year. She had been a friend of both Craig's and mine, but she was a lawyer, too. When I moved out of Seattle we lost touch. I figured she had gravitated over to Craig's side of the breakup because she hadn't bothered trying to get in touch with me again.

"Hello?" My voice was scratchy, and I forced myself to sit up and lean back against the headboard. I punched the speaker function, and as I held the phone up, with my other hand I reached for the bottle of water on my nightstand. I slugged back the drink, soothing my throat.

"Hi, Maddy. I know you're probably surprised to hear from me. It's been a long time, but I felt like I had to call you. It's about Craig."

"If you want to convince me that he's a stellar guy and he did nothing wrong, you can stop right there." It would be just like him to use a mutual friend to try and squirm his way out of his responsibility.

"No, it's nothing like that. I wanted to warn you. Craig just got out of jail, and I think he may be headed your way."

I stared at the phone for a moment. What fresh hell was this?

"Um...Scarlett, it sounded like you just said that Craig just *got out of jail*? What the hell did he do now? He showed up at my house the other day, telling me that he had got himself involved with some loan sharks while we were married and that they had my name, too. I kicked him out and told him to take care of the problem."

"I don't know anything about loan sharks, but

228

this is worse than that. Apparently, he's been under investigation for a few months. He was arrested for embezzling money from two of his clients. I guess the cops got worried that he was going to try to skip the country, so they closed in on him Thursday morning."

I wasn't sure what to say. I knew Craig was underhanded, and I knew he was a jerk, but I had never dreamed that he would steal from his clients. "You said he's out of jail?"

"He bailed himself out last night. I guess he put up his house as bond. I heard through the grapevine is that he's blaming you for some debt that he owed."

"That would be the loan shark incident."

"Well, whatever the case, Craig's really gone off the deep end. He's irrational. And he's disappeared. The cops came asking if we knew where he was this morning." Scarlett took a long breath, and then, before I could respond, added, "I'm sorry that we lost touch and I'm sorry if I ever took Craig's side over yours. He painted a pretty awful picture of you and I didn't bother to find out on my own. I felt like I owed you to call you about this."

"Thank you for telling me. He was over the top when he came here the other day. My boyfriend showed him the door."

"Just be careful. He's really angry."

I sighed. "My guess is that he tried to embezzle enough money to leave the country before the loan sharks caught up with him. No doubt he was planning to liquidate all his assets. It doesn't cost much to live in Mexico, and he always talked about moving there."

Scarlett and I chatted a bit longer, then I took a shower. I glanced outside at the sky. It was stormy, and the rain was starting to come down hard. I slipped into a pair of jeans and a warm cowlneck sweater the color of rich merlot. I brushed my hair, pulling it into a high ponytail, and took the time to fully do my makeup. I wanted Gregory to see me looking my best.

As I came out of my bedroom, Luna and Bubba behind me, Gregory was peeking out of his.

"Morning, Maddy, how did you sleep?"

"Oh, not too bad. Come on let's go get breakfast."

As we headed down the stairs, I heard a loud crash and then Kelson, cussing.

"Maddy? Hurry up into the living room. We've got a problem."

I was hearing that way too often. Taking a deep breath, I sprinted down the rest of the stairs, praying that pretty soon I would have my normal life back.

AS I RACED into the living room, I found Kelson kneeling on the floor, staring at Franny's painting. The frame had broken, and shattered glass littered the floor.

"What happened?"

"I don't know," Kelson said, looking up at me. "I was afraid to touch it, because Franny's trapped in there. I don't know what the glass breaking did to her, if anything."

I let out a sigh and knelt beside her. "I don't know either. And I can't sense anything because of that shot that Jordan gave me."

I cautiously moved a couple of the bigger shards of glass out of the way, then carefully picked up the broken frame. The painting looked intact, although the frame was cracked around the edges and the glass was gone. Standing, I carried the frame over to the coffee table and set it down. Gregory was standing at the door of the living room, watching us.

I glanced over at Kelson. "Why don't you clean up the glass while I try to figure out if this has affected things." I leaned over the painting, searching for any sign of Franny. "Franny? Are you there? Franny?"

Nothing. Radio silence.

Gregory joined me. "Is that the painting she was trapped in?"

I nodded. "But I can't feel anything now—magical or otherwise. Can you tell if she's still in here?"

"Do you have another frame? One that's got glass? Maybe if you transfer the painting to it, we can see if she's attached to the actual painting or to the frame itself."

When Kelson returned, Gregory took the dustpan and whisk broom from her. "I'll sweep up the glass."

She glanced at me.

"Kelson, could you see if we have any other frames this size? I don't care if you have to take another painting out of it. We want to see if Franny's attached to the painting itself or the frame."

As Kelson disappeared out the door, I gently removed the painting from the frame and examined it. I couldn't see anything out of the ordinary. The painting was still in one piece and hadn't been damaged. I set the frame to the side, just in case Franny was still connected to it. I didn't want to throw it away until we knew what we were dealing with.

Gregory jumped. "Did you see that?"

I whirled, looking around the room. Then, I saw what he was talking about. A shadow lurked in the corner, tall and human shaped. Unfortunately, I couldn't get a bead off the energy. But Gregory put down the dustpan and broom and stepped between me and the shadow.

"Whatever it is, it's not friendly."

"Probably Etum. I wonder what he's up to now." I really disliked not having my powers to fall back on.

Just then, Bubba came racing into the room. He skidded to a halt beside Gregory, staring at the corner. He let out a loud hiss, and a yowl, and the shadow went racing into the wall again. Gregory stared down at Bubba, his eyes wide.

"He's not just a cat, is he?"

I shook my head. "I guess I forgot to tell you. Bubba's a cjinn. He's been with me since I was young. I found him when he was trapped in a burning barn. He was just a little kitjin."

"Well, he certainly threw the shadow for a loop."

"Thank gods for that."

Just then, Kelson returned. She took one look at Bubba, Gregory, and me and scanned the room. "He was here, wasn't he?"

"Yep. Etum is still running around the house, apparently. Did you find a frame?"

Kelson handed me a simple wooden frame. "It's not fancy, but it has glass and will fit the painting."

"Hopefully, that's all we need right now."

Kelson used window cleaner and a paper towel to wash the glass, drying it thoroughly before she handed it to me. I fit the glass into the frame, then carefully placed the painting over the glass, taking care to tuck the cardboard firmly in place behind it before fastening it shut. Then, turning it over, I stared into the painting, hoping to see Franny looking out.

There she was, pounding against the glass. She didn't look happy.

"Oh, thank gods you're all right." Relief flooded through me. As Franny continued to rail against her prison, I caught a few choice words that I was surprised to see come out of her mouth. "I didn't think you used that kind of language."

She shut up, blushing. Obviously, she hadn't realized I could read her lips.

"One thing's for sure," I said to the others. "Until the ritual is over, we're carrying Franny's painting everywhere we go. We're not giving Etum another chance to mess things up for her."

A thought occurred to me. What would happen if I tried to take the painting outside, with Franny attached to it? She was trapped by the curse laid on her, but what about now? I thought about giving it a try, but then decided not to make matters worse.

And with that, we headed into the kitchen for breakfast.

Chapter 13

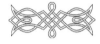

SANDY AND MAX joined us around three o'clock. Gregory and I had spent the day walking around the yard, leaving Kelson to watch over Franny's picture. I had shown him the campground in progress and had offered to drive him around the island, but he wanted to spend the time just talking.

"I'll come back soon, and play tourist," he had said.

We had caught up on all the little things that you never think about when you live with someone day-to-day or know them throughout the years. Favorite foods, times in our lives that were relatively unimportant to other people, but that had mattered to us, people we had known and loved. I told him all about Fata Morgana, and he was quite silent for a while afterward.

Then he said, "She sounds lonely. I know we

love whom we love, but you don't think you could ever return her passion?"

I shook my head. "I've just never had a romantic bent toward her. I've slept with women over the years, and have had relationships with some of them, but although I consider myself pansexual, I do tend to be more attracted to men. And Fata... There's always been something about Fata that made me nervous, as much as I cared about her."

"Nervous how?"

"I suppose even back then, I could sense the process of transformation working on her. She came in on a wave, crashed against the shore where I was standing. When someone appears in your life in a mystical way like that, well, I don't know if you ever see them as quite human. You know what I mean," I said, shrugging.

"I suppose I do. I don't know if I'll ever marry again. I've had several failed marriages, and to be honest, I pick the wrong kind of women and I know that. But like a moth to a flame, I find it hard to steer away from them. I'm content in my ways and I don't like changing for others. So I date casually, but I don't expect that to change."

He looped his arm through mine, pulling me close. "I wasn't sure what to expect when I arrived, but this is going so much better than I thought it would. You really do feel like my sister. And that's nice." He broke into a wide smile that warmed my heart.

When Sandy and Max arrived, Max and Greg began to chat while Sandy and I moved into the kitchen, leaving them in the living room. Kelson had emptied just about every cupboard. Food covered the counters, and dishes were piled in the sink. Franny's painting was sitting in the middle of the kitchen table where she could see everything that was happening.

"Kelson, what are you doing?"

"I figured it was time to do a thorough cleaning. Since we don't have any guests right now, this is the perfect time to go about it before the holidays hit."

"I suppose you're right. Hopefully, if the ritual goes as planned tonight, we'll be able to start booking guests again this coming week." I realize that I was tense, worried about the ritual and whether it *would* work. I couldn't permanently exist without my powers, but if the ritual didn't go as planned, I was concerned that the allergy might become permanent. Or that I'd have to sell the Bewitching Bedlam to get away from it.

"Stop worrying," Sandy said. "I can see it in your eyes. You just have to trust. That's all we can do for now—have faith. We'll worry about the future once it's over and done with. And if we're lucky, we won't have to worry about it at all."

I nodded. "You're right. Okay, we should get the parlor ready. Actually, I'm not sure where they want to hold the ritual. All Alaysia told me was they need to hold it in the house."

The doorbell rang, and I motioned for Kelson to continue what she was doing. "I'll get it."

Sandy and I found Alaysia and Leroy waiting on the porch. They were carrying large bags, probably ritual gear. I stood back, ushering them in. Max and Gregory popped out from the living room, and I introduced Gregory to the two professors.

"Greg's a bard."

Alaysia's eyes glittered. "I don't meet many bards. How do you do?"

After the pleasantries were out of the way, I asked Leroy and Alaysia where they wanted to set up. Leroy pointed toward the stairs.

"In the secret room, where else? That's the most likely place for this to work."

That was the last place I wanted to be. But I led them upstairs and Kelson followed, carrying Franny's painting. "Should we bring Aegis up here, since he was affected by the curse as well?"

"It might be a good idea."

I glanced at the clock. It was nearly four thirty. "I suppose we should we leave him locked in his coffin."

"Another good idea. Can you manage carrying it up the stairs and getting it into the attic, though?" Alaysia asked.

I glanced at Max and Gregory. "Well, we have two very strong, handsome men..."

Max snorted. "Go on, woman. All right, all right. We'll bring your boyfriend and his coffin up. But you owe me a good dinner."

"You mean a meal out, I hope. Unless you want a grilled cheese sandwich or boxed mac and cheese." I stuck my tongue out at him and he grinned. Really, Max was a good-natured guy. I was grateful that Sandy had found him.

As Gregory and Max headed toward the basement, I brought a stepstool out for Leroy so that he could open the trapdoor. When the ladder was down, we trudged upstairs and I turned on the lights. Now that the wall was down between the attic and the secret room, it was easier to see into the back corner. Kelson handed Sandy the painting and darted back down the ladder. She returned carrying two high-powered LED lamps and plugged them in toward the back, showering light into all corners.

Alaysia began opening the bags they had brought and setting up an altar in the center of the secret room. Shivering, I folded my arms across my chest and wandered over to one of the walls, staring at the cuneiform writing. Now that I knew what it said—at least paraphrased—it made me more nervous than it had before.

"Are you sure you're ready for this?" Sandy said, standing beside me as she held onto Franny's painting. Franny was staring out of the glass, looking more frustrated than ever.

I nodded. "I have to go through with this. I have no idea what's going to happen, but I hope to hell that I come out the other side."

By the time I turned around, Alaysia had set up an elaborate altar. She had set up a folding table, and over it she had placed a deep shimmering purple tablecloth with gold trim. In the center she had placed an amethyst chalice, and encircled it in a ring of obsidian and moonstone spheres. To the left side of the chalice she placed a black obsidian dagger, and to the right side, a bowl for incense. She took what looked like a human skull from her bag and set it in front of the chalice, then scattered blood-red rose petals around the table. Their scent filled the air, heady and intoxicating. On the right side of the skull, she placed one carved out of clear crystal, and on the left side, one carved out of obsidian. From a second bag, she shook out a long purple gown and handed it to me. It looked similar to the gown I wore for ritual, only this one had gold trim and a gold sash that tied at the waist.

"Please dress in this. Wear nothing else, and go barefoot. Take off all your jewelry as well. You'll want to take a ritual shower beforehand, using this soap." She pressed a cake of lotus-scented soap into my hand and motioned for me to leave. "Once you're done, stay in your room until we come for you."

I headed down to my bedroom, passing Gregory and Max in the hallway. They were carrying Aegis's coffin. I wasn't sure how they were going to get the coffin into the attic, but I left them to figure that out and went to my room.

I stripped off my clothes and tossed them on the bed, then carefully laid out the dress and sash. Entering my bathroom, I turned on the water and stepped into the shower with the soap. As I lathered up with it, I realized I was slipping into a trancelike state. I hadn't expected that, given my lack of magical powers. Making sure I was squeaky clean, an important part of formal rituals, I then toweled off.

As I dressed, I was startled to find that the top of the dress was composed of two thin straps that covered my nipples, leaving the rest of my boobs exposed. They crisscrossed my chest, looping over my shoulders to attach to the back of the dress, which barely covered the upper part of my butt. The material was filmy and as I tied the sash around my waist, I thought about using quake wax to keep the straps in place. But Alaysia had told me to wear nothing else. Feeling exposed, I sat at my vanity and brushed out my hair, then waited for them to come get me.

"Please, Arianrhod, Great Goddess of the Silver Wheel, let this work. Let us get back to normal and everything be all right in our household." But even as I whispered the prayer, I wondered if she could hear me.

IT WAS SANDY who came to fetch me. I opened the door when she tapped on it and was surprised to see that she was carrying a circlet, a necklace, a wand, a ring, and a pair of golden slippers.

I started to speak, but she held up her hand for silence. She entered the room and without a word decked me out with all of the gear. She placed the circlet on my head last, and a shiver ran through me. I wasn't sure what it was from, but everything became very real at that moment.

She motioned for me to follow her down the hall to the ladder. Leroy was standing there, holding a goblet filled with steaming liquid. He handed it to me and I glanced at him, questioning. He nodded for me to upend it.

I drained it, then handed it back to him, grimacing at the cloying taste. It tasted like honey and corn syrup and saffron all mixed together. He held his fingers to his lips, and I nodded, keeping the silence. Then he motioned for me to climb the ladder. Once I was in the attic, Leroy joined us, followed by Sandy. They joined Max and Gregory, who were standing to the side.

Alaysia was beside the altar wearing ritual robes, ornate and embroidered with metallic threads. They were black and silver, and the heavy pall of magic that hung around her penetrated even my magic-blind state. She motioned for me to kneel on a pillow that was on the floor in front of her, and I did so.

As I waited, she began to intone a chant that sounded as ancient as Ereshkigal herself. I closed my eyes, drifting on her words. I couldn't understand the words she was singing, but the music caught me up and I soon found myself drifting on the musical currents.

The incantation seemed to drone on and on, but at one point, I realized I was beginning to understand what some of the words meant. Alaysia was singing to Ereshkigal, asking her to open a gateway.

A moment later, there was a sudden hush as Alaysia's song drifted away. I opened my eyes and found the room was filled with mist. The only person I could see was Alaysia. Beside her shimmered a vortex, reminding me of a magic mirror. She bade me to stand and I did.

"Are you ready to face the dread goddess Ereshkigal, Queen of the Underworld?"

It was as though every ounce of courage in my heart drained away, but in its place was utter resignation that this was what I was meant to do. I was terrified, and yet I had no other choice.

"I'm ready. What must I do?"

"You must face the guardians of the gates. Do as they ask, even though it may lead to your death. I ask a second time, are you ready to face the dread goddess Ereshkigal, Queen of the Underworld?"

"I'm ready." I recognized that this was a formal challenge, a required part of the ritual.

"I ask a third time, are you ready to face the dread goddess Ereshkigal, Queen of the Underworld?"

"Yes. I'm ready."

A hush fell through the room, and the mist grew thicker.

Alaysia motioned toward the doorway. "Then step through, and face the seven gates of Ereshkigal. Return if you can."

My stomach tied in knots, I stepped toward the portal, the mist frothing around my feet. I could see myself in the reflection, looking almost like a queen, and I caught my breath at how beautiful I felt at that moment. And then the mirror fell away, opening up into a dark chasm, and I stepped through.

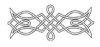

I FELL, NOT sure how long I was falling. Eventually, I came to rest, standing on a dark stone staircase. The dropoff was steep on both sides, and down below, energy roiled in shades of blue and purple and white. The steps themselves were narrow, barely eighteen inches wide, and the sandals I was wearing were slick against the stone. Shaking, terrified I was going to lose my balance and fall over the edge, I began to descend.

I don't know how long I went down the staircase, using my arms to keep my balance, but finally, up ahead, I saw another portal similar to the one I'd stepped through. And at the gateway stood a tall figure, as dark as the stone steps themselves, looking carved from the very foundations of the earth. Indeed, I thought perhaps he was stone, this guardian who was every inch ten feet tall. Sparks flew with every movement he made. He was standing in front of the portal and as I approached he held out his hand, warning me to stop.

"Who approaches the Queen of the Underworld?"

"Maudlin Gallowglass. I come to make a plea of the great goddess Ereshkigal." I wasn't sure if that was what I was *supposed* to say, but since Alaysia hadn't prepared me for this part, I had to wing it.

"As payment for passage, as a symbol of your humility, give me your wand." He held out his hand.

Suddenly, I realized that I really was in the middle of the descent of Inanna, and now I really was well and truly scared. I handed him my wand, saying nothing. He took it and stood to the side, motioning to the portal.

I stepped through it and fell again until I found

myself on the staircase once more. Below was another portal, with another guardian. At this portal, I was asked for my ring, and I handed it over. Again, I was escorted through the gateway, and yet again found myself on another staircase. The third time, the guardian asked for my shoes. At the fourth, I offered up my necklace. At the fifth gate, I was asked for my sash and I untied it, handing it over.

By the sixth gate, I was ready. The guardian asked for my dress and I slid it over my head, standing naked with just the crown left. By now I was shivering, goose bumps rising all over my body.

I had no magic to protect me, and I was naked, with nothing between me and the elements. But I had to go on trust. The guardian guided me through the portal, and once again I was on a staircase. This should be the last one. Seven gates had the goddess Inanna gone through on her descent to visit her sister, Ereshkigal. At each one she had been stripped of a symbol of her power until she stood naked before death itself.

At the seventh gate, I handed over my crown, leaving me thoroughly bare. The guardian looked at me, through those dark and silent dark eyes, then pointed toward the portal.

"Do you still wish to visit the dread goddess Ereshkigal, Queen of the Underworld? Speak now, or forever leave this realm."

I wasn't even sure I *could* leave this realm if I wanted to. But it didn't matter. I had come here to plead with Ereshkigal for my household, and for my loved ones.

"I do."

"Then step through, and face the Queen of the Underworld."

The portal flared, sputtering with energy. Blue and purple, white, and then red flames came roaring out of the portal, then vanished.

Naked, terrified, I stepped through the vortex. The world shifted once again.

THE CHAMBER INTO which I stepped seemed unending, filled with fog and mist. But I noticed nothing else, for in the center of the chamber sat a massive throne carved out of black onyx and marble.

Atop the throne was the winged goddess, her skin the color of hematite, her eyes shimmering white. She wore a flowing skirt with a belt of silver, leaving her breasts bare. Her wings spread out, massive and bat-like, and she radiated the energy of the grave.

Her hair hung to her knees, in massive braids that snaked on their own, and she wore a necklace of skulls and a headdress made of bone and stone and crystal. Her lips were full, and she towered over me, at least twenty feet tall.

She watched, laughing, as I approached. Her voice echoed off the sides of the chamber, reverberating deep within my core, almost stilling my heart.

And then the next moment, she was standing before me, now seeming to be barely taller than I was, but her power still overwhelmed me, and it took everything I had to keep on my feet. I knew that here, even Arianrhod could not save me.

My existence and my return to my home depended solely on Ereshkigal.

"What is it you seek?" Her voice rumbled through the chamber. I heard moans and groans coming from the fog, and the sounds of bones clicking, and the ghostly rattle of death throes.

My stomach lurched. I struggled to find my voice, struggled to figure out what to say. Now that I was here, my mind went blank. Finally, I cleared my throat.

My voice came out in a whisper. "I come to ask for your help."

"And what help would you ask of the goddess of death?"

I took a deep breath. "An ancient sorcerer runs through my house. He's there because of a curse you laid on him, condemning him to a half-life. He was in an urn, and someone broke it, freeing him. He's hurting my family. He's hurting my friends. He's hurting me. He doesn't belong in our world and I have come to you asking you to take him. I ask you to undo your curse and summon Etum to the Underworld, where he belongs."

I wanted to close my eyes, to squeeze them shut in case she struck me down for being so presumptuous. But I couldn't. My gaze was fastened on the brilliant goddess. She was as dark as the night sky and yet she was more brilliant than the sun. She was beautiful and terrifying and seductive. And she was staring at me with those white-hot eyes.

Finally, she spoke. "I have not heard that name in a long time. So Etum runs free once more? I thought I had buried him forever."

"The people of my world seem to like digging up the past," I said.

Ereshkigal considered my words for a moment. "Sometimes, I suppose you must dig up the past in order to erase the wrongs it harbors in it."

Again we stood there for what felt like hours. I was cold, but I was too frightened to even shiver.

"When you began this journey, you must have realized that there was a chance you would never return. Why did you choose to come into my presence?"

I thought about my answer before I spoke. It had to be true. She could tell if I was lying.

"Etum is harming people I love. He's hurting me. And he will hurt others. He tried to take over a woman who's gone into hiding, who seems to be the reincarnation of his lost love. When she realized that he was trying to act through her, she vanished rather than let him use her powers. With his very presence, he threatens anyone who comes into contact with him. Since his curse is on *my* household, I'm the one who is responsible. I did not willingly free him, and the man who did so accidentally is dead. We already have one death caused by Etum's presence. I cannot let there be any more."

Ereshkigal held out her hand, and a pale light appeared in it. She stared at the light, and it did not waver. "You speak the truth of your heart. You fear me and yet you came to help save others. Perhaps it *is* time for me to bring Etum into my realm, to teach him the error of his ways. Perhaps it's time to end the curse."

I was about to speak, about to thank her, when she waved her hand. There was an explosion of light and thunder. Blinded, I fell to my knees from the shock. I found myself falling again, down a deep, dark hole, spiraling into an abyss. I screamed, and the next thing I knew, the world went black.

WHEN I OPENED my eyes, everything seemed out of focus. I blinked. Someone was lifting me, carrying me in his arms. He smelled like cinnamon and vanilla, honey and autumn leaves.

"Aegis?" My throat hurt so much I could barely talk.

"Shush. It's me. You'll be all right. I'm just carrying you to your bed."

"Everything is blurry. I can't see."

"Your vision will clear. Sandy's called Jordan."

Closing my eyes again, I slipped back into unconsciousness.

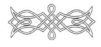

"MADDY? CAN YOU hear me?"

I squinted as I opened my eyes. This time I could make out Jordan's face. He was sitting on the bed next to me, and I was propped up on pillows, under the covers.

"Can you speak?"

I searched for my voice. "Yeah, though my throat burns. What happened? Did it work?" My memories felt scrambled. I had the vague impression of standing in front of a dark winged woman, but I couldn't remember the details of what she looked like. All I could remember was the immense power that she emanated.

"Yes. It worked. Etum is gone. Aegis is all right."

I tried to focus on Jordan's voice, but I kept wanting to sleep. The impulse was so overwhelming that I finally caved. Closing my eyes, I drifted back to sleep.

WHEN I FINALLY woke for real, it was near midnight. Aegis was sitting next to the bed, waiting for me. I groaned, pushing myself to a sitting position. My throat still hurt, and every muscle in my body ached. I motioned to the water bottle on my nightstand and he handed it to me.

"How are you feeling?"

I assessed my body, from my toes on up to the top of my head. "Like I've been to hell and back. I feel scorched, like I have a very bad sunburn on the inside."

"I'd say that's to be expected, considering where

you went." Jordan's voice came from the other side of the bed and I looked around to see that he was standing beside the door. "Considering everything that's gone on, I'd say that's the best we could expect. I'm just glad you're back."

"Back?"

"According to Alaysia, you actually vanished through the portal. You *were* in Ereshkigal's realm, body and all." Aegis was staring at me, looking more worried than I had ever seen him. "I can't believe you actually went through with it."

As the memories began to flood back, I let out a gasp. "So it really worked? She took Etum? The curse is gone?"

Jordan nodded. "Oh, the curse is gone off your house, all right. Once the medication drains out of your system, your magic will be fine and dandy. And there's something else. An unexpected side effect, one that I think you're going to like."

Curious, I cocked my head. "What is it? What happened?"

Aegis held up my robe for me. "Come and see."

I realized I was still naked, so I slipped my robe on, tying it around my waist. I was feeling weak, but Aegis carried me over to the French doors. I opened them, and he carried me out to the balcony and stood me at the edge.

"Look down there," he said, a broad smile spreading across his face.

I pressed against the screen, staring down into the back yard. There, out on the lawn, I could see a misty figure dancing around the yard. It was Franny.

Chapter 14

I COULDN'T BELIEVE what I was seeing. Franny was *outside* the house! I turned to Aegis, so excited I could barely speak.

"*How?* What happened?"

"I guess when the curse lifted on the house, it also lifted the curse on Franny. She came out of the painting and was so excited to be free that she went whirling around the living room. She accidentally careened into the wall and went right through and ended up outside. That's how we knew her curse was lifted, too."

"How wonderful. I can't believe this is finally over." I paused, then added, "Well, it will be over when my powers come back."

"They'll be back," Jordan said from behind us. "And in a few days Max will be able to change back into his tiger self as well. Everybody seems fine, so I'm heading back to my girlfriend to finish watching the movie we were just starting when Sandy called. As much as I like you, I hope I don't have to see you for a while. Unless it's a social situation."

I turned to Aegis. "Is everybody still up? I want to go downstairs. I'm so happy."

Even though I felt like crap, my heart was exploding with joy. Just seeing Franny outside had been one of the most joyful moments I'd had the past few months. She had spent well over two hundred years locked within the walls of this house, wishing she could go out. And now, she was free.

I froze as I realized what that might mean.

Franny was *free*. What if she wanted to leave? And right then I realized how accustomed to her I'd become. She was part of our household, part of our family, complaints and all.

"Do you think she's going to leave?"

Aegis wrapped his arm around my waist. "If she does, we'll have to accept it. You wouldn't blame her, would you? She's been here in this house since the day she died in 1815. I wouldn't blame her in the least if she wanted to see the world. You have to prepare yourself for the fact that she might be ready to move on. To another life, or something else."

"I don't *want* to prepare myself for that. But you're right, I can't be selfish. Regardless of what she decides, I'm grateful that she *has* a choice now."

I slid on my slippers and we headed downstairs. In the kitchen, Max and Gregory were sharing a bottle of wine. Sandy was standing out on the patio, watching Franny as she raced around the yard, leaving a trail of mist behind her.

Leroy and Alaysia were nowhere in sight.

"Where did—"

"They left about an hour ago. Once they were assured that you would be okay, they packed up everything and took off. You know what's odd? All the writing on the walls upstairs vanished when the curse lifted. Every trace of the black powder is gone. And the pottery all turned to dust and disappeared." Aegis pulled me into his arms, stroking my hair out of my eyes. "Do you realize how brave you are? How proud I am of you?"

My breath caught in my throat. "It's easy to be brave when your loved ones need you."

Memories flooded back of my journey to stand in front of Ereshkigal. And yet I wasn't ready to talk about them. The whole ritual had been so overwhelming and so terrifying that I didn't want to think about it. I wanted to let the whole matter vanish into the past.

"Not everybody would do what you did." He paused. "Go ahead, I know you want to go out and talk to Sandy and Franny. I'll wait in here with the guys." He kissed me, his lips soft against mine. I draped my arms around his neck, not wanting the kisses to end.

"I love you. You know that, right?" I whispered.

He nodded. "I know. And I love you. Now go talk to the girls."

As I headed outside, all I could think about was the fact that our house was clear. The curse was gone, and we were once again safe.

Franny saw me and raced to my side, a swirl of

mist and vapor and yet still as visible as she had been inside. "I'm free! Maddy! You freed me. How can I ever thank you?"

I wanted to tell her that I hadn't been the one to free her, that it had been Ereshkigal. But the words wouldn't come. And I didn't know if it mattered.

"Thank me by coming back to visit. *A lot.*" There was a lump in my throat as I spoke, and I realized I was on the verge of tears, overwhelmed by all that had happened.

"Come to visit? Oh! I see. Yes, I'll be leaving," she said. "Someday. But not right now. I'm going to venture out and explore the island. And I want to see the world, but that can wait awhile. I need to get my bearings first. In fact, I was going to ask if you would take me in your automobile—if you would drive me around so I could see the sights. I think it would be fun and I've never been in a car before. I've never even touched one."

I laughed, suddenly relieved. "Of course I'll take you out to see the sights, although I'm sorry but I don't think you'll be able to touch the car now, either. You're *still* a spirit. But you can probably ride in it. So you're saying that you're going to stay?"

"I will, for a while at least. I don't know how long. I don't know what I'll find out there. I don't even know if I'll be allowed to stay. But for as long as I can, the Bewitching Bedlam will be my home base." She threw back her arms and stared at the sky. "Do you know how long it's been since I've actually seen the stars? They're so beautiful, more beautiful than I remember them."

I shivered, as Sandy walked over to me. The

clouds were starting to sock in again, and the temperature was dropping.

"We should go inside," Sandy said.

"I think I want to stay out for a while. You don't mind, do you?" Franny asked.

I shook my head. "Stay out as long as you want. We'll see you in a while."

I leaned against Sandy as we headed inside, still feeling weak and exhausted. The adrenaline rush was gone, and all I wanted was my bed and a peaceful night's sleep.

BY MORNING, I was feeling back to myself. My throat was still scratchy and I still felt like I had an inside-out sunburn, but I wasn't feeling like death warmed over.

As I clattered down the stairs, Gregory was waiting in the kitchen. He had his suitcases packed and it looked like he had already eaten breakfast.

"Are you leaving already? It's only six. I don't want you to go. We haven't had nearly enough time to catch up."

"I have to, I'm afraid. In order to catch my flight, I need to arrive at Sea-Tac by noon at the latest to check in and get through security. But I had so much fun, and I learned so much. I promise you, I'll come back. And someday, you have to come over and visit me."

He hugged me, squeezing me tight. "I'm proud of my little sister. You're an amazing woman,

Maddy. Bonkers, yes, but damn, what a life you've led. Don't stop being you, okay?"

I gave him a kiss on the cheek. "Drive safe. Text me when you get to the airport. And yes, I want you to promise that you'll come back to visit for longer. When there isn't an ancient sorcerer wreaking havoc in my house."

He laughed. "I promise." As he headed out to his rental car, a tear slipped down my cheek and I realized how much I was going to miss him. It was funny. A few days back I hadn't known if I would even *like* him. Now, I didn't want to see him go.

Meanwhile, Aegis was baking up a storm. He had already made four loaves of bread, two pans of cinnamon rolls, four batches of cookies, and was now making croissants.

I stared at the bounty of goodies. "You realize that I'm gaining weight from all your baking." It wasn't exactly true, but it felt like it.

"I don't care what you weigh. All I care about is that you're healthy and happy. And that you still love me." He glanced at the clock. "I have enough time to whip up a pan of lemon bars before I have to go to sleep. I can't tell you how good it feels to be in control of my predator again. Thank you, for not taking a chance."

"I love you, but I'm not a fool. I know what vampires on the prowl are like." I was glad that we could be frank about the fact that he was a predator. That the subject wasn't off-limits.

"Max and Sandy are coming over Friday for dinner, right?"

I nodded. "They're bringing Jenna. Sandy and

Jenna and I are going to look at bridal magazines. Sandy's not sure what kind of a dress she wants to wear, and since Jen is going to be her maid of honor, she gets a say in her own dress. I'm afraid that there's going to be a lot of wedding talk the next few months. You and Max are just going to have to deal with it."

Aegis laughed. "I think we can manage. Okay, get your coffee and breakfast, woman. I want you feeling strong and healthy for tonight, because it's been a little too long since—"

"Housekeeper in the kitchen!" Kelson said, stopping him. "She knows what you mean and so do I, so no graphic explanations needed." She laughed, setting a plate of eggs and bacon on the table for me.

As I sat down to eat, I looked out the window and saw Franny in the back yard. It was pouring down rain, but she was standing out there, just gazing up at the sky. The sight made me incredibly happy and yet sad. Life was changing, and we were all changing with it.

IT WAS ALMOST three o'clock when I finally finished organizing the books and letting people know that we were open for business again. I had already booked one of our guestrooms for a week in early December when Franny showed up by my desk.

"Do you think you could show me around the

island? At least a little bit?"

I pushed away my books. The light was starting to fade, and I had promised to take her out during the afternoon.

"I'm sorry I spaced out. Of course we can go. There's still time to see some of the marina and downtown. But don't you go spooking anybody, okay?" Honestly, though, the idea of Franny scaring anybody seemed ridiculous. Besides, most of Bedlam was used to spooks and spirits.

Lanyear fluttered over, landing on my shoulder. I stared up at him.

"You want to go, too?"

I got the distinct impression that he did, so I slung my purse over my shoulder and, carrying a jacket, headed out to the car with Franny in tow. As we neared my CR-V, I paused. Something felt weird—a tingle of some sort. At first I thought my foot was going to sleep but then I realized that it was an all-over tingle. I looked around, not sure what I was searching for.

"Is something wrong?" Franny asked. She had slid inside the passenger seat, through the door and was now sitting primly there, staring at the dashboard.

I hesitated, then shook my head. As I opened the door, it still felt like something was off.

"Maybe it's my magic starting to come back. The medication that Jordan gave me might be wearing off. I just feel antsy. Kind of like someone's watching me."

"If it doesn't go away, maybe you should talk to Jordan." Franny pointed at the dashboard. "Tell me what all those dials and lights are for. And what's this?" She pointed at the radio.

As I began to explain the finer points of an automobile's anatomy, I put the car in gear and pulled out of the driveway. I was about to tell her to fasten her seatbelt when I realized how ridiculous that sounded.

"Where are we going to first?"

"I think we'll go to Bedlam City Park. It's on the shore, and it's not far from here. It's open till dusk so we've got some time. Then we'll drive downtown and I'll show you the town that you've lived in for decades, but haven't ever seen."

As I headed down the road, Franny kept up a steady chatter, commenting on the houses as we passed them. I was awash in a whirl of her voice, not really paying attention but murmuring an appropriate response here or there, when we finally came to the park.

I pulled in and parked in one of the farthest stalls. There didn't seem to be anybody else there given it was raining, but I didn't mind. I was in an introspective mood.

Franny was out of the car and running down to the shore before I could even unbuckle my seatbelt. I stepped out into the rain, pulling my hood over my head, but staying next to the car as I watched her dance along the shore and wade into the ocean. At least she wouldn't get cold or drown, I thought. Lanyear flew down to the beach beside her, swooping and gliding on the currents of wind.

I felt awash in a tangle of emotions. I was still stunned and shell-shocked from my visit to Ereshkigal. And I was grateful that the curse had been lifted, grateful that I would be getting my magic back, ecstatic that Franny was free from her curse. All the conflicting emotions had wound themselves up into one big ball.

So deep in my thoughts, I barely noticed when another car eased into a parking spot behind us. Watching Franny, I tried to give my thoughts a rest, breathing slowly and deeply. As the cool air hit my lungs, it calmed the inner burn that plagued my lungs and my throat.

A crunch on the gravel behind me startled me, and I turned to see who was there. As my eyes met Craig's, I let out a shriek and stumbled back.

"So, Maddy. You didn't expect to see me so soon again, did you? Surprise, surprise!"

The next moment, he lashed out, hitting me so hard against the side of my head that I tripped and fell. As I hit the gravel, everything went blurry and I realized I was about to pass out. I tried to scream again, to beg him not to do whatever it was he was planning, but the next moment he leaned down and hit me again, and I lost consciousness.

WHEN I WOKE up, I was laying on the ground, in a puddle of water.

It was dark and we were on a cliff that I recognized as the parking lot at Beachcomber Spit, a steep shoreline park on the east side of the island. There were catacombs below these cliffs, but what mostly worried me was that there were also a lot of very sharp rocks down below. One misstep could lead to a deadly end.

My wrists were tied together with a scratchy length of rope. Craig was sitting near me on a rock, drinking out of a whiskey bottle as the rain poured down around us. He was soaked through, but he didn't seem to notice. Groaning, I rolled to a sitting position.

"Craig? What the hell is this? You need to let me go. What do you want?"

"What the hell is this? What do I want? What I want is to get my old life back. I want my condo back that you took from me. I want my job back." The bitterness in his voice cut through the air like a knife.

"I didn't do anything to you. *You're* the one who chose to embezzle your clients. *You're* the one who took the loan from the loan shark because *you're* the one who wanted the cabin. Let me go and I'll try to help you." I stopped, suddenly realizing that it might not be the wisest idea to point out his faults at this time.

"Can't do that, Maddy. I'm sorry, but I can't. My life started downhill the day I met you. I thought you were a goddess, I thought you were sexy and beautiful and funny and witty. You were my fantasy woman. What happened?" He sounded angry and lost, and I realized he'd never accept responsibility for destroying his own life.

"I'm a *real person*, Craig. You built a fantasy up in your mind of what you wanted me to be. You had this vision of your ideal woman, but nobody can ever match up to a fantasy. I'm strong and I have my own needs and my own desires. I wasn't a blowup doll or a robot there to service you. You wanted a trophy wife. I can guarantee you, I'm not a trophy, and I never have been."

"Well, you've got that right. You're certainly no prize." He let out a snort, then paused. Then his tone took on a different note. "I found out something recently. Something you never told me. I found out that vampires *love* witches' blood—it's an aphrodisiac for them. You never bothered to fill me in on that little secret."

"There's a good reason for that." I didn't like the tone of his voice. He sounded crafty, dangerous.

"We could have made a killing by selling off your blood once a month. Ah, well. Water under the bridge. However, I met a vampire who belongs to an underground club and they'd love to have a juicy witch in their stable. They're going to give me $100,000 to hand you over to them, and you're going to become one of their bloodwhores. And I will have the money to get out of the country before my trial. I can't tap into my bank accounts, I can't even pawn my Rolex without the cops coming down on me. But $100,000 will get me to Mexico. And Mexico spells freedom."

I began to panic. He was right. There were rogue vampires who would just love to have a witch for a bloodwhore.

"Craig, don't do this. I swear, I'll help you escape if you untie me." Using my feet, I pushed myself back against the car to brace myself as I stood up. I was woozy from the hit on the head, but I had to do something.

"Oh no, you're not going *anywhere* without *me*. And every time I get angry, I'll just think about those vampires bleeding you dry and fucking you so hard you scream, and I'll laugh." And then he did laugh, sounding manic and driven. He also sounded drunk.

I knew that I had to act, because once he got me into that car, I wasn't going to be able to get free. I still didn't have my magical powers back, and there wasn't much I could do, as bruised as I felt. So I began to run toward the edge of the parking lot, trying to get out into the road where somebody might see me. I screamed as I ran, howling like a banshee.

"Come back here, you bitch!" Craig launched himself after me, but by the sound of his footsteps I could tell he was lurching around, probably because of the booze. I tried to zigzag to throw him off so that he would trip and fall. But as drunk as he was, he was still quick, and he caught up with me, grabbing hold of my hair and yanking so hard that it felt like my neck cracked. I screamed again as he flipped me around, letting go so that I went plowing face-first into the gravel.

I rolled over, trying to work my hands free so that I could fight back.

Craig loomed over me and kicked me, giving me a nasty blow in the side.

"That's for being a bitch." He kicked me again. "And that's for leeching me dry." He was about to kick me again when a woman's voice echoed out.

"Get him, Lanyear!" It was Franny, racing along

the cliff toward us.

Lanyear swept down out of the sky, raking across Craig's face, leaving a long scratch that began to bleed profusely. Craig screamed, turning as Franny came up behind him. He hit out at her, but his hand passed through and he screamed again.

Lanyear turned on his wingtip, barreling down to claw him from behind. I struggled to get up but I was hurting so badly that I could barely move. Just then a car came screeching into the parking lot and before it even came to a stop the door opened and Aegis jumped out.

"I warned you," was the only thing Aegis said before he launched himself onto Craig, taking him down, biting deep into Craig's jugular. Craig let out a painful shriek that hurt to hear. Aegis reared up, his mouth bloody and his eyes crimson. He stood, yanking Craig up by the throat. "You hurt the woman I love for the last time."

Craig swung his leg, kicking Aegis right in the nuts. Aegis just stared at him, then with one good throw, tossed Craig across the parking lot. Craig went rolling into the grass that skirted the edge of the cliff, managing to stop himself before he toppled over the edge. He dragged himself to his feet as Aegis began to stomp his way over to him.

"Stay back—stay back, I warn you. I've got a gun!" Craig pulled a gun out of his jacket, holding it up with shaking hands.

At that moment, Franny appeared behind Craig. He hadn't noticed her yet, but I could see her from where I was laying. She leaned forward, and then, in a loud voice yelled, "Boo!"

Startled, Craig stumbled back through Franny.
She moved delicately to one side as he wavered on the edge of the cliff, and then toppled over the edge. We heard one loud shriek, and then the night was silent.

Chapter 15

BY THE TIME we finished talking to Delia, the coroner was on the way to the hospital with Craig's body, and it was almost nine P.M.

Against my wishes, they also insisted on taking me to the hospital to get x-rayed. I had a broken rib, a bruised hip, and more lacerations and contusions than I could count. Jordan just stared at me as he taped my ribs and tended to my wounds.

Sandy was there with me. Aegis had called her, not wanting to come into the hospital so he wouldn't frighten anyone. Franny had gone back to the house with Lanyear.

By the time we got home, the only thing I wanted was a pizza, a glass of wine, and some peace and quiet. The glass of wine would have to wait, though. Jordan had nixed it, given the pain pills he had given me for my ribs.

Kelson just stared at me, giving me a look much

like Jordan had.

"Well, that ends an era of my life. Craig's dead. I can't believe it. I can't believe he was going to sell me off to a vampire club as a bloodwhore." I broke down in tears. "I'm so tired."

Aegis rubbed my shoulders. "I know, sweetie. I know. I want you to rest and get better. Kelson and I will take care of all the business for the next few weeks. You need a long vacation."

"I've got some good news," Kelson said. "I got a call from Henry. He's coming home tomorrow. I told him about Franny and he's truly happy for her. He doesn't blame her in the least for his stroke."

Grateful for small favors, I accepted the cup of peppermint tea that Kelson made me as Aegis ordered a couple pizzas. Sitting back, in the glow of the kitchen, the only thing I could think about was that I was in the home that I loved, with the man that I loved, and my best friend sitting by my side.

OVER THE NEXT couple weeks, Henry returned. He was doing well, all things considered, and he and Franny were back to being friendly, although I had the feeling their friendship would never be quite what it was. But they seemed to be enjoying each other's company again, and I was grateful for that. Franny was exploring the island, whisking this way and that way, coming back with all sorts of things to tell me that I already knew about, but that were so new to her. But I listened, excited because she was excited. She hadn't mentioned leaving yet, in fact she hadn't talked about it at all, and I was in no hurry to ask her about it.

Aegis and Max had painted the attic and what was no longer the secret room, putting up drywall to turn the entire attic into an actual usable space. They had hung new lights so that it was bright and cheery, and nothing remained to remind us of Etum and the curse.

Gregory had made it back to London. His conference had gone extremely well. He was already planning his next trip over, which he wanted to make in March.

As far as Craig's death went, I was still sorting out my feelings on it. I wasn't distressed, although I was truly sorry that he had fallen to such depths. At one time I had loved him, though that had died along with the marriage.

Thanksgiving was a quiet affair. We had encouraged our guests to go to the community meal so that we could have a quiet evening at home with just Sandy, Max, Jenna, Kelson, and Henry. Bubba and Luna were busy picking over their share of the turkey.

Sandy and Max were in the living room with the others, but I had opted to take a little time to myself. I was sitting in the kitchen, in the rocking chair, holding Drofur—my stuffed unicorn. Aegis entered the room.

He sat down beside me, taking my hand in his.

"What are you thinking about?" he asked, scooting closer.

"Thanksgiving. Craig and everything that happened with him. The curse. You. Everything that's happened over the past year. My life has turned upside down and inside out. Some of it's been bad, but some of it—you and Franny and Lanyear and moving to Bedlam—have been the best choices I've ever made."

Aegis nodded, his eyes warm. "Maddy, I want to ask you a question. I've been thinking about it for a while, but I think it's time."

A sudden fear froze my heart. He sounded so serious.

"What is it?"

"I've been thinking about Max and Sandy and what they have together. And I've been thinking about us and what we have together."

He reached in his jacket pocket and everything began to shift. As he pulled out a little black box, I caught my breath. He opened it, holding it forward, and the glitter of sapphire and diamond sparkled in front of me.

"I know that a year is a short time in our life spans, but it feels like it's been longer and it feels like we've known each other before. We've been down this road before together, even though we don't know where it was or when it was. Will you make me the happiest vampire in Bedlam? Will you marry me?"

As I slid into his arms, crying, I realized that it felt right. It all felt so right and everything had led up to this moment. He slid the ring on my finger as I looked up into his eyes. He might be a vampire, and maybe I was one of the best vampire slayers in the world, but love transcended so many different chasms.

I nodded. "Yes. I'll marry you." As my lips met his, Sandy, Franny, and Kelson came bounding out from the living room, cheering. Bubba and Luna began to chase each other around the room. Max followed, helping Henry. As I looked around, I realized *this* was my family. All of them. And even Fata Morgana. They were my family of choice. And Gregory would become part of that.

"You may be the happiest vampire in Bedlam, but I'll tell you this, Aegis. *I'm* the happiest witch alive." And then I kissed him again.

If you enjoyed this book and want to read the rest of the series, then come meet the wild and magical residents of Bedlam in my Bewitching Bedlam Series. (It's lighter-hearted but still steamy paranormal romance.) Fun-loving witch Maddy Gallowglass, her smoking-hot vampire lover Aegis, and their crazed cjinn Bubba (part djinn, all cat) rock it out in Bedlam, a magical town on a magical island. BLOOD MUSIC, BEWITCHING BEDLAM, MAUDLIN'S MAYHEM, SIREN'S SONG, WITCH-ES WILD, BLOOD VENGEANCE, TIGER TAILS, and THE WISH FACTOR are available.

You might also enjoy my new series The Wild Hunt. Urban fantasy/paranormal romance, the first three books are out: THE SILVER STAG, and OAK & THORNS, and IRON BONES. A SHADOW OF CROWS will be available later this year, and there will be more to come!

If you like a far darker read, my Indigo Court Series is once again available in e-format. Dark fantasy/steamy hot paranormal romance, you will find the series available for your e-reader: NIGHT MYST, NIGHT VEIL, NIGHT SEEKER, NIGHT VISION, NIGHT'S END, and NIGHT SHIVERS.

I also invite you to visit Fury's world. In a gritty, post-apocalyptic Seattle, Fury is a minor goddess, in charge of eliminating the Abominations who come off the World Tree. The first story arc of the Fury Unbound Series is complete with: FURY RISING, FURY'S MAGIC, FURY AWAKENED, and FURY CALLING. The second story arc will begin later this year with FURY'S MANTLE.

If you like cozies with teeth, try my Chintz 'n China paranormal mysteries. The series is complete with: GHOST OF A CHANCE, LEGEND OF THE JADE DRAGON, MURDER UNDER A MYSTIC MOON, A HARVEST OF BONES, ONE HEX OF A WEDDING, and a wrap-up novella: HOLIDAY SPIRITS.

The newest Otherworld book—HARVEST SONG—is available now, and the last, BLOOD BONDS, will be available in April 2019.

For all of my work, both published and upcoming releases, see the Bibliography at the end of this book, or check out my website at Galenorn. com and be sure and sign up for my newsletter to receive news about all my new releases.

Playlist

I often write to music, and here's the playlist I used for this book.

A.J. Roach: Devil May Dance
Al Stewart: Life in Dark Water
The Alan Parsons Project: Breakdown; Can't Take it With You
Alice in Chains: Man in the Box; Sunshine
The Asteroids Galaxy Tour: X; Sunshine Coolin'; Heart Attack; Out of Frequency; Major
AWOLNATION: Sail
Beck: Broken Train; Devil's Haircut
The Black Angels: Don't Play With Guns; Always Maybe; You're Mine; Phosphene Dream; Never/Ever; Indigo Meadow
Black Mountain: Queens Will Play
Black Sabbath: Lady Evil
Boom! Bap! Pow!: Suit
Broken Bells: The Ghost Inside
Cake: Short Skirt/Long Jacket; The Distance
Clannad: I See Red; Newgrange
The Clash: Should I Stay or Should I Go
Cobra Verde: Play with Fire
Crazy Town: Butterfly
David & Steve Gordon: Shaman's Drum Dance
Donovan: Sunshine Superman; Season of the

Witch

Eastern Sun And John Kelley: Beautiful Being

Eels: Souljacker Part 1

FC Kahuna: Hayling

Foster the People: Pumped Up Kicks

Gary Numan: Down in the Park; Cars; Soul Protection; My World Storm; Dream Killer; Outland; Petals; Remember I Was Vapour; Praying to the Aliens; My Breathing

Godsmack: Voodoo

Hedningarna: Ukkonen; Juopolle Joutunut; Gorrlaus

The Hollies: Long Cool Woman (In a Black Dress)

In Strict Confidence: Snow White; Tiefer

Jessica Bates: The Hanging Tree

Jethro Tull: Overhang; Kelpie; Rare and Precious Chain; Something's on the Move; Old Ghosts; Dun Ringall

Julian Cope: Charlotte Anne

The Kills: Nail In My Coffin; You Don't Own The Road; Sour Cherry; DNA

Leonard Cohen: The Future; You Want It Darker

Lorde: Yellow Flicker Beat; Royals

Low with Tom and Andy: Half Light

M.I.A.: Bad Girls

Marilyn Manson: Arma-Goddamn-Motherfuckin-Geddon; Personal Jesus; Tainted Love

Motherdrum: Big Stomp

People In Planes: Vampire

R.E.M.: Drive

Rob Zombie: Living Dead Girl; Never Gonna Stop

Saliva: Ladies and Gentlemen

Seether: Remedy

Shriekback: Underwaterboys; Over the Wire; Big Fun; Dust and a Shadow; This Big Hush; Nemesis; Now These Days Are Gone; The King in the Tree; The Shining Path; Shovelheads; And the Rain; Wriggle and Drone; Church of the Louder Light

Spiral Dance: Boys of Bedlam; Tarry Trousers

Steeleye Span: Blackleg Miner; Rogues in a Nation; Cam Ye O'er Frae France

Tamaryn: While You're Sleeping, I'm Dreaming; Violet's in a Pool

Tempest: Raggle Taggle Gypsy; Mad Tom of Bedlam; Queen of Argyll; Nottamun Town; Black Jack Davy

Tom Petty: Mary Jane's Last Dance

Tuatha Dea: Kilts and Corsets; Morgan La Fey; Tuatha De Danaan; The Hum and the Shiver; Wisp of A Thing Part 1; Long Black Curl

Wendy Rule: Let the Wind Blow; The Circle Song; Elemental Chant

Woodland: Roots; First Melt; Witch's Cross; The Dragon; Morgana Moon; Mermaid

Yoko Kanno: Lithium Flower

Zero 7: In the Waiting Line

Biography

New York Times, Publishers Weekly, and *USA Today* bestselling author Yasmine Galenorn writes urban fantasy and paranormal romance, and is the author of over sixty books, including the Wild Hunt Series, the Fury Unbound Series, the Bewitching Bedlam Series, the Indigo Court Series, and the Otherworld Series, among others. She's also written nonfiction metaphysical books. She is the 2011 Career Achievement Award Winner in Urban Fantasy, given by RT Magazine. Yasmine has been in the Craft since 1980, is a shamanic witch and High Priestess. She describes her life as a blend of teacups and tattoos. She lives in Kirkland, WA, with her husband Samwise and their cats. Yasmine can be reached via her website at Galenorn.com.

Indie Releases Currently Available:

The Wild Hunt Series:
The Silver Stag
Oak & Thorns
Iron Bones
A Shadow of Crows

Bewitching Bedlam Series:

Bewitching Bedlam
Maudlin's Mayhem
Siren's Song
Witches Wild
Casting Curses
Blood Music
Blood Vengeance
Tiger Tails
The Wish Factor

Fury Unbound Series:
Fury Rising
Fury's Magic
Fury Awakened
Fury Calling
Fury's Mantle

Indigo Court Series:
Night Myst
Night Veil
Night Seeker
Night Vision
Night's End
Night Shivers

Otherworld Series:
Moon Shimmers
Harvest Song
Earthbound
Knight Magic
Otherworld Tales: Volume One
Tales From Otherworld: Collection One
Men of Otherworld: Collection One

Men of Otherworld: Collection Two
Moon Swept: Otherworld Tales of First Love
For the rest of the Otherworld Series, see Website

Chintz 'n China Series:
Ghost of a Chance
Legend of the Jade Dragon
Murder Under a Mystic Moon
A Harvest of Bones
One Hex of a Wedding
Holiday Spirits

Bath and Body Series (originally under the name India Ink):
Scent to Her Grave
A Blush With Death
Glossed and Found

Misc. Short Stories/Anthologies:
Mist and Shadows: Short Tales From Dark Haunts
Once Upon a Kiss (short story: Princess Charming)
Once Upon a Curse (short story: Bones)

Magickal Nonfiction:
Embracing the Moon
Tarot Journeys

For all other series, as well as upcoming work, see Galenorn.com

CPSIA information can be obtained
at www.ICGtesting.com
Printed in the USA
LVHW04s0250141018
593522LV00002B/300/P